Fringe Benefits

Also by Sandy James

Fringe Benefits

SANDY JAMES

FOREVER
YOURS

New York Boston

Copyright © 2015 by Sandy James
Excerpt from *The Bottom Line* copyright © 2014 by Sandy James
Cover design by Elizabeth Turner
Cover image by Shutterstock
Cover copyright © 2015 by Hachette Book Group, Inc.

Forever Yours
Hachette Book Group
1290 Avenue of the Americas
New York, NY 10104
www.hachettebookgroup.com
www.twitter.com/foreverromance

First published as an ebook and as a print on demand edition: April 2015

Forever Yours is an imprint of Grand Central Publishing.
The Forever Yours name and logo are trademarks of Hachette Book Group, Inc.

The publisher is not responsible for websites (or their content) that are not owned by the publisher.

The Hachette Speakers Bureau provides a wide range of authors for speaking events. To find out more, go to www.hachettespeakersbureau.com or call (866) 376-6591.

ISBN: 978-1-4555-3337-4 (ebook edition)
ISBN: 978-1-4555-3338-1 (print on demand edition)

*Although I've dedicated a book to my husband in the past,
I have to let him know that this book is also in his honor.
Recently diagnosed with cancer, he has shown courage
and grace in the face of adversity. I not only love him
with every piece of my heart, but I also admire
him from the depths of my soul.*

So this one's for Jeff . . .

Acknowledgments

When the editor of my first three Ladies Who Lunch books left Forever Yours, I was worried I'd be "orphaned." Instead, I found myself working with one of my dream editors—Leah Hultenschmidt. I can't thank her enough for taking me on!

Big thanks to Dana Hamilton for her insightful editorial notes on this book. She made it a stronger story.

As always, I'd be nowhere without my agent, Joanna MacKenzie, and the other Browne & Miller agents, Danielle Egan-Miller and Abby Saul. Love you!

And last, but most certainly not least, to my critique partners— the ladies who save my butt over and over again. Love to Cheryl Brooks, Leanna Kay, Nan Reinhardt, and Sandra Owens.

Fringe Benefits

Chapter 1

One more day.

That was all Danielle Bradshaw had left. One more day before the school year started and her life would become a routine that made an air traffic controller's day seem relaxed.

Up at five in the morning. A five-mile run. Shower and pour some coffee down her throat—maybe finding a moment to choke down some oatmeal or granola—and then get herself dressed and get her fanny to work. Teach six sophomore English classes, usually with at least thirty kids in each, and head home to do some laundry and try to make a dent in the eternal pile of student papers to grade. Once spring rolled around, she could add after-school track practice and meets to her agenda, since she served as the coach for the distance runners.

And the next day?

Do it all over again.

"Danielle?" Her principal's call kept her from leaving the main office.

She'd made a quick trip to the heavily guarded supply closet to grab a fresh gradebook and was heading back to her room to prepare to face her new students. Her clean escape had just been thwarted. "Yes?"

"I need your help." He turned to motion to someone in his office. "Nathaniel? Come on out here. I want you to work with Ms. Bradshaw."

Oh no.

She had no doubt what Jim Reinhardt wanted from her. The department was getting a new teacher. Finally. That would mean some relief from the onerous number of kids the teachers of Stephen Douglas High School faced on a daily basis.

But with that blessing came the need to break in a newbie. Since she'd been promoted to department head this school year, a position that came with an embarrassingly small raise and a hell of a lot more responsibility, she'd have to be the one to show the new teacher the ropes. No doubt this was a kid fresh from college, because there was no way the corporation would spring for someone with experience. The administrators were too cheap.

Her day was now shot to hell.

Her biggest concern, aside from having to spend every minute of her work day spoon-feeding some newbie, was that as department head she should've been included in the decision on which teacher to hire. Since her summer had gone by without a single word from her boss about interviews, she'd simply assumed that the school corporation hadn't scraped together enough funds to hire a new English instructor.

With a sigh, she tried to paste a smile on her face to welcome the poor guy who now faced the most challenging nine months of his life. "Hi, I'm—"

The words froze in her throat as she took in the man standing in front of her, flashing her a smile that damn near stopped her heart before sending it slamming against her ribs.

He was blond, his hair close-cropped and slicked down with the right amount of gel. He wore a dark suit and red tie as though a born executive. His eyes were the most fascinating shade of blue, the color of the clearest of the Caribbean waters. And exactly like those waters, Dani could feel herself drowning in them.

"Nathaniel Ryan," he said, holding out his hand. "But I prefer Nate."

Somehow, she was able to force herself from her stupor to shake his hand. "Dani…um…Danielle. Bradshaw."

Jim cuffed Nate on the shoulder. "Dani will get you introduced and give you a tour of the place." His gaze shifted to her. She knew that expression well. It was the same guilty grimace he gave her whenever he knew he'd just given her yet another nearly impossible task.

And breaking in a new teacher the day before school qualified as a "nearly impossible task." The only thing that kept her from being furious with Jim was the fact that he was the best principal she'd ever worked for.

She found her voice. "What room will he be in?"

"Nate's going to be in the empty room at the end of the English hall."

"Um, okay." The last time anyone had used the room was five years ago. Since then, it had been a place to store all the broken desks. The teachers in her department called it the "Black Hole of Calcutta."

"Don't worry, Dani," Jim said. "I already had the custodians clear it out. Nate, Dani's going to be your mentor this year. She teaches sophomore English—same as you. She'll help get you ready for tomorrow, and my office door is always open if you need me. We'll both be observing you in action a couple of times this year—once in the first week or two, so be ready."

On that, he strode back to his office, leaving her to gape at the new teacher.

God, her friends would be laughing their asses off at the way she gawked at Nate Ryan. The Ladies Who Lunch, her closest friends, loved to joke about how nonchalant Dani always acted around handsome men. Even though all three of her friends were happily married, they had an eye for good-looking men and ogled any hunk who passed them while Dani rolled her eyes at their brazenness.

If they could only see her now...She couldn't even put together enough words to make a coherent sentence.

She should be talking a blue streak right now, telling this guy—Nate Ryan—about the ins and outs of Stephen Douglas High School. She should be explaining how to set up his electronic gradebook and attendance file and then joking with him about why he had to keep a paper gradebook and attendance file as well. She should be doing something productive rather than standing there staring at a man who had to be almost ten years younger than her own thirty-one. Thirty-two in a matter of weeks.

A decade ago, she'd been standing where Nate Ryan stood, ready to take on the students. Ready to teach kids and believing she had the power to change the world, to reach each and every student and help them learn to love reading and writing every bit as much as she did.

Ten years at Douglas High School had seasoned her. She wasn't entirely soured on teaching—not yet—but that time was on the horizon. One of the Ladies Who Lunch had left teaching only two years ago. Juliana Wilson had been a special-education teacher who'd burned out and carved herself a profitable career as a real estate agent.

Would the four friends still be the Ladies Who Lunch once they all left the profession? They'd found each other years ago, bonding as they shared their lunch period each day. They'd weathered Juliana jumping ship, still finding time to get together a couple of times a week.

But if Dani left, too?

Who exactly was she fooling? There was no reason even worrying about leaving. As it was, she'd be lucky if she saved enough money to retire at sixty-five.

"So, Ms. Bradshaw..." Nate raked his fingers through his short hair.

Dani got a hold of herself. The poor kid was obviously nervous. "Call me Dani. Please. How about I show you your room? I have no idea what's usable in there, but the department has several sets of classroom books that I can help you carry over. We also have e-books for our kids because they all have electronic tablets instead of textbooks."

His eyes widened. "Really? Wow. That had to be expensive. I thought schools were pinching pennies like crazy nowadays."

"We are. E-books are actually more cost-effective. They're a helluva lot cheaper than hardcover textbooks. Plus the kids don't get strained backs from carrying them around." She led the way to the big double doors leading out of the main office and was pleased when Nate reached past her to pull one open for her.

The man had manners, something sorely lacking in the guys she'd dated the last few years. Not that there'd been that many.

"Follow me," she said, gesturing toward the English hall. "I'll show you to your new home."

* * *

Nate Ryan followed his new boss, trying desperately to keep from staring at her ass.

But *damn*...

He hadn't expected a department head to be so young. She couldn't be that much older than his own twenty-four. How could she already be the leader of the whole English department? His mother had retired from teaching just last spring. She was barely fifty, but she'd been her school's science department head for only three years.

Maybe Dani was the oldest in the English department. A lot of experienced teachers were leaving the profession. His mother's retirement had all but been forced on her when the school corporation sponsored a buy-out for teachers at the top of the pay scale. She'd crunched some numbers based on the money she'd saved over the years and decided that she'd do fine retiring.

His stepfather had joined her, taking his thirty-year pension from being a police detective and leaving the force. Now they worked together, writing books and running a blog about traveling in middle age. It was brilliant. Every trip they took was deductible, and they were able to go to the places they'd always dreamed of visiting.

Maybe Danielle Bradshaw had benefited from a mass exodus of older teachers with a promotion. "You seem kinda young to be department head."

Sweet Lord, he'd gone and blurted that out.

Unlocking the door, she spoke over her shoulder. "I just got the job this year. You'll be my first virgin." Her eyes flew wide as a blush stained her cheeks. "Sorry. That might've been sexual harassment..."

"No worries," he said with a forgiving chuckle. "That's exactly what I am right now. A virgin—at least in this school."

As a grin lifted the corner of her mouth, she opened the door. "Here you go. Room thirteen."

"Great," he grumbled. Being a new teacher was tough enough. The last thing he needed was to start out with an unlucky room number.

"It's haunted, you know." She tossed him an enigmatic smile he found very attractive.

"My room?"

"Yep. When the school was first built, this was a dressing area for the guys who refereed our basketball games. One of them collapsed during a game in 1976."

"Heart attack?" he asked.

She nodded. "He died right here in this room."

"Wonderful. Now I've got a ghost *and* an unlucky room number."

Her laugh was as sweet as her voice. Some women had voices that grated on him. High-pitched. Squeaky. Made him want to gnash his teeth.

Dani's voice was a pleasant register, her laugh husky and genuine.

"At least the heat and air-conditioning work in this room," she countered. "My room is like a refrigerator all winter."

"Where's your room? I mean…you're my mentor, right? Shouldn't we be close?"

"I'm in twelve. Right across the hall. Don't worry. If the kids get out of control, I've got a whip and a chair handy. Just scream. I'll come running."

His first classroom, a chance to start his career. Hopes high, Nate flipped on the bank of light switches. The fluorescent lights buzzed and popped, sputtering to life. One look around made him wish they hadn't bothered.

The place was horrible. Desks were lined up in institutional rows, all the seats a boring brown. The walls were what his mother always called "school beige," and there wasn't even a window to bring in any light.

Prisons had to be more inviting.

"Looks like I'm heading to Education Depot at lunch," he said, talking more to himself than his boss. There was a shitload of stuff he'd have to buy. Bulletin board borders. Posters. A desk calendar. He was definitely starting from scratch, since his mother had been a science teacher. None of her leftovers would work, with the exception of her "You Can't Scare Me, I Teach" poster.

"Nope," Dani retorted. "Lunch will be with our department. It's the only chance we get to meet before school starts tomorrow. You'll have to go shopping after school."

He frowned, panic tickling at his nerves.

He shouldn't even be here. Nate had already accepted a job with a department store regional office, writing copy for their advertisements. He was supposed to start tomorrow. All the teaching jobs he'd applied for had been filled during the summer months, so he'd given up hope for this school year. That was as it should be. Teachers should be hired early enough to give them time to plan lessons, decorate classrooms, and gird their loins to face the students.

Instead, he'd received a phone call from Jim Reinhardt yesterday morning. Hoping to put his degree to better use than enticing people to buy things, Nate had interviewed right after lunch and signed his contract first thing this morning. He didn't have a damn thing ready for the kids who'd step across the threshold to room 13 tomorrow to greet their new English teacher.

How in the hell am I going to do this?

"I'll help as much as I can." Dani laid her hand on his arm. "I've got your back."

So he'd spoken the question aloud. Not a surprise. His former fiancée said it was one of his less-endearing habits. Of course, she had her own bad habits, one of those being becoming annoyed with him easily and often.

Dani drew back her hand and spun toward the bare teacher's desk with the grace of a ballerina. Her hair made him think of a dancer, too. Blond, even a lighter shade than his own, and she'd pulled it into a tight bun that accentuated her slender neck.

He suddenly wanted to see how long her hair was, whether it would be naturally straight if she let it down. And when she fixed her intense blue eyes on him, every thought he'd had seemed to fly right out of his brain.

Nate had always been drawn to older women, probably because girls his age were so damned flighty. His one serious relationship had almost resulted in marriage, but her behavior had changed abruptly after an unplanned pregnancy and sudden miscarriage. She'd started going to parties, saying she needed to be young, that losing their baby had made her realize exactly how close she'd come to having to grow up before her time.

They'd broken up after dating less than a year.

Every date he'd had since then had left him fearing he'd never have another serious relationship. Did all twentysomething girls think going out and drinking themselves stupid was the only way to celebrate a weekend?

No, girls his age didn't interest him.

But Danielle Bradshaw?

She interested Nate. A lot.

For all he knew, she was happily married with five kids. And she was his new boss, the woman who'd be evaluating him to see if this would be his one and only year teaching at Douglas High School. He had no business thinking of her as anything but a colleague.

The weight of the world suddenly settled on his shoulders. Tomorrow, six classes of eager new students would be sitting in those stark desks, expecting him to have a syllabus, a set of class rules, and a lesson to teach them.

What he had was jack shit.

Dani stepped over to one of the desks, letting her fingertips brush the surface as her gaze swept the room. "I don't know about you, but I hate having rows like this. I put my desks in pairs."

"I can move things around?" Nate asked. The only classroom he'd spent time in had been the one he'd student-taught in, and his supervising teacher hadn't wanted Nate to do anything to personalize the room. That only emphasized the fact that it wasn't Nate's classroom.

She laughed at his question, and he felt his mouth twitch, threatening a grin in response. "It's your room, *Mr. Ryan*. You can move the desks, the bookshelves, the—"

"Should be easy since they're empty," he drawled. "Not sure I'll ever get used to Mr. Ryan."

She chuckled again. "When you hear it a hundred times a day, you will. And no worry on décor. I've got a ton of posters you can use."

"Posters?"

"One of our teachers left a couple of years ago. Went on maternity leave and never came back. She left all of her stuff, and I didn't toss it."

"Typical teacher."

She cocked her head. "Pardon?"

"You're a pack rat."

A smile lit her face. "I resemble that remark. But how do you know that? This is your first job, right?"

He nodded. "My mom was a teacher. I don't think she's ever thrown anything away. Always said she might need it for her classroom."

"If she's like me," Dani said, "she never uses any of it. Right?"

"Right."

"Let's go to my room." She herded him toward the door and flipped off the lights.

"Aren't we coming back?" he asked.

"Of course."

"Then why turn out the lights?"

Her laugh eased some of his crippling anxiety. "Old habit. The corporation went hog wild trying to save money and trained all of us to turn out lights whenever we leave the room, even if only for a few minutes." She inclined her head toward her room. "C'mon, Nate. Let's get you some stuff to brighten up your room—other than turning the lights back on."

Although he appreciated her help, he had something more pressing. "I'd rather you hand me a stack of lesson plans for the week. I've got nada, not even a copy of the texts and novels I need to use."

She shut the door to his room behind them. "Don't worry. I'm the other sophomore-level teacher. We need to sync our lessons, so for now, I'll share all my plans and assignments with you. As the year goes on, we can start to work on things together."

Surely he'd heard her wrong. Share all her lesson plans? All her assignments? She couldn't mean that. Most teachers seemed to guard their materials as if they were printed on gold tablets. "Really?"

"Really. We've spent the last couple of years aligning curriculum. All of us share so we're teaching the same things at the same time."

"Thank God." Right after the words fell out of his mouth, he realized how desperate he sounded.

"C'mon." She headed across the hall, the heels of her shoes clicking against the terrazzo floor. "Let's go see what we can scrape up for this nightmare of a classroom."

Chapter 2

Dani would've felt sorry for Nate Ryan if she'd had the time. The whole day was eaten up babysitting him. The only thing that kept her from blaming him was that it truly wasn't his fault. Jim owed her a hell of a favor for tossing the guy in her lap only hours before the school year began.

As she sipped her iced tea, she watched Nate over the rim of her glass. When the department members arrived at Chili's for their late lunch—or early dinner, depending on how one looked at eating at four in the afternoon—she'd introduced Nate to the other English teachers. There were five people, including her, in the department. Nate made six. Only one other man worked in language arts, so he and Nate were definitely outnumbered. They'd all been cordial because Nate's presence meant their class loads would drop. If Jim had not brought him on board, each of the English teachers would have had to absorb one of the sophomore classes. Now they could focus on their own grade levels.

Nate was quiet. Shy? She wasn't sure yet. Although he seemed to be paying attention to the conversations, he had a wide-eyed and rather overwhelmed expression on his handsome face.

Handsome. That adjective had crossed Dani's mind on more than one occasion since meeting him. Ludicrous on her part. Not only was she now his boss, but he was also far too young for her.

Mary Henry leaned closer to Dani. "So what do you think?"

Dani wouldn't participate in Mary's kind of gossip. "About?"

Mary snorted. "The new guy, of course."

"I think he's got a master's degree from Indiana University, so he must know at least something about teaching English."

"And?" Mary prodded.

Setting her drink down, Dani knit her brow. "And what?"

The sigh Mary breathed betrayed her frustration. "What do you *think* about him?"

Dani knew what Mary was asking, whether she considered Nate to be good-looking. No matter what she thought of him, she wasn't about to get drawn into some juvenile discussion about how cute the new boy was. "He seems eager to get going. God, were we ever that young and naïve?"

"Stop being obtuse," Mary scolded. "At the risk of being labeled a 'dirty old lady,' I'll admit I think he's gorgeous. Just what I would've gone for. Forty years ago. And that dimple?" She let out a heavy sigh.

Since Mary was only two years from Social Security, Dani had no reason to be jealous.

Jealous? Of a guy she'd only met a few hours ago?

Shit, I need a drink.

Something stronger than iced tea would help, and she'd be texting Beth tonight to try to exorcise some of this weird attraction out of her mind by letting her best friend tell her she was being an idiot for panting after a guy so young.

"Earth to Dani," Mary said with a chuckle. "Nate asked you a question."

Cheeks flushing warm, Dani said, "Sorry. What did you ask?"

"You forgot to tell me about lunches," he said. "Is there a teachers' cafeteria? Where I student-taught—"

"Where was that?" Mary interrupted, as was her exasperating habit.

"Bloomington Central," he replied. "They had a great cafeteria. Ate there almost every day for only two-fifty."

Dani shook her head. "I wouldn't advise that at Douglas. God love 'em, the cafeteria ladies try, but...all the rules about what they can't serve kinda ties their hands behind their backs. Most of us bring our lunches."

"Especially Dani and the *Ladies*," Mary quipped, gesturing air quotes on the last word.

Nate quirked a tawny eyebrow. "Ladies? Do most of the women eat together or something?"

Before Dani could brush off the question, Mary jumped right in. "Dani and her friends have been eating together for just about forever. They call themselves the Ladies Who Lunch. Come to think of it, so does everyone else. You know, after *Company*."

"After what company?" Nate asked. "I feel like I'm missing the punch line of the joke."

"*Company* is a musical," Dani replied. "Let it go."

As if Mary would ever surrender the spotlight. She had Nate's rapt attention now, which meant she'd never stop talking. "There's a song by that name. Dani, Bethany Rogers... er...Ashford, Mallory Hamilton...er...Carpenter, and Juliana Kelley...damn. It's Wilson now, isn't it? I'm never gonna get their new names right. Geesh, Dani. Are you the only Lady who hasn't landed a husband yet?"

Not about to dignify that absurd question with a response,

Dani sipped more of her drink, wondering why Nate looked like he even cared about Mary's stupid gossip. The woman couldn't even get their names straight, for God's sake.

"You're not married?" Nate asked, digging around his salad with his fork. Since he was staring at her and not Mary, Dani assumed he was talking to her.

She shook her head.

"Jules is gone now," Mary announced. "Left teaching. Lucky woman. She still comes a couple times a week to eat with the Ladies, though. They always eat in the upstairs workroom. Most of the rest of us eat in the downstairs lounge."

* * *

Nate couldn't figure out why Dani's face had turned so red. Perhaps because she was embarrassed to be part of what sounded like an adult version of a clique? Were these Ladies Who Lunch nothing more than the school bullies? Hell, no one even wanted to eat with them.

That was hard to imagine after spending so much time with Danielle Bradshaw. She had patience to spare, and she didn't act as if telling him everything he needed to know about how Douglas High ran was a chore. If only his supervising teacher at Central had been half as solicitous, he'd have had a better student-teaching experience.

"I need to head back," Dani announced, slipping some bills into the black folder holding her check. "I didn't get as much done as I needed to." She rose, slung her purse over her shoulder, and smiled. "See you all in the morning."

Nate scrambled for his wallet, stuffed money into his own folder, and sprinted after her. A glance back made his stomach knot. Everyone gaped at them. His chasing after Dani like a puppy would surely be fodder for gossip.

Who the hell cares?

He needed Dani's help. He had a bunch of work yet to do on his room, and he had no idea how to get back inside the building. Principal Reinhardt had ordered Nate's electronic entry card from the tech director, but it wouldn't be ready until tomorrow. There might still be people in the building, but it was getting late, close to five. The doors would be locked, and he sure didn't feel like pathetically pounding on one of the doors until someone took pity on him and let him in.

"Dani!" he called, jogging toward her Honda Civic. "Wait!"

She stood in the open car door. "Nate. What's up?"

"I need to head back to school, too. I still have stuff to get done before tomorrow morning."

"Don't we all?"

"I don't have a keycard yet. Can I follow you so I can get back in?"

Her rather exaggerated sigh almost made him take a step back. Had he misjudged her patience?

Great. He'd only spent a day with her, and she was already annoyed with him. Sure he'd needed her help today—*a lot* of her help—but she was his boss. Helping her new department member get acquainted with the school was part of her job.

Nate's annoyance quickly ebbed, and he had to admit she'd gone above and beyond. Hell, she'd spent the whole day in his room. She'd shown him the best way to arrange the desks to maximize his limited space. She'd carried almost as many books as he had, and she'd probably put up more posters.

His shoulders slumped. "I'm sorry."

"Pardon?"

"I've taken up all your time today. No wonder you look like I asked you to loan me money."

Another sigh escaped her lips. "I'm the one who should be apologizing."

"Why?"

"All you did was ask me to help you get into the building, and I acted like...well, like you asked me to loan you money."

Nate grinned at her. "You really are a great boss. I'm just sorry I abused your kindness. I imagine you've got a shit... er...crapload of stuff to do, too."

"A shitload and a half," she replied with a beautiful smile. "Meet you at the door we exited through." She slid behind the wheel and shut the door. The Civic roared to life.

Scrambling back to his own car, Nate hurried to follow.

* * *

Dani stepped into the teacher workroom, not a bit surprised to see Nate standing sentry over the copy machine. In her career, she'd been in that same place more times than she cared to remember, trying not to fall asleep as the machine spit out paper after endless paper in a hypnotizing rhythm. He was so still, she wondered for a moment if he had drifted off, asleep on his feet. Heaven knew she'd done just that before.

Time to wake him up. "I wonder how many months of my life I've wasted in front of that copier," she quipped.

When he jumped, she tried not to laugh. That was another thing that happened to her regularly. The machine made a person forget there was life outside the school. Perhaps the captivation was a form of teacher meditation—watching the copies spit out and out and out...

"You scared a year off my life," he grumbled. "Enjoy sneaking up on a guy like that?"

"I thought the building was empty. I think we're the only two left. I can't leave until I get copies of my class rules made." She couldn't help but explain. "I had them done until the administration changed the dress code this morning. Teaches me not to be so organized."

"Sorry to hog the copier. I just need to finish getting my syllabus printed, and then I've got one set of assignments to run. That's all I had time to get ready, and that's only because you've been so generous."

Being more than a little anal retentive about preparing for her students, she understood the touch of panic in his voice. "Here's a piece of hard-earned advice. Take it one day at a time, Nate. First year is difficult enough without preparing too far ahead. Get things ready for the next school day, and we'll work together on helping you have lesson plans scheduled for a week or so at a time."

"Awesome. I feel so scattered. I'd resigned myself to not teaching this year."

She pulled a chair away from the table, spun it to face the copier, and took a seat. "I'm rather amazed you were even available. I saw your transcripts and your résumé. Can't believe some other school didn't snap you up."

"Yeah, well…it's a little harsh out there right now. School budgets are tight. I had interviews, but…the master's degree didn't work in my favor. They have to pay me more." He shrugged as he picked up a stack of finished copies from the output tray, loaded a new project into the scanner, and hit the start button. "Soon as this is done, the copier's yours."

Dani wasn't in a hurry. Something about watching him relaxed her. A rare talent. He'd ditched the suit jacket, loosened his tie, and rolled up his sleeves. His forearms were sublime. Tan, muscled, and covered with light hair that looked so soft she wanted to stroke it like a cat's fur.

With his back to her, she had a hard time not staring at his slim hips and squeezable butt. The only thing that prevented her from doing so was the mesmerizing width of his shoulders. "Distracting" didn't come close to describing Nate Ryan. Did he lift weights? Jog?

It would be great if he was a runner. Maybe they could run together in the mornings and…

She gave her head a shake. Not only was he closer to her students' ages than hers, but she'd also vowed never to get involved with someone at work. When Juliana had taught at Douglas High, so had her ex-husband. The Ladies heard more than their share of how miserable it was to have to see someone from a past relationship every weekday. Dani wasn't about to think of spending unnecessary time with Nate, even if he managed to notice her as something more than his new department head.

"We have a fantastic workout room," she said, trying to keep herself focused. "And the indoor track's open year-round if you jog."

The copier sputtered to a halt. Nate checked the small control screen. "Damn. Out of toner."

"Oh, no worries." She grabbed the lanyard holding her keys. "I'll get some from the supply closet and switch out the cartridge."

"Wait, I thought you said I wasn't supposed to do anything to the copier like add toner or clear a jam."

"I did." She moved to the door of the large supply closet and unlocked it.

"You said there was a secretary who handled all copier emergencies, that I should let her know."

"I said that, too. But she's not here. No one is, and I'm not letting that stupid rule keep me from being ready for tomorrow. Besides, it was mostly for the idiots who think they know how to fix problems and don't. I do." The supply closet was fairly large, and finding something in it was akin to the quest for the Holy Grail. But the copier needed toner, and she needed to get her work done so she could go home and try to get some sleep.

Nate followed her. "Anything else in there I might be able to use?"

"Definitely. That's why the closet's locked. Jim likes for us to beg for stuff we need. Grab some dry-erase markers," she replied, habitually kicking the plastic stop under the open door and beginning the search for toner. "If you can find any. Damn. Someone rearranged everything." Her gaze flitted along shelves, finding nothing really useful. No dry-erase markers. No hall passes. And definitely no toner cartridges. Just pile after pile of old carbon paper discipline slips no one used anymore and school stationery that dated back to before the school logo changed ten years ago. "See any toner?"

His back was to her, but she could hear the frustration in his voice. "Nope. Not much of anything useful." A few moments passed in silence until he said, "Let me check the shelves behind the door."

Arms folded over her chest, Dani let out a sigh as she glared at the useless supplies. If there wasn't any toner, she was royally screwed. "Fine, just be careful and please don't let it—"

Nate shut the door, the echo of the latch clicking as loud as a gunshot.

"—close."

He cocked his head. "Why not?"

"Because now we're locked inside."

Chapter 3

Nate tried the doorknob, but it wouldn't move. "What do you mean 'we're locked in'?" He jiggled it again, harder, hoping Dani was wrong.

"What I mean is exactly what I said. We're locked inside now. The stupid thing locks behind people, which is why I kicked the stop under it and told you not to shut it."

"You might've told me that *before* it was almost shut."

"*Everyone* knows it locks." Her matter-of-fact tone made him want to growl at her.

"Except new teachers." He dragged his fingers through his hair before putting his hands on his hips. "Who in the hell thought that was a good idea—having a door to a supply closet that can't be opened from the inside?"

Dani let out a weary sigh. "I really am sorry. I should've told you to be careful. I'm just...tired."

The resignation in her voice made Nate feel contrite. They were only in this predicament because he'd kept her here so late. "Probably from having to teach me everything about this place in such a short time. No, it's my fault for not listening to you. Question is, how do we get out?" He patted his pockets. "Left my cell on my desk. Got yours?"

"Nope. Mine's in my purse, locked in my closet." Dani checked her watch. "It's just after eight. The night custodian comes in at nine. We'll have to wait 'til he makes his rounds and checks the copy room."

"How do you know he'll come here?"

"We left the light on. Goes against school policy, remember? Poor guy spends half his shift turning off lights people left on."

Nate tried the door again, even knowing it was a waste of his time. "Shit."

"More like double shit. We're here until he lets us out, Nate. Might as well make yourself comfortable."

He turned to find Dani kicking off her shoes. She grabbed some of the yellowed stationery, plucked a pencil from her hair, and grinned. "Wanna play tic-tac-toe?"

"Seriously?"

"Look, if you're gonna be a good teacher, you have to learn to roll with the punches. Being locked in a supply closet might be a pain in the ass, but it's not a catastrophe. Wait 'til you come in the wrong door sometime and set off an alarm. That happens, you have to wait patiently while the cops come with sirens blaring and your boss arrives to turn it off."

"You did that?"

Her smile lit the entire room. "Sure did. First year, too. I honestly thought I'd get fired because of it."

"You obviously didn't."

"Obviously," she drawled. "Remember, this, too, shall pass. It'll get you through a rough year."

Trying to take Dani's advice, Nate resigned himself to the situation. There was one bright side to being locked in the damn closet—he could spend time with her. Maybe once he got to know her a little better, his weird fascination with the woman would dim.

"Tic-tac-toe, huh? Be warned—I'm a champion at it."

She drew out a grid and pointed the eraser end of the pencil at him. "A competitor. I like that. Everything I do tends to end up a competition."

Plucking the pencil from her fingers, he drew an X in the best place to start a winning game. "So do I. Mom says it's because I was the younger brother, that I always have something to prove."

Her chuckle was warm and inviting—just like the woman herself. With no hesitation, she took the pencil back, made her mark, and handed it back. "That explains being a teacher. Babies of the family tend to make great teachers. Did you take any psych classes in college?"

He nodded.

"Remember Adler?"

The name rang a bell.

No, stupid. That was Pavlov.

Then Nate remembered, mostly because of the fun his professor had with the topic. "The 'compensation' guy, right? The one who said guys with small dicks drive big trucks." The words slipped out before he caught himself. "Sorry."

"For what?" she asked. "You're right. He was that guy. He also did research into birth order affecting personality. Youngest kids are more social and love to prove themselves. Makes them great teachers."

"Where are you in the pecking order?" he asked, a bit surprised that he wanted to know everything there was to learn about Dani Bradshaw.

"No pecking order. Just me, which made me always feel like I had to prove myself, to show them how great I was."

"Lots of childhood baggage?"

"Not really. My parents were pretty typical Midwesterners, so we had a classic family relationship. Mom, Dad, and kid in the suburbs. They moved to California when my mom developed rheumatoid arthritis. The weather's easier for her."

And so the conversation went, each sharing little things, safe things, as they played games and waited for rescue.

* * *

This will be a great story to tell the kids one day.

Why that ridiculous thought kept tumbling through Nate's head was beyond him. But it did.

Your mom and I got locked in a supply closet together. That's when we decided to start dating.

There was a stack of papers they'd used to play what seemed like a million games of tic-tac-toe, which had been followed by hangman. Over an hour had passed, and there was no sign of the custodian.

Funny, but he no longer minded losing all that time to get things ready for the first day of school. Instead, he found himself drawn to his pretty, witty boss.

He recognized her perfume. Angel. Once, he'd gone to the trouble of picking a perfume he thought was the perfect scent and bought his fiancée what the salesman called a "recruitment set." The bundle of Angel products had everything from the perfume in a star-shaped bottle to body lotion.

Kat had hated it.

Obviously Dani liked it as much as he did. Everything about her appealed to him and—

Jesus have mercy. She was his boss. So why did he keep forgetting that?

"My legs are getting stiff." She struggled to stand, groping for one of the shelves. A hiss fell from her lips. "Shit."

The pain on her face hit Nate hard, and he grabbed her arm to help steady her. "What's wrong?"

"Cramp. Leg cramp." She leaned heavily on him as she got to her feet and immediately stuck out her right leg, pointing and flexing her foot. "Damn, that smarts."

"Where?" He didn't want to start pawing her leg, but he wanted to help.

"Calf." Dani's face tightened into a grimace again.

Nate eased down on one knee and started rubbing her leg. "Nice knot you've got there."

"I think I'm dehydrated." As he kept working on the knot, she flexed and extended her foot. "Left my water in my room."

"Yeah, well, neither of us expected to be here so long." The muscle relaxed under his kneading fingers. "Getting better?"

"Much."

So why couldn't he stop touching her? When it dawned on him that he wanted to trail his fingers up her leg, to her slender thigh and beyond, he slowly stood. Her eyes were locked with his, and tension rose between them as he gently put his hands on her waist, easing her forward.

Her head cocked just enough to show that she would allow him to kiss her. With a smile, he lowered his face to hers.

With a loud rattle of the lock, the door suddenly swung open, and the sixty-something custodian stared at them wide-eyed. "What in the hell are you two doing?"

* * *

Dani had never been so mortified in her whole life. She quickly stepped away from Nate, stumbling and landing against one of the shelves. Several boxes of discipline slips tumbled to the ground. Bending down to pick them up, her head collided with Nate's so hard she saw stars.

He rubbed the heel of his hand against his forehead and groaned.

"Weren't bored in here, were you?" The custodian laughed, making Dani wish she could find her "teacher voice" to give him a good scolding. But she was too rattled to say a word. Then again, she was honest enough to admit, if only to herself, that she'd be laughing, too, had she caught a couple of teachers kissing in the locked supply closet.

The reason they were in that closet came rushing back. "We got locked in."

Nate was picking up packages of staples. "It was my fault."

"No, it was mine," she countered. "I should've warned you."

"Good thing I saw the light on in here or I wouldn't have caught, er, *found* you." The janitor shook his head as he chuckled his way out of the teachers' lounge. "Turn out the lights when you're done," he called as he disappeared down the dark hallway.

"Where's the toner?" Dani shouted.

"Behind the copier."

Nate put the last box of staples back on the shelf and stepped out of the closet as she hurried to look behind the machine. A single box labeled *toner* waited there.

"Son of a bitch," she mumbled under her breath. After changing the toner, she closed the door and the copier began spitting out papers again as though nothing had ever happened.

Nate leaned his hip against the machine, appearing totally unaffected by the night's events.

How could he be so damned calm?

Her heart was hammering, and sweat trickled between her breasts and down her spine. Her face was so hot she wondered why she didn't spontaneously combust. There was no way she could get out of this without some kind of explanation to him.

Or could she?

Nate grabbed the last of his papers, picked up the stack he'd set aside earlier, and said, "If all the excitement's over, I'm leaving." His gaze settled on her. "Good night. I'll see you in the morning." On that, he strode out of the room.

Dani stood alone, wondering when her life had become an episode of *Candid Camera*.

When she finally made her way home and to bed, she dreamed a foolish, girlish dream of a maiden stuck in a tower—only in this version, a knight in shining armor was trapped in there with her.

Funny, when the knight lifted his visor, he looked an awful lot like Nate Ryan...

Chapter 4

"I miss this so much." Dani sealed her now-empty plastic container and shoved it in her purple nylon lunchbox. "Sure we can't talk you into coming back to teaching, Jules?"

Juliana Wilson let out a loud laugh. "Hell, no. I miss lunch with all of you, but come back to a classroom? Never. I've found a new calling selling houses."

"Besides," Mallory Carpenter added, "her husband would never allow it." She gave her friends one of her impish smiles. "He'd be lost without Jules—both at work and at home."

"How's that 'manny' working out?" Dani asked.

The Wilsons' twin boys were close to three years old now and only stopped moving when they fell asleep. The frazzled parents had recently lost their nanny to an out-of-town college and had hired a male au pair.

"Stefan is great," Juliana replied. "Beth drops Emma off every morning, and Stefan takes care of her, too."

That news came as no surprise. The Ladies always supported each other. Through thick and thin. Through cancer and childbirth. Through despair and elation. They were closer than most sisters.

When Beth lost her younger sister and became her niece's adoptive mother, Jules had been the one to help Beth cope with instant parenthood. Of course she would let her "manny" babysit Emma. Beth had agonized over whether she could keep teaching and worried about finding good child care. Jules had taken away that concern by offering her manny, so Beth had decided to teach at least one more year.

Bethany looked up from her cell phone. "Looks like Emma's down for her nap."

"Did Stefan text you or something?" Mallory asked.

"Or something," Beth replied with a chuckle. She held her phone so they could see the screen. The image was of the large nursery at the Wilson home, and Emma and the Wilson twins were sleeping peacefully on their small daybeds.

"Ain't technology grand?" Beth quipped. "I can see my baby all day long. Did I tell you she's calling Robert 'Daddy' now instead of Bobber?" Her eyes filled with tears.

"Don't you dare cry," Mallory scolded. "That's *happy* news."

As the Ladies chattered on, the door to the workroom opened and Nate Ryan walked in.

The conversation immediately stopped, and Dani's three friends stared at him. No wonder. He was wearing a baby blue polo that showed well-toned arms. His navy pants left no doubt that the rest of his body was every bit as fit. Damn, but she could stare at his butt forever and never get tired of the view.

The normally confident Nate suddenly faltered, walking ever so slowly toward the copier and resembling a gazelle that had spotted a pack of hungry lions. "I...um...need to make some copies?"

Dani almost laughed at his nervousness. "Are you asking us or telling us?"

"Um…asking? I don't want to interrupt."

"Copy away!" Jules said. "Copies wait for no one. You're a newbie?"

He nodded.

"Then are you looking to buy or rent a home?" A business card with a large shamrock logo seemed to instantly appear in her hand. "I can help. I have a lot of great properties I could show you. There's a special HUD program for teachers who buy repos."

Nate got the copier in motion before taking the card from Jules. "Actually, I *am* trying to find a place of my own. I'm in a long-stay hotel for the month, but I'll need a more permanent place. This job sort of came out of the blue. I didn't have time to find anything else."

"The Stay-Put Inn?" Jules asked.

"That's the one."

"We'll get you out of that pit."

"It really isn't…good," he admitted. "I'd be grateful to have somewhere else to call home."

Hoping to put him at ease, Dani gave the introductions. "Everyone, this is Nate Ryan. He's my new sophomore English teacher. Nate, these are my friends." She nodded at Jules. "Juliana Wilson. She used to be a special-ed teacher here. Now, obviously, she handles real estate." She smiled at Beth and Mallory. "And Bethany Ashford and Mallory Carpenter, who you'll see around school. They teach here, too."

His eyes shone with understanding. "Ah, I see. You're the Ladies Who Lunch. Mary told me all about you."

"Mary Henry?" Mallory asked.

"That's the one," he replied.

"Biggest gossip in the school," she said with a dismissive wave. "Despite what you've probably heard, we're quite harmless."

"Where are you from, Nate?" Beth asked with one of her almost nonstop smiles.

Dani was pleased to see him relax, if only a smidge.

"Indiana," he replied. "Went to Indiana University."

"Is this your first job?" Mallory asked.

"Yeah. Student teaching was great, but I'm still trying to get my sea legs."

"It gets easier," Mallory promised.

"So Dani keeps telling me." He gave Dani a lopsided and entirely too handsome grin. The dimple was almost more than she could take.

At least his responses weren't clipped, and hopefully he saw the Ladies' questions as polite rather than an interrogation.

The copies ceased. Nate grabbed the stack of papers. With a saucy salute, he said, "A pleasure to meet the infamous Ladies Who Lunch." A glance to the clock. "Oh, and two minutes 'til the bell." He shut the door softly behind him.

"Wow." Jules shifted her stare from the door to Dani. "Seriously. *Wow*. He's a cutie."

"Absolutely delectable," Mallory added, her knowing gaze also on Dani.

Beth joined in the stare-down, her eyes searching for something Dani wasn't sure she was ready to admit to herself, let alone to her friends.

Beth slapped her palm against the table. "You like him!"

So like Beth to figure it out.

"Oh, puhleeze…" Dani rolled her eyes, hoping to dissuade them from pursuing the topic. "I'm technically his boss, and I'm his mentor for this school year."

"Sounds like a perfect way to spend time together," Jules said.

Mallory, as usual, added to Jules's thought. The two were every bit as in sync as Dani and Beth. "Plenty of forced contact. Up to you to turn it into quality time."

Beth kept on grinning as she packed up the litter from her lunch. "You know, that basement apartment of yours might be the answer."

"Answer?" Dani quirked a brow. "To what?"

"To Nate's problem. And yours."

The gleam in Beth's eye alerted Dani to her friend's thoughts. "Oh no, no, *no*." She gave her head an emphatic shake. "I am *not* asking Nate to take that apartment. That's for when I host foreign exchange students."

"Which you aren't yet," Mallory pointed out. "Beth's right. Invite him to stay with you while Jules helps him find a house."

While a part of Dani wanted to immediately embrace the idea of Nate Ryan sharing her home, the saner part of her brain screamed not to do it. Beth's husband, Robert Ashford, was a custom builder. He'd built Dani's house, and at her request, he'd turned the basement into a nice one-bedroom suite. Her reasoning had been that she wanted to host students from other cultures at Douglas High for a year of school. When she'd been a teenager back in Chicago, her parents had hosted three different kids from overseas. Sweden. England. Germany. Each of their guests had been a delight. To this day, they still hosted students, although it was now in their California home.

Dani wanted to continue the tradition. Her parents were still in touch with each of the students who had called the Bradshaw house "home." Maybe the exchange students were their way of coping with having an only child, one who'd followed several miscarriages that had left them bereft of having the large family they'd wanted.

Her apartment was supposed to host a teenager. Not once had she anticipated having a man like Nate living so close.

"Oh yes, yes, *yes*." Beth grinned. "Think about it. The poor guy's stuck in that ratty place."

"It'll only be a month or so," Jules added. "I'm really good at my job, and I'm sure I'll get him a great place quickly."

"Why bother?" Mallory asked. "Once he sees Dani's place, he'll want to move right in."

Hating being trapped in a corner, Dani waved her hand in dismissal. "I'll think about it." Their scoffs made her add, "I will. I'll think about it."

"That butt is just begging to be squeezed." Beth winked at her.

"I'm telling Robert you said that," Dani joked. "Even if you're right, Nate Ryan's too young for me."

Three snorts sounded right before a merciful bell rang, ending lunch.

"Bring him to the barbeque Sunday." Mallory tossed her trash in the wastebasket. "We'll check him out."

Dani shook her head. "You'll do no such thing."

"Bring him," Jules insisted. "I could use the business." She winked.

Without waiting for a reply, Jules and Mallory strolled out of the workroom.

"You really should invite him to the barbeque," Beth said. "I can tell you like the guy. It's a great kind of nonthreatening date."

It was Dani's turn to snort her derision. "Nonthreatening? I'd be feeding Nate to the sharks. Not only will the Ladies be there, but your husbands will give him a hard time."

"What better way to find out if he's right for you than to toss him in the deep end?"

As far as Dani was concerned, she and Nate were already swimming in treacherous waters. The near kiss was all she could think of when she wasn't focused on students.

"Why are you blushing?" Beth asked as they walked toward her classroom.

Since Dani had prep period right after lunch, she was in no hurry. The area around them was free of eavesdropping students, so she let her guard down for a moment. "Nate and I stayed really late last night to get some work done. We got locked in the supply closet when we were looking for toner."

"How romantic! Is that what's making you blush?"

"Yeah, well…We almost kissed."

Beth cocked her head. "You were trapped in a closet and you almost *kissed*? Weird reaction."

"I know. I know."

"And?" Beth prodded.

"And I certainly wouldn't mind if he tried to kiss me again."

Chapter 5

Noise assaulted Dani's ears the moment she opened the doors to the gym. One thing she could say about Douglas High—the students always turned out to support their sports teams. Even a sport that seemed less popular, like volleyball.

Scanning the bleachers, she was relieved none of the usual school gossips were there for the match—especially Mary Henry. After Dani had been locked in the closet with Nate, Mary had somehow found out and the story had spread like a rampant virus. While the grapevine at Douglas was extraordinarily efficient, it was also highly inaccurate. By the time someone worked up the guts to tease Dani about the closet incident, the tale involved them not just kissing but shoving their tongues down each other's throats and having their hands in inappropriate places when the principal happened to discover them.

The reason she'd decided to come to Nate's volleyball match was to show that they were nothing more than colleagues. Friends. When people saw them being cordial yet distant, the stories would finally die, hopefully replaced with more juicy gossip about other people that was every bit as exaggerated as the "closet clinch," as it had come to be called.

The announcer, fellow English teacher Jeremy Pratt, was introducing the players, so Dani worked her way up the bleachers to sit by herself in what she hoped was a rather inconspicuous place—where if she were seen, no one would think anything of it. Just a teacher out to cheer for her students. As she settled herself on the uncomfortable seat, Nate's gaze caught hers as though he'd somehow known she'd arrived.

A smile, dimple and all, lit his handsome face. He hadn't shaved in a couple of days, judging from the light brown stubble covering his cheeks and chin. The rugged look suited him, and damn, she really needed to stop thinking about him with any inclination toward romance.

Why? Beth's voice echoed in her head. *What harm would there be in getting to know him?*

The harm would be if their names were linked often enough that the administration got wind of it. Nate was a new teacher, which meant he needed to prove himself. Dani was the new department chair, which left her in the same position—trying to show the principal that she could handle the job.

It simply wasn't the right time to even *consider* getting involved.

He tossed her a goofy half-wave and then focused on talking to his team.

Volleyball. The poor guy had clearly been roped into coaching the sport, judging by how uncomfortable he looked pointing to his clipboard and trying to explain something to his girls. One thing that was expected of new teachers was to fill any openings in extracurricular activities. She'd coached everything from cheerleading to academic teams to the philanthropy club. All in their season, and each easily passed on to a newer or more enthusiastic teacher. With the exception of training the spring distance runners, Dani had shed all her extracurricular responsibilities, and she'd become selfish with her personal time.

The match was close, and she lost herself in cheering for the students she either had in class or had taught in years past. Breaks between sets were filled with kids who scrambled up the bleachers to greet her and talk for a moment or two. Although she wasn't the most popular teacher at Douglas, she did like the fact that her students sought her out to ask advice, tell her some news, or just chitchat.

When the match ended, with Nate's team winning, she worked her way down the bleachers, not sure if she should head out without at least speaking to him for a bit. As he packed things into his bag, he glanced back at where she'd sat, his eyes widening and then scanning the gym. The panic in his expression eased as his gaze caught hers.

Wait for me? he mouthed.

At least he hadn't shouted. Dani inclined her head toward the exit, and he nodded, zipping his bag and striding toward the hallway that led to the locker room, most likely for the after-match debriefing of his team.

The night was sultry, a typical late August evening in Illinois. Cicadas buzzed in the trees that bordered the far side of the baseball field, and a nice breeze kept the evening from being too warm to enjoy. She took a seat on one of the wooden benches right outside the big double doors, hoping he wouldn't be too long.

Nate strode through the doors a brief ten minutes later. "Hey," he called as he headed toward her. "You came."

"Just showing my school spirit," she replied, knowing her flushed cheeks had to make him think otherwise.

"Have you eaten?"

She shook her head.

"Wanna go get a burger?"

The hopeful tone in Nate's voice made Dani feel guilty turning him down. "That's probably not a good idea."

"Why? You a vegan or something?"

"No. It's just…people are already talking."

He rolled his eyes. "The 'closet clinch'?" A snort slipped out. "People really do have vivid imaginations around here. Mary Henry ought to write romance novels. She has a way of embellishing that most authors would envy."

Dani smiled. "That she does."

"C'mon, Dani. Let's get a burger. I'm starving, and I still want to talk about the unit we're starting on *To Kill a Mockingbird*."

Her heart sank. After all her worrying about the spark between them whenever they'd been together, she'd misjudged the attraction. Nate only cared about being a good teacher, not about anything that might or might not happen between them.

"It'll be fine," he said. "We can go to Aspen Grill."

His suggestion confused her. "A great place to eat, but it's a long drive."

"Not that long, especially if we want some privacy."

"You want privacy to talk about *To Kill a Mockingbird*?"

He took a slow look around the entrance and then his gaze swept the parking lot. Too many ears to say what he wanted?

Dani stared up at him. "I guess Aspen Grill would work."

"Great. I'll drive."

* * *

Aspen Grill was almost empty. No wonder since it was almost eight. The drive to Ellisville had eaten up a good half hour, but Nate had scented Dani's fear.

However, he didn't share it. They taught at the same school. So what? Teachers dated other teachers all the time. Sure, Douglas High was a small school in a tiny town, but there had to have been other teachers who forged relationships in the microcosm of Cloverleaf, Illinois.

He held the door open for her, letting his hand rest on the small of her back as if it were the most natural thing to do. A waitress led them to a booth, handed them menus, and then took their drink orders. In a short time, they were sipping soda and waiting for their burgers.

"Let's talk themes for *Mockingbird*," Dani said. "I love the coexistence of good and evil that the story—"

Nate held up a palm.

"What?" she asked. "I've got some great insight into that book. It's one of my favorites. And we get to teach *The Hobbit*."

"We're not here to talk about Atticus or Scout or Jem or themes from *To Kill a Mockingbird*."

"*The Hobbit*, then?" The gleam in her eye made him happy. She was finally relaxing with him.

"No matter how much I love it, not even *The Hobbit*."

"But I thought you wanted to get in synch with what we were teaching about *Mockingbird*."

"I want to talk about us and the closet."

Dani glanced away. "Nate…"

Sitting back, Nate folded his arms over his chest and stared at her. He didn't know her. Not really. Sure, they spent time together in school, working through their lesson plans and coordinating the sophomore classes. And she'd been a great mentor, showing him the ropes and making him feel welcome despite being dumped in her lap with no notice.

No, he didn't know her.

But he wanted to.

Now he needed to figure out if he was stuck in a one-sided attraction and whether that chemistry he'd felt had been his and his alone.

"What are you so worried about?" he asked.

Slowly, her eyes came back to his. "The kids have to take the Illinois sophomore literature test in November."

"You told me that."

"*Mockingbird* is a great book to prep the kids for that test."

"You told me that, too."

Her brows gathered.

"I don't want to talk about school anymore."

Her blue eyes widened. "I'm not sure that's a good idea."

Nate took a breath and blew it out slowly. For a while, he'd thought she'd simply been playing coy. On the drive there, they'd talked about the volleyball match and the upcoming Open House evening. Not a thing was mentioned about the fact that they'd come so close to kissing.

Now that they were someplace private, Dani acted as though she had no idea why he'd dragged her out of town just to get a burger. No wonder. She really didn't know what he wanted from her.

She wasn't being coy after all.

"I want to talk about what happened…well, what *almost* happened when we were locked in the supply closet."

The speed that her face flushed red made him smile. "I thought we'd put that behind us."

"I don't *want* to put that behind us."

Fiddling with her silverware, she said, "Nothing happened. Not really."

Nate laid his hand over one of hers. "You're right. Nothing

happened. But I brought you here to tell you that I wanted something to happen." He smiled when she finally looked him in the eye again. "I think you did, too. Did you want me to kiss you, Dani?"

Even though her teeth tugged hard on her bottom lip, she nodded.

"There. Was that so hard to admit?"

"Yes!"

"Why?"

Dani eased her hand back. "Why? You have to ask me *why*?"

"Since I have no idea what's going through your head right now, yes. I have to ask you why."

"I'm your boss, Nate."

"You're my department head. While that might technically be my *boss*…"

She let out an inelegant little snort.

"Fine. You win. You're my boss. But that only means you get to do a couple of evaluations of my teaching. That's all." Trying to get her to relax, he waggled his eyebrows. "Unless you think your lust for me would keep you from impartially judging my teaching abilities."

At least she smiled.

"Seriously, Dani. If you weren't my department head, would you at least give me one date? Just one date to see if whatever it was that we felt back in that supply room might lead to something…more?"

"I don't know, Nate…"

The waitress interrupted, putting their burgers in front of them.

They ate in silence, although Nate didn't feel any kind of awkwardness between them. He hoped to hell that meant she was thinking things over. A good thing since he wasn't about to give up on her simply because she'd have to give her opinion of the kind of teacher he was.

It was time Dani learned he had a stubborn streak a mile wide.

After wadding up his napkin and tossing it onto his empty plate, he rubbed his belly. "That was great. I'm definitely full." Her plate was empty, too. "Want some dessert?"

"Nah. You said you were full."

"You're not?"

She shrugged.

"You never cease to amaze me," he said, meaning every word.

"Because I eat like a real person and not a rabbit?"

"That, among other things. You're just not like other women. In a good way."

Over Dani's protests, he paid their check and they headed to the parking lot. It wasn't until he was opening the car door that he realized he was missing what might be his last chance to have her alone, away from the small-town prying eyes.

Nate laid a hand on her shoulder, turning her gently to face him. "Wait."

* * *

Dani knew better. She did. But the plea in Nate's voice was her undoing.

Instead of shaking her head, getting in the car, and hightailing her ass back to Cloverleaf—away from temptation—she did the stupidest thing she could think of. She put her arms around his waist and pressed her lips to his, knowing she would savor his surprised expression for a good, long while.

His lips were soft, his breath sweet. His kiss gentle. Until he wrapped his arms around her and held her tight against him as he thrust his tongue between her lips. The kiss he gave her was anything but gentle.

Heart pounding, Dani fisted her hands in the back of his shirt and let go of her tight self-control, if only for that moment. She was rewarded with the kind of kiss she'd always dreamed of, one that seemed to suspend the laws of time and space and made her wish for one of those impossible happily-ever-afters.

Her common sense returned in a rush, making her turn her head and ease her hands between them.

Nate resisted her push against his chest for a moment; then, with a sigh, he released her.

"We should get back." Her voice was husky and full of need she hoped he couldn't hear.

With a nod, he let her into the car and shut the door. Moments later, they were on the road back to Cloverleaf.

Nate slid her a glance. "So have we solved the problem?"

"I beg your pardon?"

"The 'you're my boss' problem. Have we solved it?"

Dani understood exactly what he was asking, but it was easier to play dumb. "It was just a kiss, Nate. Just one stupid kiss. Nothing special." The hangdog look on his face made her regret the lie. "We're colleagues. Friends. Can't we just leave it at that?"

His sigh hung heavy in the air, but he never answered her.

It wasn't until they were back at Douglas to pick up her car that she spoke again. "Look, how about you come to a cookout this weekend?"

"I thought you said we weren't—"

She dismissed the thought with a wave of her hand. "Not as a *date*. It's just the Ladies having a relaxing Saturday together. It'll give you a chance to get to know Mallory and Beth. They are teachers at our school, after all."

"Fine. When and where?"

"Just like that?"

"Just like that."

Chapter 6

Wow. What a cutie." Bethany nudged Dani with her elbow. "I see why you brought him today. Makes a great first date with so many guys for him to talk to."

"It's not a *date*," Dani insisted. She smoothed her hand down her white capris and adjusted the spaghetti strap of her purple top since it kept dropping to one side. "The poor guy was just shell-shocked after the first weeks at school, and he needed a place to relax. He doesn't know too many people in town." She shrugged, causing the strap to fall against her upper arm again. "I'm just being nice."

Juliana sat down on one of the seats in the new gazebo Robert had recently completed. She popped open her Diet Coke as Mallory took the opposite side. Both were dressed as casually as Dani, probably to avoid the heat. Beth wore a pink sundress that suited her dark hair and complexion.

The manny was inside the house with the Wilson twins and Beth's daughter, Emma. They'd exhausted themselves on the enormous jungle gym and were all napping in earnest. Made for a nice, quiet, and rather lazy afternoon.

"Did you card him, Mal?" Jules smirked. "Don't want to get arrested for serving beer to a minor."

Dani followed the gazes of the Ladies to Nate. He stood with the other men, holding tight to a bottle of Miller Lite and chuckling at whatever they were talking about. "A few of the teachers haven't met him yet, so he keeps getting asked for a hallway pass."

"A definite baby face on that one," Beth said. "Have you asked him to move in yet?"

"For pity's sake, Beth." Dani shot her a frown. "He wouldn't be 'moving in.' He'd be my tenant."

She was an idiot for even thinking about having him so close, but ever since their night out, she could think of nothing but having Nate live in her basement.

I'm an idiot.

Problem was, she was fascinated by him. Each school day, they shared a common prep period, which gave them time to plan for their sophomore classes. They could also talk books, something few of her friends, even the Ladies, could manage. To have someone share her hunger for literature was rare. And special.

And there was, of course, the kiss that had curled her toes and haunted her dreams with images of the passion she thought she might find in his arms.

A real idiot.

"Move in. Become your tenant. Pure semantics," Beth countered. "He'd be upstairs with you for stuff like laundry. And you didn't answer my question."

"Her lack of answer *is* the answer," Jules said. "She wants him there but can't find the courage to ask. Want me to talk to him? We're going out to see a few houses Monday after school. Could discuss renting then. I'll even draw up a contract for you."

With a shake of her head, Dani decided to stop being passive-aggressive. She was a grown-up; it was time to start acting like one.

She wanted him close? Fine. She'd admit it, if only to herself. So she'd offer him a way to be near that didn't threaten their working relationship. "No. I'll ask him when I drive him back to his hotel." The thought of him going back to that pit made her stomach knot. "Definitely asking today."

"He'll be a helluva lot happier with you," Jules said. "Your apartment is great—"

"Because my husband's a genius," Beth said with a smile.

"—and he can stay there while we search. I've got several places that are perfect for him, but it'll be at least three weeks before we can close any of them. Most are fixer-uppers, so he might want to get a few things updated before he moves." She fixed her intense green eyes on Dani. "You really are helping him out. That long-term place is—"

"Horrible." Dani couldn't help but feel guilty for not suggesting her apartment sooner. "I know. I know. I'll ask. I promise."

Three weeks. The perfect amount of time to decide if this infatuation was simply that.

* * *

Nate smiled at something Ben Carpenter said. The man had a great sense of humor, as did the other two guys who were clearly taking Nate's measure.

He tried to keep all their relationships straight in his mind. Connor Wilson belonged to the redhead, Jules. They were parents to the two dark-haired boys. They sold real estate, and she was taking Nate out to look at houses Monday. Seemed like a nice couple for salespeople. Most were pushy; these two weren't. Very, very helpful, but definitely not pushy.

Ben went with Mallory, the thin lady with the great smile. She'd helped him with locker duty, and for a tiny thing, she could use her voice to get a kid's attention pretty damn quick. Ben was the one who was going to help if Nate got a fixer-upper. Since he couldn't afford something like the Ashfords' home, he hoped Ben was as frugal as Nate's mother had taught him to be.

The cute brunette with the curly hair—Beth—was married to Robert Ashford. He was the one Dani said used to be a teacher but now built homes, and Beth still taught at Douglas. He'd constructed Dani's house. Maybe one day she'd let Nate take a tour so he could judge the quality for himself.

"I should've asked for an ID," Ben quipped as he pointed at Nate's longneck.

Connor grinned. "You hear that all the time, don't you?"

"Yeah." Nate took a pull of the beer. "But it's my face, so I'm stuck with it."

"You'll be glad in ten years." Ben raked his fingers through his dark hair, drawing Nate's attention to the gray at the temples. "Another five, I'll be entirely gray."

Robert shook his head. "Takes longer than that. I had gray at your age. Over forty now, and"—he rubbed his temple—"hasn't gone beyond my sideburns."

"Besides," Connor added, "he's a blond. Won't go gray as fast as guys like us with dark hair."

Ben scoffed as he flipped a slab of ribs. "We sound like a bunch of women, bitching about our gray hair. Next thing you know we'll be talking about gravity making our boobs sag and how bad our hot flashes are." He inclined his head toward where the four women sat in comfortable chairs at the far end of the deck. "Uh-oh, Nate."

The teasing tone of Ben's voice kept Nate from being concerned. "Uh-oh what?"

"All four of them are staring at you. There's mischief afoot."

"He's right." Robert grabbed a beer from the cooler. "The Ladies can get themselves into a jam eight ways from Sunday, especially if they're conspiring."

"So the Ladies are troublemakers?" Although that had been his original guess, it didn't jibe with what most of the people at school had to say about them. The women were well respected, as were their husbands.

When Dani had extended the invitation to come to the cookout at the Ashfords' house, he'd jumped at the chance to spend more time with her. She might be resisting going on a serious date, but he would wear her down. It had been a long time since he'd felt such a strong attraction to a woman. Only Kat had ever gotten that kind of reaction.

Kat had been his one and only long-term relationship. He'd only dated sporadically in high school, and he was the polar opposite of a ladies' man. Plagued with awkwardness his first three years of high school, he'd waited a lot longer than most guys for his growth spurt. Between his junior and senior years, his body had cooperated, adding five inches of height and destroying his knees in the process. He didn't truly hit his stride until college, and he'd met Kat not long after he'd started classes at IU. She was the only woman he'd ever loved, and at the time, Nate had thought she was "the one."

He'd been dead wrong.

"Did you like IU?" Connor asked.

"Yeah," Nate replied. "Liked it enough to stay almost six years."

"Change majors?"

Nate nodded. "Senior year, I had an epiphany when I took a work study as a teaching assistant for one of my professors. I loved being in front of a class. It felt…right. Since I was almost done with the requirements, I went ahead and got my bachelors in English; then I decided to go back for a teaching license and a master's in education. My mom objected, but I knew what I wanted."

"She's a teacher, isn't she?" Ben asked with a grin. "Mallory keeps telling Amber to do anything *but* teach. My daughter's got a mind of her own, though. Seems like every teacher is steering college kids away from the profession."

"Can you blame them?" An acerbic chuckle slipped from Robert's lips. "I sure as hell don't miss the bullshit. You know, teaching used to be a great profession. Now it's just mountains of paperwork, crappy pay, and people thinking a computer can do your job better than you."

"Easy, boys," Connor cautioned. "You're gonna scare the kid."

Kid? Was it a blessing or a curse to always look younger than he was? He was twenty-four, and everyone told him he acted a lot older. But that damn baby face…

Nate tried to turn the topic. "Amber?"

"My daughter from my first marriage. She's a sophomore at Douglas this year. Wants to be a teacher, no matter how much Mallory tells her not to."

Nate snapped his fingers. "Amber Carpenter. Fourth period. Didn't make the connection 'cause I'm still learning names."

"Takes a few weeks," Robert said. "I sure don't miss having to memorize a hundred-plus new names every year."

"Not talking about the students," Nate teased. "Talking about all of you."

At least the men laughed.

"Why'd you leave teaching?" Nate asked Robert.

Shooting a grin at Connor, Robert replied, "This cocky bastard breezed into town and turned my life upside down."

Connor let out a chuckle. "Now, Robert...you need to blame Tracy as much as you do me. Barrett Foods is what turned your life upside down."

It wasn't hard for Nate to fill in the rest of the story. "Barrett Foods. I've got tons of kids whose parents work there. I take it you built most of their houses."

Robert replied with a nod.

"Do you like being a builder?"

"Love it," Robert replied. He inclined his head at Ben. "We both thrive on breathing sawdust and sheetrock powder."

"I envy that," Nate said. "My dad isn't very handy with tools. My stepdad is, but he and Mom travel a lot. If I'm gonna buy a house, I can guaran-damn-tee you it'll need work, so I'll have to get my hands dirty. Doubt my stepdad will be able to help much. He and Mom are usually on the road to somewhere new."

"I'll be glad for any help you wanna give, and I'll teach you anything you want to learn." Ben slathered a little more barbeque sauce on the ribs and then shut the lid to the stainless steel grill. Then he sat down on the bench and glanced at Robert and Connor before he leveled a hard stare at Nate. "Time for the tougher questions."

Bracing himself, Nate took a long swig of his beer. "You want to know about me and Dani."

Connor let out another laugh. "Damn, kid. You really cut to the chase."

All Nate did was shrug. He'd learned quite a bit from watching his parents' marriage fall apart. The biggest lesson was to always be honest, something his father had a hard time doing, even with his sons. "There's nothing to tell. Not really. Dani and I are colleagues. Technically, she's my boss. Or so she keeps reminding me..."

"Heard you didn't worry about that when you got locked in the supply closet," Robert drawled. "Got quite cozy, didn't you? And then you took her on a date to Aspen Grill."

So the Ladies shared information not only among themselves but also with their husbands. Another shot of envy sliced through Nate. How wonderful would it be to have friends? Especially friends who could be trusted with secrets?

Nate's closest friend had always been his brother, Patrick. Come to think of it, Nate had been such a horribly shy geek and had never made any close friendships. Unless he counted the people he killed daily in online role-playing games. Cyberfriends hardly counted.

One of the reasons he'd chosen to be a teacher was because he wanted to help kids who were like he'd been. Alone. Feeling like a misfit. Wondering when or if life would really begin.

"No girlfriends back at IU?" Connor asked.

Nate shook his head, biting his tongue against the overwhelming need to talk to someone about Kat.

"You're holding back," Ben insisted. "What don't you want us to know?"

"Mind you," Connor added, "keeping secrets has a way of biting a guy in the ass."

That was a loaded line if he'd ever heard one. "It's...embarrassing. Makes my life sound like a soap opera."

Robert plopped onto the bench next to where Nate had taken a seat. "We love soap operas. So spill."

"Would you believe my ex-fiancée is now my stepsister?"

The three men stared at him in stunned silence.

Nate let a wry grin spread over his face. "I know, right? Very Greg and Marcia Brady." He figured now that he'd opened the can of worms, he might as well tell them the whole story. "Kat and I had no idea our parents had even *met* when we started dating. My mom hit it off with her dad when we were a world away in Bloomington. I liked a girl in class and worked up the guts to ask her out, and we clicked. Imagine everyone's surprise when we all got together for Parents' Day lunch."

Ben let out a low whistle. "Oh boy. Fireworks?"

"Like the Fourth of July." Funny, but the memories made Nate smile now. It had been almost four years since he and Kat had called it quits. Maybe he'd finally moved on for good.

"No women since then?" Connor asked.

"Dates, but nothing serious." Nate's gaze was drawn to the Ladies, who were meandering from the gazebo to the deck. He'd wondered if he'd ever get close enough to Dani to tell her everything about his relationship with Kat. Looked like he might have to since he'd shared it with the guys, which made his heart beat just a little faster.

What would she think?

The kiss they'd shared haunted him, but that wasn't the only reason he wanted to know Danielle Bradshaw better. The more chances they had to chat, the more he realized exactly how much they had in common.

Both were morning runners, enjoyed listening to R & B, and worshiped Mexican food. Then there were books, something he loved sharing with her. They could talk plots and themes and characters in a way he'd never known with anyone else. Nate wanted to learn more about Dani because he'd loved everything he'd seen so far. And he'd only scratched the surface.

And that kiss…

"Ladies." As Ben lifted his beer in a toast to the women, he grinned. "You're joining us at the perfect time. We were playing Twenty Questions with Nate, and he was just telling us about being engaged to his sister."

So much for deciding when to share the story with Dani…"*Step*sister," Nate hurried to explain.

While the other Ladies' reactions might have been humorous, all Nate cared about was the stunned expression on Dani's face.

"What the heck?" With a cock of her head, Jules gave him a goofy grin. "Are you from Kentucky or something?"

"Ha-ha, Jules," Nate said dryly. He explained the situation, hoping Dani wouldn't think poorly of him.

"That sounds like a bad Lifetime movie plot," Beth said. She sat down next to Robert and leaned against him as he draped his arm over her shoulder.

At least they were teasing, which meant they weren't condemning him. "Let's just say we were the butt of quite a few jokes."

Mallory tossed her can into a green recycle container in the corner of the deck. Then she nodded at her husband as he held up a can of Diet Coke he'd fished out of the cooler. "I can't imagine what family holidays are like for all of you."

"It's really not that bad now," Nate said. "Kat's off 'finding herself' overseas."

Robert gathered his brows. "What about your dad? What's he got to say about all this?"

"He's kinda out of the picture," Nate replied. "He and the trophy wife are busy raising my brothers. They're only six and three."

"And what exactly does one say to that?" Ben said.

"What did Kate's—" Connor began.

"Kat," Nate corrected.

"Kat's mom say?"

"Hell, what did her *dad* say?" Robert asked. "I'd think he'd want to skin you alive."

Since the Spanish Inquisition had clearly been revived, Nate went with the flow. "Kat's mom passed away when she was in high school. She had cancer."

The color drained from Mallory's face, and she went to her husband, settling herself in his lap while Ben wrapped his arms around her.

Nate felt like an idiot. "I said something wrong."

"Not at all," Mallory said, leaning her head against her husband's shoulder. "I'm a breast cancer survivor. It's just hard to hear about people who don't make it."

His face flushed hot, and he wished one day he'd actually learn not to insert his foot in his mouth so damn often. "I'm so sorry. I didn't…I shouldn't…"

"It's fine, Nate. Really it is. You couldn't have known."

"Tell us about Kat's dad. Your stepfather," Ben said, steering the conversation away from the hot-button topic.

"He wasn't too keen on Kat and me, but Mark—my stepdad, Mark Brennan—got over it." While there was more to the story, Nate was quite ready to stop being the center of attention.

He might have designs on dating Dani, but he didn't have a clue as to whether she was entirely interested in him. There was that fantastic kiss, but nothing since. No sign that she wanted more from him. Sure, she'd invited him to this cookout, but that might have been because she felt sorry for him. He was all alone in Cloverleaf, living in a fleabag extended-stay hotel.

Beth smiled sweetly, looking as innocent as a child. From what he'd learned, she was Dani's best friend and a person who bordered on sainthood. "Since we're putting poor Nate under the microscope, Dani," she said, "perhaps now is a great time to ask him to move in with you!"

him to move in with you?"

Chapter 7

The flush started on Dani's cheeks before spreading out to her
ears and down her neck. "Bethany!"

There was absolutely no doubt that Beth had worded her
outburst perfectly to give Nate the wrong impression. The
man wasn't an idiot. He had to know that Dani wasn't really
going to ask him to move in with her, but there was a note of
confusion on his handsome face. As well as a subtle hint of a
smile.

"Are you looking for a roommate?" he asked, his tone full of
hope.

"Yes. Um, no. Um…" Dani took a deep breath and tried to
tamp down her embarrassment. "I have a basement apartment
and—"

Nate jumped to his feet and held out his hand as though he
wanted her to shake it. "Taken! When can I move in?"

She clasped her hands to keep from immediately taking his
and begging him to move in today, to get his stuff right that
very moment.

The implications stopped her.

Cloverleaf was a typical small town, rife with gossip. If she offered her basement to Nate, everyone at Douglas High would know about the arrangement in three minutes flat. Added to the "closet clinch," they'd be the center of conversation all the way to Christmas break.

There were also meals to consider. Dani's basement had been designed to house exchange students, not a full-time tenant. She'd wanted the students to have privacy, but she'd also wanted them to have the complete experience of being part of an American family. While the "family" would only be her, she planned on her exchange students spending time with her at meals, going to events, even riding to school. So she'd left out the one important thing that would make her basement a true apartment—a full kitchen. Although there was a small kitchenette, she'd wanted most meals to be shared in her gourmet kitchen.

Her feelings about Nate moving in were in direct opposition. Part of her wanted to see his face every day; part of her feared what would happen if she spent that much time with him. She already craved his company almost as much as she did chocolate.

"What's the matter?" Nate awkwardly withdrew his hand and knit his brows.

"Um…" As if she could be honest with him.

You scare the shit outta me, Nate Ryan.

He held his hand over his heart. "I promise the following: no wet towels on the floor, no unfolded laundry left in the dryer, no leaving the toilet seat up, no—"

With a shake of her head, Dani held up a hand. "Stop!"

"I mean it, though," he insisted. "Every word of it. I'll be the perfect tenant."

She should turn him down. She should just shake her head and be done with it. She should use a little common sense and let Jules help him find a new place. What fell out of her mouth was as much a surprise to her as it probably was to everyone else at the cookout. "It might work…"

"You said you needed the money," Mallory chimed in.

"Yeah," Jules added. "You're supposed to be saving for your grand tour of Europe."

They had her there. Although she was paid more than the poor newbies like Nate, the money would come in handy. Seeing places like London and Paris with her own eyes was at the top of her bucket list.

Nate took her hand, stroking her knuckles with his thumb. "I'd be really grateful, Dani. And it will only be temporary." His eyes shone with humor as the corner of his mouth rose with a lopsided smile. " 'The charity that is a trifle to us can be precious to others.' "

The man could fucking quote Homer. How could she ever turn him down?

"Fine. You can live in my basement."

* * *

"This is the best way for you to get inside for now. I'll talk to Ben about getting you a private entrance." Dani tried to control the nervous tremor in her voice. She punched the code into the remote garage door opener and waited while the door rose.

"Don't go to any trouble. I'm fine with this." Nate followed her through the garage, stopping to stare at the empty pegboard and shelves. "You don't have any tools?"

"I've got a hammer, a couple of screwdrivers, and a wrench.

They're in a drawer in the kitchen." She shrugged. "Haven't really needed anything else."

"That's 'cause this place is new. Trust me, you'll need more as it ages." His gaze returned to her, his eyes capturing hers. "Sorry. That was too pessimistic, wasn't it?"

Unnerved by his intense scrutiny, she went to the door and opened it. "Not pessimistic. Realistic. A trait we share. I guess I always thought I'd have Ben or Robert to call on if I needed any help." She stepped into the foyer and held the door for him.

Nate followed her, moving out of the way so she could close the door. Then he looked around her two-story foyer, eyes wide. "Wow. This place is amazing."

Although she thought so, too, she didn't want to sound as though she were bragging. "Robert builds amazing houses."

He pointed at the etched glass chandelier. "I love the light fixture. So modern."

They evidently had the same taste, because she'd loved it from the moment she saw it in the lighting store.

"Did Robert pick it out?" He brushed his foot across the ceramic tile lining the foyer's floor. "And this? The color's fantastic."

"He pointed out some choices for me."

"So *you* picked it."

Since Nate had made it a statement, Dani wasn't sure whether she should respond. It was easier to continue the tour. She was too rattled having him in her house to hold a genuine conversation.

That didn't bode well. If he took the basement, he'd be in her house all the time.

Grow up, Dani. You're not sixteen anymore.

On that admonition, she got her pluck back. "Want to see the basement?"

"Nope." He headed right to the staircase, running his fingertips over the carved cherry banister. "I want to see the whole house first. This place is a masterpiece!" Before she could say a word, he bounded up the stairs.

Dani loved his enthusiasm for her home. Robert worked miracles, no doubt about it. He'd helped a single woman living on a teacher's salary build a beautiful, spacious home. A part of her enjoyed the fact that Nate felt comfortable enough with her to give himself an impromptu house tour.

He was waiting at the top when she followed him up the staircase. "I'm sorry. I'm being rude. If you don't want to show me the house…" His fingers raked through his hair. "I shouldn't have gone nosing around."

"It's fine, Nate. Really. I'm happy you like my house."

Each room earned more praise as she led him through the bedrooms and baths. When she'd picked out the design, she'd known she might never have a need for four bedrooms. She'd decided a long time ago never to have kids of her own. She made her living with children. Day in, day out, her life was a revolving door of educating—and sometimes mothering—young people. That left her emotionally depleted. Her personal life would only include adults. And maybe a dog.

Not that she didn't want a family. It was that her definition of the word was nothing more than a husband and wife. Two people who would share their lives, spending time traveling and seeking out all the experiences the world had to offer.

Maybe she'd chosen four bedrooms because in the back of her mind she was thinking about the Ladies Who Lunch. Or maybe because four was her lucky number.

The longer Nate was in her home, the more Dani relaxed. By the time she led him back downstairs and to the kitchen, things between them seemed natural. Easy. Exactly like at school.

"And here's the *pièce de résistance*," she said, sweeping her arm toward the kitchen.

Nate strode to the enormous island, smoothed his hands over the gray granite, and gaped like a child seeing the bounty left by Santa Claus on a Christmas morning. "My, oh my…" He glanced at her, smiling. That dimple was going to be the death of her. "Did I tell you how much I love to cook?"

"No, you didn't." They'd talked. A lot. About books. About music. About running. Although she was getting to know him better, there was still much about Nate Ryan she needed to learn.

"Well, I do."

"So do I."

He turned and put his hands on her shoulders. "Hope the apartment's kitchen is half this nice."

"Um, about that…" She nibbled on her bottom lip, feeling guilty.

His touch turned to a caress as he rubbed her bare upper arms. "What's wrong?"

"I didn't tell you, and I probably should have, especially since you're so excited now…"

"Tell me what?"

She couldn't speak; she was simply too tongue-tied. He was sure to be disappointed that she hadn't told him, probably doubly disappointed since he enjoyed cooking so much.

That, and his touch evoked memories of his kiss—that incredible kiss that Dani wished she could forget.

But she couldn't.

"C'mon, Dani. It can't be *that* bad."

The best thing to do was just spit it out. "There's no kitchen in the basement."

Nate blinked a few times. "You built an apartment without a kitchen?"

Dani shook her head. "I wanted to host exchange students. The basement would give them privacy."

"So exchange students don't need a kitchen?"

"Well, yeah. But—"

Mischief filled his features. "Pretty damn cruel to bring exchange students all the way over to America and never let them eat."

"They'd eat up here. With me. In my kitchen. And the dining room, too." Great. Now she was babbling. "Look, there's a sink, a dorm fridge, and a microwave. But that's it."

A few long seconds passed before Nate said, "Then what's the problem?"

"What do you mean?" She was having a hard time following how quickly his mind jumped from thought to thought, so she tried to clarify. "If you stay in my basement, you won't have any place to cook."

He gave the kitchen a good, long look as he rubbed his chin. "There's a sink?"

She nodded.

"And a fridge?"

"A dorm fridge."

"There's a microwave, too?"

"Yes."

"Do they all work?" he asked, the teasing plain in his voice.

"Of course they work."

"Then I'll be better off than I am now. But there is one thing that would help—one thing you can do to make me feel more at home."

* * *

Nate savored the confused expression on Dani's face.

She'd sounded so forlorn when she'd admitted her basement didn't have a full kitchen. He'd been disappointed for a few seconds before he realized that her revelation wasn't a disaster. There might not be a gourmet kitchen, but a kitchenette would do just fine.

It also left the door open—hopefully literally—for him to spend time upstairs, using her kitchen. He could cook enough to shove some meals in the freezer; then he'd be able to warm them up during the week. Maybe she'd even let him create special meals for her so they could talk some more about their favorite books. They might be able to share some mealtimes, something that bordered on intimacy.

In his mind's eye, he could see them now, standing side by side at the big island, cutting vegetables. She'd dip one of her long fingers in a special sauce and offer it to him. He'd lick it off before tugging her into his arms and kissing her.

Yep. He had it bad for her. And for the time being, he didn't intend to let that bother him one bit.

"I want to be able to use this kitchen," he said. "As part of the deal, I want you to let me cook in this awesome kitchen."

"B-but…" Dani kept opening and closing her mouth like a kissing fish.

"Don't worry. I promise I'll clean up after myself."

"Then you're okay with just having a kitchenette?" she asked.

He swept his hand out toward the six-burner gas stove. "I am if you'll share this. And if you'll let me cook for you from time to time."

"Of course!"

"Well, then…I'm anxious to see my new place. How do we get to the basement?"

She pointed at a door.

"Let's go." Taking her hand, Nate dragged her there and then let her lead him down the stairs.

The basement was no less dazzling than the rest of the house. Instead of being decorated in boring neutral colors, the walls popped with red and white. An enormous flat-screen TV was mounted on one wall, and a black leather sectional gave whoever was watching something a great place to kick back and get comfortable.

Nate skipped his fingers across the back of the couch. "I won't even need my beat-up old sofa."

Tucked away under the stairs was the kitchenette—a small stainless steel sink, a thigh-high fridge, and microwave. "It's not much…"

"Like I said, it's better than what I've got now."

"You still want to stay here?" Her incredulous tone made him worry for a moment that she wasn't nearly as attracted to him as he was to her.

Then he remembered their kiss, remembered how passionately she'd melted in his arms. No way she could've faked that kind of attraction.

"Gotta see the bathroom first. No stand-up shower is a deal breaker." He peeked into the large bedroom, pleased with the size; then he poked his head in the bathroom. "Oh, yeah. This'll do nicely."

A large vanity gave him plenty of room for his stuff. The subway tiles in the shower had to have taken forever to arrange into the intricate herringbone pattern. Hell, this basement would probably be the nicest place he'd ever call home, even if he lived to be ninety. At that moment, he made himself a promise that if he did decide to stay in Cloverleaf, he'd find a way to get enough money scraped together to have Robert Ashford build a house for him.

"I'm ready to move in right now," he announced.

"Nate, I'm not sure—"

"Wait. Before you say anything...there's something important I have to do."

"What's that?"

"Time for some major league begging."

"Begging?" Her brows knit.

He loved keeping her off balance. "Yeah, begging. Shameful, pitiful begging. This place is amazing. If I have to go back to that long-term hotel after having this carrot dangled in front of me, I'll just curl up into a ball and die."

The confusion on her face morphed into a smile. "That bad, huh?"

"The ninth circle of hell."

"The ninth? Wow. That's pretty bad."

"Really bad. Have I mentioned the noise?"

"Nate..."

Getting down on one knee, he clasped his hands. "Or the smell?" He raised his hands as if seeking divine intervention. "Dear God, the smell!" When she laughed, he knew he had her. He clasped his hands and held them to his chest. "Do I get this gorgeous basement as my new home?"

"I should be 'deaf to pleading and excuses. Nor tears nor prayers shall purchase.'"

It was his turn to laugh as he got to his feet. "What if I told you that women who quote Shakespeare make me hot?"

"I'll have to reconsider letting you have my basement."

"Then women who quote Shakespeare no longer make me hot."

"Good." Dani glanced around her basement. "So you'll take it?"

"Oh, yeah," Nate replied.

* * *

Although Dani was happy, she was also terrified. "I haven't even told you the rent yet."

"Can't be any worse than the long-term place. Trust me, this is a huge step up in my world." His smile slowly bowed to a frown, but the spark of humor remained in his eyes. "There's only one problem that I see."

How easy it would be to become accustomed to the way he loved to tease her. "Problem? Hmmm…" She deliberately waited a few moments. "Sorry. I can't think of a single problem…besides having to use the upstairs kitchen from time to time."

"It's not that."

Although she would probably regret asking, she did anyway. "Then what's the problem?"

Nate grabbed her wrist and tugged her toward him hard enough she ran right into his chest. He slipped his arms around her waist, giving her little choice on what to do with her arms—either shove him away with them or loop them around his neck.

Dani chose the latter.

"The problem is"—he kissed her nose—"I won't be able to keep my hands off you."

Before she could say a word, his mouth was on hers.

She'd almost forgotten how wonderful his lips felt pressed against hers, how much those lips could make fire shoot through every limb. And when his tongue tickled the seam of her lips, she stopped thinking and tried to just…feel.

Her heart hammered a rough beat as her tongue rubbed against his. No man had ever made her so hot so quickly. Her breasts tingled as her nipples tightened, and her core throbbed with want.

The kiss ended only long enough for her to catch a breath. At least her pride was saved since Nate panted for air as well. Then his mouth was on hers again, his tongue probing and teasing and raising her desire to a fever pitch.

Dani couldn't stop a soft moan when he slid his hands down to cup her backside and pulled her pelvis hard against his, letting her feel his erection.

Nate kissed his way across her cheek and traced the ridges of her ear with his tongue before burying his lips against the sensitive skin of her neck. Each little nip and soothing lick sent her head whirling.

"I want you, Dani," he whispered, his voice ragged and full of need.

Good sense came back in a flood that felt like being dunked in cold water. "Stop."

Easing back, he knit his brows and stared down at her. "What's wrong?"

"J-just stop." She put her hands against his chest and pushed.

He only resisted for a heartbeat or two before releasing her. "I don't understand."

With trembling legs, Dani made her way to the stairs. "We can't do this again, Nate."

"Are you saying you don't want me?"

She let out a sad little snort. "Of course I want you."

"And you know I want you. So what's the problem?"

"Problem? Try *problems*."

"You're still stuck on the you're-my-boss crap?"

"It's not crap!" Fisting her hands to keep from shouting, she tried to explain her tumbling emotions. "I *am* your boss. I'd think that growing up with a teacher would've ingrained the teaching hierarchy in you."

He shrugged. "Department head really isn't that big a deal. You know it, and I know it. I sure didn't see any rules about teachers being forbidden from dating other teachers. Aren't there even some married couples teaching at Douglas?"

He had her there. "There are. And you're right; there's no rule against it. But there is common sense. You're new, Nate. The first two years are probationary. You don't want to give them any reason to look at you too hard. Sure, being department head isn't a big deal, but it's important to *me*. I want to move up in the world, hopefully be a principal one day. You think the school board would approve me for any administrative job if I got involved with someone under my supervision?"

Nate's lips thinned to a tight line.

"And you and I both know that there's also a difference in our ages, and not just a year or two."

"Not enough to matter to me," he insisted.

"It's eight years, Nate. That's a lot in my book."

The frustration of desire unquenched was bad enough, but now she had to deal with something she wasn't at all used to.

Self-pity.

Dani folded her arms under her breasts. "I don't want to fight about this anymore."

"We're not fighting," he said. "We're ... *discussing*."

"We're *fighting*," she insisted. "Which is exactly why we can't do this. We have to work together, and now we have to live together. It's better if we don't complicate things. Okay?"

He reached his hand out. "Dani, please."

"I mean it. We can't do this. Not now. Not ever."

Nate heaved a sigh before he gave her a curt nod. "Fine. We'll do it your way. I'll be nothing but your colleague and your tenant. Happy now?"

Dani nodded, glad she'd won.

So why did she feel like crying?

Chapter 8

The next Saturday, Dani stepped out on her porch, cradling her cup of coffee between her hands. It was moving day for Nate, and she was worried about meeting his brother.

A blue pickup was backing into the driveway as he signaled directions to the driver. A walnut bedroom set, a thick mattress, and a box spring were piled in the truck bed. Since the basement was furnished in every room but the bedroom, those items would be all he would need to settle in.

"That's it!" Nate smiled as he hopped up the porch steps. "Do I need a key?" His smile was better than caffeine to perk her up. "Or did you leave the door open?"

"No key needed this time," she replied. "But I do have your spare. It's sitting on the kitchen island with the garage door remote. There's a Post-it note on it with the keypad code."

A brunette with short, stylish hair exited the passenger side of the pickup while a tall blond guy jumped out of the driver's side. The man looked like Nate with glasses, which meant he had to be his brother. She blinked, trying to clear her sleep-fogged brain so she could remember his name.

Patrick.

At least she wasn't so old her memory was starting to go.

The woman came to join Dani and Nate on the porch while Patrick popped open the truck's tailgate.

"You must be Nate's mom." Dani smiled, not sure whether she should shake the woman's hand. Since she hadn't known his mother was coming, she wasn't at all prepared for what to say.

"Guilty," the woman replied, returning the smile. "I'm Jackie Brennan. You must be Danielle."

"Guilty," Dani echoed. "Would you like a cup of coffee?"

"Oh, hell yeah." Jackie nodded toward the truck. "Nate, go help your brother." Then she glanced to Dani. "Where's the door to the apartment?"

Having no idea what Nate had told his mother about the basement suite, Dani could only reply honestly. Thankfully, he beat her to the punch.

"There isn't a separate entry, Mom. We can just carry stuff through the front door." Directing his attention to Dani, he added, "We brought extra rugs to put on the floor to protect it."

"Thanks, but there's no need," Dani replied. "Robert brought over shrink wrap that movers use about half an hour ago. It's ready to go."

Damn. Now Jackie probably thought that she was OCD about her home. She was, but she didn't want to start off on the wrong foot with Nate's mother.

"Good thinking." Jackie's tone seemed genuine. "Now, about that coffee…"

Relieved yet still nervous, Dani led Jackie to her kitchen. After setting down her own mug, she grabbed another from the cabinet and filled it. She slid it in front of Jackie, who'd taken a seat on one of the barstools that pulled up to the kitchen island.

Dani put the ceramic container with sweetener closer to her guest. "Would you rather have sugar?"

"No, the pink stuff's great." Tearing two packets open, Jackie let the white powder sluice into her mug. "Do you have any half-and-half?"

"Can't drink coffee without it." Dani retrieved the carton from the refrigerator and set it next to the sweeteners. She also fetched a clean spoon. "Can I get you some breakfast? I have cereal. There's oatmeal or—"

Jackie waved the question away. "Thanks, but no. Patrick and I stopped on the drive over. The coffee's great, though."

Silence reigned between them until Jackie had taken a few sips of her drink. Cradling her cup much the same way Dani did, Jackie let her gaze bore through Dani. "So you're Nate's boss?"

"I'm his department head. You were a teacher, right?"

Jackie nodded. "I have to admit, I'm a little…concerned."

Cocking her head, Dani set her nearly empty mug aside. "Concerned? Why?"

"This is Nate's first job."

"And?"

"I don't want him living with you if you're going to be thinking about him as an employee while he's here."

Unsure of what Jackie was implying, Dani had to ask, "Are you telling me Nate is different in his personal life than at school? Should I be worried about noisy parties or—"

Another wave of Jackie's hand dismissed the thought. "No. No. Nothing like that. I just know how hard that first year of teaching can be. I want him to have a place he can relax and not worry about keeping on that 'teacher mask.' Make sense?"

This, Dani understood. "Yep. Sure does. He can be himself here. No worries."

"If he has to see you every single time he comes home…" The thought was left hanging in the air.

Part of Dani wanted to reply with typical sarcasm. *He can't see me if I'm upstairs. Or doing laundry. Or out in the yard. Or plain not home.* But it probably wasn't a good thing to piss off Nate's mom when they'd just met. "I'm sure we'll learn to give each other space. Nate didn't seem to mind that there isn't a kitchen in the basement."

Jackie's eyes flew wide. "Wait…what?"

"The suite doesn't have a full kitchen, but—"

"He won't have a kitchen?" Jackie hopped off the barstool and hurried away, leaving her barely touched cup of coffee behind. "Please excuse me, but I need to talk to Nate."

She was out the door before Dani could explain.

Great. It only took two short minutes to make Jackie Brennan hate me.

* * *

"Uh-oh. Here comes trouble."

Nate was trying to hold on to the dresser and had absolutely no idea what had made Patrick stop and issue that warning. While he stood on the driveway, Patrick was supposed to be lifting the other end down off the truck. As it was, it seemed like Nate was bearing all the weight. "C'mon, Pat. I don't have time for teasing. This sucker's heavy. Let's get it out of the truck."

"Nathaniel, may I have a word with you?" From the volume of his mother's question, she had to be standing right behind him.

Not that he could see her. His cheek was pressed against the dresser as he held up his end. "A little busy, Mom."

"There's no kitchen?"

"Mom...kinda busy here." At least she held the door open for him. When he and Patrick reached the basement door, Nate said, "Need a breather, Pat. Put it down for a second."

"Sure thing."

Once Nate had a moment to rest his arms and gather his thoughts, he finally turned to his mother. "There's a kitchenette. It'll be fine."

Patrick snorted. "Like Mom would know whether it's a good kitchen or not. We all know she can't cook to save her life. Have you forgotten the first Thanksgiving with Mark?"

A smile spread over Nate's face. "Forget that fiasco? Never."

"What happened?" Dani asked.

Since he hadn't seen her come up behind him, he jumped at her question.

Her hand settled gently on his arm for a quick moment, and she offered him a sweet smile. "I didn't mean to scare you."

He tossed her a wink in return. "No worries."

"So tell me about Thanksgiving."

Jackie folded her arms under her breasts as her eyes shot daggers at her sons. "Hasn't that story grown stale by now?"

"Not in the least," Patrick replied before glancing at Dani. "She set the turkey on fire. Nate had to jerk the smoke detector off the wall to get it to stop blaring at us."

"We ended up eating side dishes for Thanksgiving dinner," Nate added. "And my stepfather wasn't even scared away by it. He actually proposed to her that day."

"The man's obviously a glutton for punishment," Patrick said before Jackie playfully punched his upper arm.

Had his mother not been standing right there, Nate had no doubt that Dani would have burst out laughing. As it was, she was pursing her lips tightly, and her eyes were bright. In the time he'd spent with her, he'd enjoyed her sense of humor. Hopefully his mother would learn to enjoy it as well, because he planned on seeing exactly where his attraction to Dani might lead.

He just had to convince Dani to give him a chance first.

"We should get this downstairs so we can get the bed next," Nate said. "I need a place to sleep tonight that doesn't have as many lumps as Mom's mashed potatoes."

Jackie let out an indignant gasp. "Who decided this was pick-on-Jackie day?"

"Didn't you hear?" Patrick asked, tossing a wink to Dani. "Congress passed a resolution that every Saturday is pick-on-Jackie day!" He hefted up his end of the dresser. "Let's go. You're slacking, little brother."

With a grunt, Nate lifted his end. At least the dresser was the only truly heavy piece of furniture. The rest would be easy. Not that there was a lot to move anyway. The basement had great furniture, and he almost felt guilty that he was going to be the one to break it all in.

There had been a small quarrel between him and Dani over the rent. What she'd proposed had seemed ludicrously low, and Nate, wanting to be fair, told her what he thought he should pay. They finally settled on a price somewhere near the middle.

He was getting the better end of the deal, and he damn well knew it. He also appreciated that she clearly remembered how difficult it was living on a first-year-teacher's salary. The price was more than reasonable, especially for a furnished suite in such a great house.

After they set the dresser in the bedroom, Nate waited while Patrick bounded back up the stairs. His mother stayed downstairs, a familiar expression fixed on her face that said she needed to dispense what she always thought was worldly wisdom. Nate would let her have her say; then he'd probably set her opinion aside.

Although Jackie Brennan was a very intelligent woman, she often let that intelligence get overrun by her emotions, especially where her sons were concerned. What she had to remember was that Nate and Patrick weren't children anymore. It was no longer necessary for her to protect them; she needed to let go.

"You really think this is a good idea, Nate?" his mother asked.

At least Dani had remained upstairs and didn't have to hear the worry in Jackie's voice. He sure didn't want her to think his mother's concern was personal. "Yes, Mom, I do. A *very* good idea. I'll be able to save enough money to consider buying a house in the near future instead of pouring money down the crapper of some shitty apartment or rental house."

"I know that extended-stay hotel wasn't great, but there have to be other alternatives."

"You do realize how small Cloverleaf is, don't you?" he asked.

"Of course I do."

"Then you know why I made this choice. The only decent apartment complexes have six-month-plus waiting lists because of the Barrett Foods factory bringing in so many new employees."

"What about a house?"

He shook his head. "I'm not discussing this anymore. I made my decision."

"You don't even have a kitchen."

Grabbing her shoulders, he turned her toward the kitchenette. "Sure I do." Instead of keeping up the verbal fencing, Nate cut to the chase. "What's the real reason you're against this move?"

Jackie crossed her arms under her breasts. "She's your boss."

"So what? It's not that unusual to rent an apartment from

someone you work for. Didn't Patrick and Caroline live in his supervisor's rental house?"

"Well, yeah, but—"

"You worry too much, Mom. This will be fine. No, *more* than fine. This will be perfect for me." He put his hand on his mother's shoulder. "I mean it. Perfect."

Jackie thought it over a long time before she spoke again. "You like her, don't you?"

Seeing no reason to deny it, Nate nodded.

"I just worry about you. You had such a bad time after Kat."

"Of course I had a bad time after Kat. We lost a baby together."

"I know that was rough, but I'm not talking about the baby. I'm talking about how horribly sad you were when you two broke off the engagement. I don't want to see you go through something like that again. That's all."

While he loved that she cared enough to be concerned, he also needed her to ease up and let him live his life. "Relationships don't come with guarantees."

She rolled her eyes. "Don't I know it."

Nate squeezed her shoulder. "Spit it out, Mom. Quit beating around the bush."

"Fine. She's older than you are. A lot, judging from her being department head."

"Yep. She is."

Why did she always have to look so shocked when he was honest? "I mean…she doesn't look *that* old. But she's got to be well into her thirties if she's chairing the English department."

Whistling a happy tune, Patrick came down the stairs carrying the nightstand.

When Nate recognized the song, he leveled a frown at his mother. "For God's sake, what did you tell him?"

Her brows knit. "What are you talking about?"

"He's whistling 'Mrs. Robinson.'"

"Sure am," Patrick said as he walked past them to put the nightstand in a corner. "Quite a cougar you've got there, bro." With a grin, he started singing, "*'And here's to you, Mrs. Robinson...'*"

Jackie frowned. "I can't help believing this is a big mistake."

"Seriously?" Nate dropped his hands to his hips, wanting to shout at her, yet knowing he couldn't. Not only would Dani hear, but also Jackie was his mother and deserved his respect. That didn't mean he wasn't going to set her straight, though. "First of all, I'll remind you it's *my* life."

"I know that," she snapped.

"Do you? 'Cause it sure doesn't feel like you're letting me live it." His stance relaxed, as did his anger. "Second of all, she's really not that much older. Even if she were, none of this really even matters. We haven't even been on a date yet. How about you relax and just wait and see what—if anything—happens?"

Jackie closed her eyes and took a deep breath. "I'm sorry, Nate. You're right. It is your life. I shouldn't be sticking my nose into your love life. Sometimes it's so hard to remember that you and Patrick aren't kids anymore."

She sounded forlorn, so he gathered her into his arms and gave her a hug. "It's okay. You're only looking out for me." After she hugged him back, he turned her loose.

"I'm going to go finish the coffee Dani got for me. You can get your bed put together and get some clean sheets on it." As she trotted up the stairs, she passed Dani, who was on the way down.

"Want some coffee?" Dani held out a travel cup. "Just sugar, right?"

Nate took the cup and sipped the drink. "Perfect. Thanks, Dani."

She cast a glance back toward the stairs. "What's up with your mother? She doesn't seem to like me much."

"It's not you. Not really. She's just a little overprotective."

Although Dani didn't look at all convinced, she nodded. Turning on her heel, she tried to take a step away.

Snaking a hand around her upper arm, Nate stopped her. "So after we get everything set up, do you wanna…maybe go out for a bite to eat?"

"With your family?"

"I imagine they'll want to get back on the road soon."

At least she thought it over before she shook her head. Then she softened the blow. "How about I fix us something here instead?"

"Sounds like heaven."

Chapter 9

Dani was slicing a zucchini when Nate came through the basement door. *His* door. It was sure going to take some time for her to get used to seeing him move so freely around her house.

"Brought some music," he said as he headed into the great room. "Is that okay?"

"Sure. Is it on an MP3?" she asked.

"Yep."

"Then use my sound system. It's on the shelf just to the left of the TV."

"Saw it earlier."

All she could see was his back as he fiddled with her equipment. He'd dressed casually—a polo and khaki shorts.

She'd chosen an outfit every bit as relaxed. This wasn't a date, she had to remind herself. They were only sharing a meal, something they'd probably be doing from time to time. The tone needed to be companionable, not romantic.

"This setup is amazing," Nate said.

"My dad got it for me."

The elaborate entertainment equipment had been a gift from

her father, but as always there was guilt attached. When the house was finally finished, her parents had come all the way from California to see it and brought along the present of cutting-edge technology. Of course, Dad had to comment on how he'd originally planned on buying her everything she and the husband she really didn't need would require when they started a family.

Could've used this money for the perfect nursery, Dani-girl, he'd said, as though buying something solely for her was a waste of his hard-earned cash. It wasn't as though he didn't have plenty to spare, so why the guilt trip?

Accustomed to her father's snark, Dani had reacted in her usual way. She'd let his criticism slide. He loved her. But being his only child put a lot of pressure on her to be what he wanted her to be.

Her mother never pressured her to settle down and have babies, probably because she knew her daughter well enough to understand that Dani was exactly like her father and couldn't be nagged or bullied into doing something she simply didn't want to do.

"This is an amazing sound system," Nate said a moment before strains of "My Girl" filled the house.

Quirking a brow, she asked, "Motown fan?"

"Hell yeah." He joined her at the island and planted his palms on the granite surface. "What can I do to help? Or are you a cook who prefers working solo?"

"Feel free to jump right in. I'm going to sauté some vegetables to go with the chicken. I tossed that in the oven not too long ago." She picked up her cutting board and slid the slices of zucchini into a bowl. "I think I'll add some yellow squash if you like it."

"Yep," he said with a charming grin. "Never met a vegetable I didn't enjoy." A thoughtful tilt of his head. "Unless jalapeños are vegetables. Can't stand those." He picked up the bottle of salad dressing. "Planning a salad? Can I help with that?"

"Sure. Grab the romaine from the fridge. You can wash it and rip it up."

The man sure made himself at home quickly. Moving around her kitchen, he acted as though he'd always cooked there, not even tossing her awkward questions. He seemed to instinctively know where everything from the colander to the knives waited.

"Big or little?" Nate held up the freshly washed head of lettuce.

"Pardon?"

"Big or little pieces of lettuce?"

"Oh…little."

That damned dimple…"A woman after my heart. I can't stand huge pieces of lettuce in my salad. I always end up feeling stupid when I stab one with my fork and then try to open my mouth wide enough to shove it in without looking like a baby bird that's expecting to be fed." He got right to work.

Accustomed to the Ladies' husbands rather reserved natures, Dani enjoyed Nate's tendency toward the same kind of companionable silence. When he did have something to say, it was succinct. A few words about school or about his students. Dani kept working on supper, finding herself smiling at the humor Nate tended to toss into his dialogue. She loved his voice, a light tenor that would make him a great audiobook narrator. Eager young women would flock to that voice.

Young.

Was she ever going to get past him being younger? Why couldn't she look at Nate as just a guy?

She'd heard Patrick's teasing that morning, calling her "Mrs. Robinson." While he'd only been kidding, the implication had been crystal clear. Dani was too old for Nate. End of story.

As "Tears of a Clown" poured out of the speakers, Nate started singing along. After only a few lines, she stopped working on the food and watched him.

In rhythm with the beat, he prepared their salads, stopping every now and then to add a spin or a couple of dance steps. When he glanced over to catch her staring, he didn't blush. And he didn't stop. Instead, he picked up the pepper grinder and sang into it as if it were a microphone.

"You've got a great voice," she commented when the song ended, replaced with "You Can't Hurry Love."

He went right back to work. "Thanks."

"No, I mean a *really* great voice. Hasn't anyone told you that?"

"My choir teacher. My dad." His eyes caught hers. "Don't be so serious. It's not like I'm ready for *American Idol* or anything." He shrugged. "I just like to sing."

"Well you do it very well."

Eyes bright with humor, he said, "Does that mean if I want to woo you I should sing to you?"

"Woo?" She let out a giggle. "Did you honestly just say 'woo'?"

"I know. It's old-fashioned. Everyone tells me I should've been born in another era. Kat used to—" He never finished the thought.

Kat. Dani had heard that name from him more than once, and it was a name his mother had whispered that morning. Kat was a woman who obviously meant something to Nate, probably even a great deal.

"Kat used to what?"

"Nothing. Hey, got any cucumbers?"

"Bottom drawer of the fridge," Dani replied. "So I take it Kat is a closed subject?"

Nate fetched the cucumber and set it next to the rest of the salad fixings. "She's not necessarily a closed subject, only one I'm ready to leave behind me."

Dani got the message loud and clear, so she dropped the subject…for now. They worked together as he hummed along to a couple more Motown songs. She even joined in when he sang the last one—until the oven timer let loose with its annoying tone.

"Want me to grab the chicken?" he asked.

Since he was already pulling on an oven mitt, she nodded. Then she turned off the burner and set the pan with the vegetables aside. "Do we go formal and put everything on platters? Or keep it simple and fill our plates from the pans?"

"Pans. Definitely. Less cleanup."

* * *

Nate had never felt as relaxed around a woman as he did spending time with Dani.

After supper, she'd suggested they walk the community trail to downtown Cloverleaf and get some frozen yogurt for dessert. He loved that her home was less than a mile from the quaint older part of the town. The evening was warm, and the stars were just beginning to dot the sky as they strolled along the paved trail. A light breeze ruffled her bangs, and she brushed them back with her long, slender fingers.

"You never finished your story about Kat," Dani said.

He'd wondered when or even if she'd get around to asking.

"Ah, yes. The infamous Kat. Sure you want to hear it? I mean, it is a rather sad tale."

"If it makes you uncomfortable…"

"No, it's fine." And it was. Talking about his dead-and-gone relationship no longer caused him pain. A good sign that he was ready for a new woman in his life. "We dated for a few months after Mom and Mark got married that Christmas. Then…" He rubbed his hands over his face, a little embarrassed at his immaturity. "Kat and I weren't as careful as we should have been. I mean, don't get me wrong. Most of the time we used condoms. One night one broke and…"

"There are a lot of oops babies in the world. Don't think you're in that boat all alone."

"I know. The memory bugs me mostly because I see how stupid we were sometimes."

Her laughter eased his awkwardness. "Weren't we all at that age?"

"I asked her to marry me, wanting to do the right thing."

"You didn't love her?"

That question required a little thought. "I did—in a nineteen-year-old's way. We got engaged, but we didn't tell our parents. It seemed romantic at the time, keeping it just between the two of us."

"You were only nineteen?"

He nodded.

"Then quit sounding so embarrassed. At that age it probably *was* romantic. Everything is."

"Kat had a miscarriage."

She stopped and took his hand. "I'm sorry. That must've been difficult for both of you."

That spontaneous show of comfort pleased Nate immensely.

Dani had a soft heart, something she seemed to want to keep hidden, something she must've thought made her appear less than a strong, independent woman. But not with him. When she was with him, she seemed more open, more vulnerable. "It was difficult for me, not for Kat, though. She was…well, honestly, she was relieved."

"I don't know what to say to that."

Keeping a grip on her hand, he started walking again. He couldn't help but grin when she didn't pull away. "What is there to say? After that, Kat turned into a party girl. Now that I've got some time and distance, I think she was celebrating that she didn't have to instantly grow up like she would've if we'd had the baby. The relationship went downhill after that."

"How long were you together?"

"Almost another year, more out of habit than anything. I finally said enough was enough."

When the walking path met Main Street, she eased her hand away. "The yogurt shop is there." She pointed at one of the many historic buildings lining the street. "Jules and Connor live there." Her finger indicated a redbrick structure on the other side of the street.

WILSON REALTY was written in gilded letters across the largest window. "They live in their office?"

"The office is downstairs. They made a really nice home on the entire second floor."

They waited in line at the yogurt shop, neither saying much. Nate wasn't sure if Dani had grown quiet because of all the people around them or because she was upset over his reckless past.

After they purchased their cones, Dani led him back to the trail, and they walked in silence as they ate. It wasn't until they were almost back at the house that she spoke again.

"Do you need anything tonight? I mean like sheets or towels. I didn't figure you'd have time to unpack your stuff."

"I'm fine," he replied. "I really don't have all that much to unpack. I made the bed and unpacked my towels. That's all I need for tonight."

She punched the code on the garage door opener. "Feels kinda…weird." She led him to the door.

He reached around her to open it. "Ladies first."

"How about age before beauty?" she teased.

By the time they'd kicked off their shoes and left them on the mat in the mud room, Nate's curiosity got the better of him. "You didn't tell me what feels weird."

"Coming home like this. Together."

"Good weird or bad weird?"

At least he got her to smile. "I haven't decided yet."

It was time to part ways. This was the moment he'd known would be most awkward, and it didn't disappoint. What he wanted to do was drag her into his arms and kiss her senseless, but something told him that wouldn't be the right tack. He'd kissed her. Twice. But she still had reservations, especially about their ages, about her being his supervisor. Forcing the issue would only make her dig in her heels.

Despite the way she'd teased him about saying "woo," that was exactly what Dani would need. Wooing. Coaxing. A slow and easy courtship. Maybe then he could get past all the reticence she nurtured about the two of them.

They'd be good together. Nate had no doubt of that. Dani was everything Kat wasn't, and there was no way he'd let her slip away without at least giving a relationship a chance.

Age is only a stupid number.

Despite what he wanted, he gave her what she needed.

A kiss on the cheek.

"See you at breakfast." On that, he headed to his new basement home.

A quick glance before he shut the door made him smile.

Dani had laid her hand against her kissed cheek, a bemused smile on her face.

Chapter 10

Fancy meeting you here."

Dani had been bent over, hugging her knees as she stretched her hamstrings when Nate's cheerful voice greeted her. Straightening up fast enough that she got dizzy, she stared at him.

Dressed in a neon-yellow shirt, black shorts, and the brightest teal Nikes she'd ever seen, he looked ready to go for a nice jog. His heart-stopping grin and singsong voice made her frown. He was too damn chipper for this early in the morning.

While she'd already had her first cup of coffee, mostly because she couldn't even function without one, she always saved her second for after her run. Somehow it was easier to run when she wasn't entirely conscious.

"Wasn't sure what time you ran," he said. Then he lunged forward, stretching his leg.

"The earlier, the better." It was difficult to have a conversation when her brain wasn't quite awake. He'd been in her basement two weeks, and he suddenly wanted to run with her?

Why?

He switched to lunge with his other leg. "Hey. Me too. Boy, we've got a lot in common, don't we?"

"Not if you're a morning person. I don't even wake up until the second or third mile."

He let out a small chuckle. "Guilty as charged. Used to drive my mom crazy when I'd be up wanting breakfast on weekend mornings before the sun even rose." Nate planted his heel and straightened his leg to stretch out his calf. "How far do you usually go?"

"Not far. Four or five miles a couple of times a week. I save Sundays for my longer runs."

"Four or five is perfect. Just enough to get the muscles warmed up and the blood pumping." He worked on his other calf. "How far on this longer run of yours?"

"Usually eight. Sometimes I find a nice groove and go a little bit farther."

They continued stretching in quiet until Dani couldn't stand it any longer. What was it about Nate that unnerved her so much?

Was it the way he'd eased right into every aspect of her life? Was it that they shared so many interests? Was it that he was too handsome to ignore?

All of the above.

"You're going to run with me?" she asked, her voice rising to an anxious squeak. Running was her Zen, her chance to escape into her music, get into a zone, and just...*be.* How could she enjoy that if she was with Nate and worried about how sweaty she was getting or whether a fart slipped out once or twice?

"Well...yeah," he replied. "I figured you could show me some great routes." With a frown, he smacked the heel of his hand against his forehead. "Sorry."

Mind still reeling with the idea of him running alongside

her, she had no idea where that statement had come from. "For what?"

"When I was little, I had a bad habit of inviting myself places. If I wanted to play with some other kid, I'd trot right over to his house and talk myself inside. I'm doing the same thing to you now. If you prefer running alone…"

The way he hung his head as though the memory made him sad made her heart clench. "No, that's fine. We can go together."

"You don't have to say that just to be polite, Dani."

"It's okay, Nate. You're right. I can show you some good places to run."

Raking his fingers through his blond hair, he frowned. "No, I'm imposing. You want privacy, not the new guy in town tagging along like a puppy dog."

The forlorn tone of his voice and the image he'd invoked made her beckon him with a flip of her hand. "You're not imposing. C'mon. Let's get going before I wake up all the way and talk myself out of it. You'll have to forgive me if I need to listen to music."

"Running doesn't lend itself to great conversation." He pointed to the armband for his iPhone. "I have a great mix to help me keep my pace up."

With a brisk nod, she shoved her earbuds in her ears and headed for the trails.

A glance over her shoulder saw him mimicking her actions with his own headphones before he took off after her.

* * *

Smiling to himself, Nate fell into step with Dani. He truly had no shame. When he wanted something, he went for it. And right now he wanted to see where the connection he felt with this beautiful woman would lead.

Did she gravitate to the sport of running for the same reason he did—to be a part of a team without having to get too physically close to people?

He'd been too lanky for football, and the idea of getting stuck under a pile of sweaty bodies was about as appealing as grading six classes' worth of research papers. Baseball? Boring. Swinging a golf club felt unnatural.

So back in high school, he'd run cross-country. The sport appealed to him since he'd always been a bit of a loner. When he went to Indiana University, he'd kept running as a way to handle the stress of college—stress that had risen to a crescendo once he'd started dating Kat. She'd always thought of running as a waste of time and energy.

But Dani loved to run—just another thing that made her so appealing.

The woman was quick, her pace bordering on brutal. Nate had to push himself to keep up with her. After that fifth mile, he came close to stopping. Thankfully, a second wind kicked in, so he made it back to the house. Tomorrow, his muscles would be screaming.

Back in the driveway, he walked in circles, hands on his hips as he panted for breath.

"You okay?" She might not be as breathless as he was, but at least she sounded a little winded.

"Fine." With a groan, he gave in to the urge to flop onto the grass, spread eagle. "Fine for a guy who's having a heart attack."

Her laughter made him smile. She came closer, standing over him. "Need me to perform CPR?"

"Nah. But I'm fine with mouth-to-mouth, if you'd like to give it a whirl."

With a shake of her head, Dani stepped back. "Seems like you're breathing fine—a little fast, but fine. How about I make you breakfast instead?"

Getting back on his feet was more difficult than Nate had expected, and it was a bit humiliating that he had to take the hand she offered to help him up. He'd have to get in better shape if he was going to keep up with her. "Breakfast sounds great. Starting with coffee."

With a sparkle in her eye, she tossed last night's teasing back in his face. "Absolutely!"

* * *

Dani folded the omelet in half and set the spatula aside. "Cheese?"

"Sounds good," Nate replied. He took the full cup of coffee from the Keurig, set it aside, and popped a fresh canister in place. "Love these machines."

"Amen to that." She used the spatula to cut the omelet in half. "Hope you don't mind. I made one six-egg omelet for us to share."

"Mind?" He blew a raspberry. "You're making me breakfast. Why would I mind?"

After putting the half omelets on plates, she sprinkled shredded cheddar cheese over them. "Grab that coffee, and we'll eat right here." She dropped the plates in front of the barstools that pulled up to the island.

Nate set the coffee cups by the plates. "I'll grab the silverware."

With a nod, Dani took a seat on one of the stools and took the cutlery he held out to her.

They ate and sipped their coffee in companionable silence until he suddenly jumped off his chair. "I know what's missing!"

"Missing? What are you—"

After opening the refrigerator door, he snagged the bottle of ketchup. "This!"

"You're kidding, right?" There were lots of things that tasted great with ketchup, but eggs? That was a new one.

"Nope. Where ketchup is concerned, I'm always deadly serious." He popped the lid open and squirted a generous amount over his omelet.

Dani's first reaction was a near gag.

"You should try it," he insisted.

"I'll pass." She wrinkled her nose when he spread the ketchup around with his fork. "That looks so gross."

All he did was shrug and shovel his ketchup-coated food into his mouth.

They worked on cleanup side by side, and while Nate finished drying the last pan, Dani rinsed out the sink. "I need a shower; then I should get started on laundry." When it dawned on her they were sharing the washer and dryer now, she had to add, "Unless you were planning on using it."

"Nope. I finished my stuff up last night while you were out with the girls."

She whipped the dishtowel from his hand. "The *Ladies*. I'll throw this in the wash."

They stood facing each other, and she thought she should turn and walk away. There were things she needed to do, and staring at Nate Ryan too awfully long was playing with fire.

Dani wanted him. She was honest enough with herself to admit it. The way he'd made her feel when he'd kissed her haunted her each time she saw him, and it was getting harder and harder to keep from reaching for him.

Nate eased closer, and she mimicked his action until they were nearly toe-to-toe. He leaned in, his eyes searching hers.

He was going to kiss her, but he was giving her a chance to back away.

She wasn't going to. It was so easy to let him take the lead. Then she didn't have to feel bad about throwing herself at the man. No, *he* was the one in control; she was merely the target of his attention.

His face hovered over hers, making her catch and hold her breath. With a smile on her lips, she closed her eyes and waited for his kiss.

When his lips brushed her cheek, Dani opened her eyes, surprised and confused. He hadn't given her a real kiss since he moved in. Just chaste pecks on the cheek, and he was starting to frustrate the hell out of her.

Nate gave her a lopsided grin as he took a step back. "Not this time, Dani."

Embarrassment made heat bathe her face, and she found herself too flustered to say anything to his rather terse statement.

"You were waiting for *me* to kiss *you*. That's not how it's gonna be."

She found her voice. "What do you mean?"

After releasing a hefty sigh, he folded his arms over his chest. "I've made it pretty clear I'd like to get to know you better."

"Which is why I was going to let you kiss me again."

"I'm not going to lead this little dance anymore, not when I'm the only one with his feelings involved." He shook his head and headed to the basement door. "The next time we share a real kiss, you're going to have to be the one giving it."

The man had her too confused to do more than sputter.

"From the moment I met you, I've wanted to get to know you better," he said. "And not as a colleague. Not as a friend. As a man captivated by a woman who's not only beautiful but also funny and intelligent." When she tried to speak, Nate held up a hand. "But she's got it in her mind that he's too young for her and that she's his 'boss.'" He punctuated the last word with air quotes. "Silly notions, but until she gets past those and wants the same things he wants, the only kiss she's gonna get is on the cheek."

"But—"

"I'm here when you're ready, Dani. But only when *you're* really ready."

The door closed softly behind him.

Chapter 11

Ladies' Night Out.

It was usually Dani's favorite monthly event, especially when she and Beth met early to have some best friends' time. Even though they taught at the same school, their rooms were about as far apart as they could be and yet still be in the same building. Thankfully, they always met for their weekday lunches with Mallory—and often with Jules as well. Ladies' Night Out was still much more fun.

But not tonight.

Dani's thoughts kept drifting back to Nate, especially to the last thing he'd said to her.

…the only kiss she's gonna get is on the cheek.

What kind of guy said something like that?

"Dani?" Beth laid a hand on her arm. "What's wrong? You haven't said more than ten words since you got here, and those were mostly to order a drink."

Lifting her margarita, Dani gave a mock toast. "Which I need desperately." She took a sip before setting it back down and playing with the salt on the rim of the glass. "Sorry, you just became the designated driver."

"No worries," Beth replied. "It's my turn, and I honestly don't mind."

The waitress swept by their table to drop off their order of fried mozzarella sticks and two small plates. Dani really didn't have an appetite, but she picked up a plate and set it in front of her. Then she grabbed a stick and dropped it on the plate.

Beth picked one up, gingerly bit into the end, and then started fanning her mouth. "Too hot. Too hot." She set the stick on her plate as well. "You'd think I'd know better by now."

"He won't kiss me anymore," Dani blurted out.

A knowing smile filled Beth's face. "I assume we're talking about Nate, and the *anymore* tells me he's kissed you more than in the school supply closet."

Dani nodded.

"Spill!"

It felt good to tell Beth about the kisses she'd shared with Nate, even better to explain what had happened after their morning run, about how he simply wouldn't open his stubborn eyes and see that she wasn't the right woman for him.

"So?" Dani asked after she'd ended her tale.

"So...I think he's absolutely right. You're being silly." Beth waved at someone behind Dani. Before Dani could turn around, Beth said, "Mallory and Jules are here. Do you want them to know about all this kissing stuff?"

That question was pure Beth, always alert to anything that could possibly hurt someone's feelings. There were some things Dani could only share with her best friend, but if Beth couldn't understand the importance of her being Nate's boss as well as being older, maybe Mallory and Jules could.

With a sigh, Dani nodded. "We should include them. Maybe the three of you can help me figure out what to do."

"Do?" Beth let out a small laugh. "What you *do* is kiss the man!"

Mallory slid into the booth on Dani's side. "Kiss the man? Are we talking about Nate?"

Jules joined Beth on her side. "Who else would she be talking about?"

"The guy's too young for me," Dani insisted.

Damn, but she shouldn't even have to be dealing with Nate Ryan. She never should have let her friends goad her into offering the basement suite to him. If she and Nate only spent time together at school, she could resist that incredible smile, that tempting dimple. That absolutely sublime butt...

"I told you," Beth said. "You're being silly. Age doesn't matter."

Dani snorted. "Sure it does. And don't forget I'm his department head. People at school would have a field day with gossip." She adopted a deep, judgmental tone. "Look at that old lady with that young stud."

"Old woman my ass," Jules drawled. "You don't even look like you've hit your thirties. You and Nate would be great together. Two baby faces."

"He can't be that much younger anyway," Mallory said. "He said something about being in college for quite a while. What is he? Twenty-three? Twenty-four?"

"Twenty-four." Dani threw up her hands. "And I'm thirty-one. Hell, I'll be thirty-two next week. I'd look ridiculous with a twenty-four-year-old!"

The conversation stopped long enough for the waitress to take the Ladies' orders, and Dani sipped her margarita in hopes the topic would turn.

As if Beth would ever allow that. "Speaking of which...Are we doing the Crab Hut for your birthday? I could get the cake."

"It's a school night," Dani replied. "We can celebrate on the next Ladies' Night Out."

"Spoken like a true creature of habit," Jules teased. "Now... back to the topic of the good-looking hunk living in your basement—the one who's a mere eight years younger. Is he a good kisser?"

"Must be," Mallory said. "Otherwise she wouldn't be upset that he won't kiss her anymore. That is what you were talking about when we got here, right?"

Beth nodded. "He told her flat out that he liked her, but he said she'd have to kiss him first next time."

"Ball's in your court, then." Mallory glanced to her left. "Food. Thank heavens."

The waitress interrupted long enough to bring drinks and more appetizers, after which Mallory raised her cosmopolitan in a toast. "Here's to drinking just enough to trigger your libido and lower your inhibitions."

"Here, here!" Jules said before taking a sip of her appletini.

While Dani wanted to accept the age gap between her and Nate as easily as her friends did, she simply couldn't let it go. "You know, I can't believe you'd encourage me, Jules. If I did start something with Nate, we'd eventually break up. Then we'd have to keep working together. You used to be miserable at school whenever you saw your ex. Why would you want me to go through that, too?"

"I'll admit," Jules replied, "it's miserable to have to work with an ex. But you kinda have to *start* a relationship before you start worrying about how it *ends*. Nate seems like a nice guy, and he acts a helluva lot older than twenty-four. Connor likes him."

"So does Robert," Beth added.

"Mallory," Dani begged, "help me out here. Tell them it's ridiculous to go after Nate."

Mallory shook her head. "Ben thinks he's great. If you want him, you've got to let him know. What have you got to lose?"

"My pride. My self-respect."

"Your heart?" Beth smiled. "Look, we all know you're the most independent woman in the world. We get it. But you like this guy, Dani. You like him a lot. What would it hurt to kiss that toad and see if he becomes a prince?"

* * *

Ben swept his arm out to indicate the big basement. "Welcome to my man cave!"

"Thanks," Nate replied, still feeling a bit awkward.

Ben had dropped by the house as a favor to Dani to see whether it was possible to give Nate a dedicated entrance to the basement suite. Thankfully, his conclusion was that Nate would have to be stuck going in and out through the kitchen. Since Nate wanted nothing more than to spend more time with Dani, that answer suited him just fine.

Taking an empty chair, Nate was surprised to find all three men staring intently at him. He glanced down at himself and then knit his brows. "What's wrong? Do I have a stain on my shirt or something?"

Robert spoke first. "How are things going with Dani?"

"Why do you ask?"

"'Cause our women are worried," Connor replied. "If you're planning on getting serious, you'll realize pretty damn quick that when the Ladies are worried—especially about one of their tribe—everyone will hear about it."

"Especially us," Ben added.

Robert popped the top off his longneck beer. "Look, Nate... I imagine you think we're a bunch of meddling old women, but we all care about our wives and about Dani. We decided if we invited you to a night with the guys, we could figure out exactly how worried we should be."

"Gee. I thought we were just cheering for the Sox." Rubbing the back of his neck, Nate wondered how weird it would look if he simply got up and walked out. He'd never been a part of this type of friendly inquisition, especially about a woman. When he and Kat had told their families they were dating, any fireworks were dimmed by his mother's relationship with Kat's dad. Once Mark knew that Nate was serious about Kat, the only time the two men had spoken about the relationship was when Nate had to call to tell his mom and Mark that Kat was in the hospital because she'd miscarried the baby.

"You can stop looking like you're facing a firing squad," Ben said with a smirk. "We only want to know what's going on."

"If you all think I'm going to hurt her—"

Nate's words were cut off by Connor. "It's kinda stupid, I know. Dani is just... I don't know how to explain it."

"Wound too damn tight?" Robert offered.

"Yeah, she's that for sure, but I was thinking more... fragile," Connor replied.

Nate relaxed a little, realizing the men only cared about Dani's well-being. "She's both. If she were any more intense, you could put a lump of coal in her fist and by the time she finished squeezing it, you'd have a diamond."

The other men laughed, which eased a few more of Nate's worries.

"I think she likes to look strong," he continued. "But underneath she's…I don't know, but 'fragile' isn't the right word."

"Vulnerable," Robert said before taking a long pull of his beer. When Ben and Connor gaped at him, he said, "What?"

Connor grinned. "That was quite eloquent, my friend."

Robert laughed in response. "I can't take credit. It's Beth's word, not mine."

"Want a beer, Nate?" Ben asked. "The fridge behind you is stocked. There's a great microbrewery near the stadium, and I've got their autumn ale. Grab yourself a snack from the table, too."

With a nod, Nate helped himself to a beer and a bowl of fish-shaped cheese crackers before settling himself back in the recliner.

They watched a couple of innings without anything else being said about Dani. Thinking he might get through the night without any more brash questions, Nate had just put a couple of cheese fish in his mouth when Robert turned to him.

"Have you slept with Dani yet?" he asked.

Nate choked on the crackers.

Connor leaned over and slapped him between the shoulder blades as he glared at Robert. "I take back the eloquent comment."

Robert shrugged. "I made my wife a promise that I'd find out, and you know I never want to disappoint her."

With a bemused frown, Ben said, "Why not have Beth ask her, then?"

"Oh, don't worry. She will. I'm supposed to ask as insurance that she gets the truth from Dani."

Nate swigged his beer before addressing the original question. "Look, guys…I already told you, I care about Dani. Can't we leave it at that?"

All three men shook their heads.

With a heavy sigh, Nate raked his fingers through his hair. "You know, I've never really had this kind of talk with anyone before."

"You've never talked to anyone about sex?" Connor softened his incredulous tone with a grin.

"Actually, no. I haven't. At least not with other guys." How was he supposed to explain to them that he'd never really had friends to talk to?

As a kid, Nate had been almost painfully shy. He spent recesses by himself, usually reading, and lunches among the other kids had been agony. The only thing that kept him from being every bit as lonely at lunch as he was at recess was that the school had the kids sit in alphabetical order. Even then, no one ever talked to him. Nate Ryan was a skinny, geeky kid. That was all there was to it.

By middle school, he'd decided he could get by just fine without friends. Patrick was only a couple grades ahead of him, and if anyone picked on Nate, Pat would step in. The bullying stopped, but Nate really didn't have anyone he was close to; there were only classmates who probably forgot about him the moment the last bell rang.

At least in high school, he palled around with the academic team, finally finding people every bit as socially backward and geeky as he was. His height had shot up, he'd added some muscle, and he could finally blend in instead of stick out.

"Did I tell you guys why I decided to be a teacher?" Nate asked.

Ben cocked his head. "Are you trying to change the subject, or will this eventually lead back to you and Dani?"

"It'll lead back. I promise."

"No," Ben said. "You never told us why you chose teaching."

Robert let out a chuckle. "I figured it was the great pay, terrific hours, and constant praise."

The laughter eased Nate's discomfort. "I wanted to help kids who were like me."

Connor leaned back in his chair and cocked an arm over the back. "Meaning?"

"I was a nerd. A geek. A kid who never fit in and never made friends. I figured that if I taught, I could look for kids like me and help them not feel so...alone. That's why it's so weird for me to be talking to all of you about something as personal as my sex life."

Silence reigned for several awkward moments before Robert said, "You know, I was a nerd, too. The only reason I made it through middle school was because the shop teacher took me under his wing."

"My math teacher made school bearable," Connor added. "By high school, I was getting pretty good at basketball, so I suddenly had friends."

They all stared at Ben. "Sorry. No sob stories in my past. I had a lot of friends. But I do understand what it's like to feel left out."

Nate nodded. "That's why it's hard for me to talk to you guys about Dani. I'm just not used to sharing stuff with anyone—except maybe my brother."

"Well, then"—Connor clapped and rubbed his palms together—"time to get used to having people around, Nate. You're interested in one of the Ladies. You'll never be alone again."

Since that sounded more like a promise than a threat, Nate allowed himself to smile. "Thanks for inviting me."

"You're welcome," Ben said with a nod. "Now, about Dani…"

"I like her," Nate admitted. "A lot. But she's resisting my charms."

"That's our Dani," Robert said with a smirk. "Did any of you ever notice she always wears her hair up?"

Thinking about that, Nate nodded, as did the other men.

"That says something," Robert added. "At least according to Beth. She said Dani can't let her hair down. Ever."

Connor nodded again. "If anyone would know her best, it would be Beth."

"Which means I need to figure out how to get her to let her hair down—figuratively and literally." Nate's mind kept skipping back to his college psychology class, and although he wasn't sure why, something niggled at him. "A control freak."

"Pardon?" Ben asked.

"She's a control freak," Nate said a little louder. "A type A personality."

"Duh." Connor plucked a tortilla chip from his bowl and shoved it in his mouth.

Although the guys started talking about the baseball game, Nate had no interest at all because his mind was too consumed with Dani.

She was a neat freak. Whenever they cooked together, she was precise in measuring everything rather than just eyeballing the spices or ingredients. She even had a small scale to weigh the meat. On their runs, she checked her pulse and distance monitor constantly, adjusting her pace or lengthening her stride to some technological command. At school, she stayed late to grade papers on the day they were due, even if it meant working right through supper.

At home, there was never anything out of place. He could hear her running the vacuum at least twice a week, and when he went upstairs to get a snack, he'd find her dusting or straightening.

It wasn't normal.

"Nate?" Ben brought him back to reality.

Time to put these new friendships to good use. "Do you guys think Dani has OCD?"

Chapter 12

Dani didn't get home until after midnight, and she was really glad Beth had been designated driver. Most of the time she wasn't much of a drinker. Being sotted meant she said and did things she couldn't truly control, so she usually enjoyed a couple of margaritas and stopped. Tonight she'd had four, and she was feeling pretty damned relaxed.

Her frame of mind about Nate had shifted somewhere around the third drink. While she could probably blame the alcohol, the attitude change was more a product of the Ladies. They'd slowly and steadily knocked down the bricks in the walls Dani had built to protect herself from him. They'd used logic and played up her intellectual attraction instead of focusing on the physical pull. They'd talked about their own marriages, using their husbands as proof there were still good guys out there and that she might have just discovered one.

By the fourth margarita, Dani had been ready to go straight home and jump him.

"Hey." Nate sat up from where he'd been lying on the couch. He threw the crocheted afghan aside. "Sorry I fell asleep up here.

Once they get the satellite hooked up downstairs, I can watch stuff downstairs."

"I told you earlier, it's fine." She dropped her purse on one of the kitchen barstools. "I don't watch TV much anyway. Someone might as well get some use out of it."

On his feet, he folded the afghan and laid it over the back of the sofa. "Have a good time with the Ladies?"

"I did. Enjoy the baseball game?"

He stepped around to lean against the back of the sofa. "Yeah."

They stood glued to their spots and stared at each other. The air between them sizzled with anticipation as Dani silently talked herself into doing exactly what she wanted to do, which was to be in his embrace.

In the end, Nate met her in the middle. As she rushed to him, he gathered her into his arms.

"Why can't I keep my hands off you?" he asked.

"Probably for the same reason I'm gonna do this." Rising on tiptoes, she looped her arms around his neck and pressed her lips to his.

The heat rushing through her veins was incredible. What was it about this man that affected her far more than a pitcher of margaritas ever could? She quit trying to figure out the riddle of Nate Ryan and simply enjoyed him.

Before she could heighten the kiss, he let out a low growl and slipped his tongue into her mouth. She replied with a soft moan and rubbed her tongue across his. When she threaded her fingers through his short hair, she was surprised how soft it was.

He smelled so good, fresh and clean and masculine. She wanted to drown in his scent and his touch. Clutching at his shoulders, she leaned back against the kitchen island and let him rest his weight against her body.

* * *

Nate had never been a guy to question good luck, especially when that luck put Dani in his arms. Something—or perhaps someone—had helped her get past the roadblocks that had stood between them. If the Ladies had caused the change, he was going to send all three of them bouquets of roses and boxes of chocolates.

She tasted sweet, and a hint of lime was on her breath. Although she seemed relaxed, her speech wasn't slurred and she'd been steady on her feet. She wasn't drunk. Tipsy, maybe.

That thought caused him to pause. Ending the kiss, he eased back just enough to look at her.

Her lips were red, her eyes clear. A flush covered her cheeks, spreading down her neck.

Passion?

Or alcohol?

He closed his eyes for a moment and took a deep breath. When he opened them, she was smiling at him. All he wanted to do was kiss her again. "Dani…how much did you drink tonight?"

"Not much. A few margaritas."

"A few? How few?"

At least she didn't take a long time thinking about her answer. "Four. Pretty sure I stopped at four."

He had no idea if a woman her size could handle four margaritas, especially if the bartender used a heavy hand with the tequila. Despite the way his groin throbbed, he knew he couldn't take advantage of her. "I should head downstairs."

She fisted her hands in his shirt and pulled him into another heated kiss.

Dani made him so hot so damn fast, he knew when they

finally came together, it would be incredible. But he wasn't about to make an event that special become something she resented once her head cleared.

Nate let the kiss go on until he could dredge up the strength to finally bring it to an end. He loved that she followed him with her lips when he pulled back. "Oh, Dani. You have no idea how hard it's gonna be to go back to my apartment." He grabbed her wrists and gently eased her arms away from him.

She nibbled on her lower lip before she said, "You can come upstairs instead. If you want to…"

"I want to. I really, *really* want to." After brushing a quick kiss over her pouty lips, he hurried to the basement door. "But not tonight."

He passed through the door, shutting it quietly and hurrying down the stairs before he could change his mind. He almost tripped over his own big feet, making him laugh at the thought that he was going to end up breaking his neck because he'd been stupid enough to turn down sex with a woman he wanted desperately.

After getting ready for bed, he was still wound as tightly as a yo-yo. Lying on his lonely bed, he stared at the slowly rotating fan, wishing it could hypnotize him into a sound sleep. His thoughts were so full of Dani—of her taste, the scent of her perfume, and the feel of her body molded to his—that he couldn't turn off his brain. Or his body.

Nate gave serious thought to taking matters into his own hands before his mind caught on to a new topic. Back at the Carpenter house, he'd thought about all the odd things Dani did and had speculated whether she had OCD. Although the men hadn't gone out of their way to convince him that he was wrong, he did feel a little less like she might actually have obsessive-compulsive disorder.

Her habits might be extraordinarily neat, but the guys had made some great observations, pointing out that Dani was quite capable of letting go—if she had the proper motivation. Robert shared a story about how much fun she'd had when they were constructing the house. Evidently, she'd taken red paint and decorated the subfloor before the carpet was put in place. Whoever pulled up that carpet in the future would find what looked like a massive bloodstain and *Get out!* scrawled in huge letters.

Connor's story was about how Dani ran a race where people gave money to a charity by buying packets of colored powder to toss at the runners. Then she'd challenged all of her students to show up and pelt her with color. She'd spent quite a bit of the day looking as though she were wearing a rainbow.

Even Ben had shared a story about how Dani had been so exhausted from her housewarming party that she'd left the entire house a mess of dirty dishes and cups until she got a good night's sleep.

No one with OCD could tolerate one, let alone all three, of those events.

Nate might have convinced himself that she wasn't OCD, but she was a woman who kept far too tight a rein on herself, especially her emotions. If he was going to win her heart, he'd have to wage a battle to not only allow him in, but to get her to see and treat him as an equal. A very hard thing for a control freak.

How was a guy supposed to handle a woman like that?

Women like Dani needed a guy to be strong, to take the lead and show them that it was okay to let someone else be in charge. It was the only way to win her heart, and if he did, the prize would be more than worth the effort.

To make Dani his, he'd have to show her it was okay to let go.

* * *

Nate was already stretching the next morning when Dani came outside to run. "Good morning!" he called. "Ready to rock and roll?"

"Are you planning on running with me every day?"

He tried not to take offense to her disgruntled tone. "Pretty much. Unless I break a leg or something."

She came to stand right in front of him and folded her arms under her breasts. "Why are you doing this to me?"

"I beg your pardon?" When she rolled her eyes, he put his hands on his hips. "I'm not trying to be difficult, Dani. I honestly don't know what you're talking about."

Throwing her hands in the air she started pacing. "Yes, you do! You're driving me crazy! And you damn well know it!"

"I assure you. It's not on purpose."

She stopped long enough to stomp her foot. "See? There you go again."

Nate let out an exasperated sigh. "No. I honestly *don't* see. Can you stop fuming long enough to explain why you're so pissed at me? Last night, I thought things were good…or at least getting good."

"They're not good! They're confused! I mean, one minute you're acting like you want me; then you're back to this let's-just-act-like-friends stuff."

"You think I don't want you?"

"You walked away from me last night. I was ready to…" Her pale cheeks flushed red. "You know. And you turned me down. What the hell else am I supposed to think?"

Reminding himself it was time to take the lead, to show her she didn't have to always be the strong one or the one who made every decision, he caught her and pulled her into his arms. Then he kissed her soundly.

After easing back, he couldn't stop grinning as he stared down at the bemused expression on her face. "Do you still think I don't want you?"

"Then why didn't you go upstairs with me last night?" she asked, her voice barely a whisper.

"Because it wasn't the right time."

"Because I was drunk?"

Nate kissed her forehead. "You weren't drunk. A little tipsy maybe…"

Dani slid her arms around his waist and rubbed herself against his growing erection as she slipped her tongue into his mouth.

His response was passionate until he realized they were standing in the middle of the driveway. Making out in public was frowned upon in general. Two teachers passionately kissing— especially in such a small town—could equal getting fired.

Stepping back, he took deep breaths until he could regain control. Thankfully, it was cool enough this morning that he'd worn his sweats and not more-revealing running shorts. "How far today? I liked the path around the lake. We could—"

"Go upstairs. We could head upstairs and—"

He wouldn't let her continue. "No."

"Why?"

Nate raked his fingers through his hair. "Dani, I want you. I do. It's just…" A heavy sigh slipped out. "I've been down that road before—the sex before the relationship doesn't work. Let's get to know each other better first. Let's work on the relationship. The sex will come."

Dani snorted at him. "That's the worst pun I've ever heard."

At least he could chuckle, despite the seriousness of the conversation. "I meant what I said. I want us to be something more. Something other than just a couple of people who have sex and pretend they care about each other. I like you. I want to get to know you first. And I promise that if we take our time, the sex will only be better because of it." At least he hoped so. This was all too new to be sure.

She fisted her hands and closed her eyes.

"Why'd you change your mind?" he asked.

Her eyes flew open. "What?"

"Why'd you change your mind about having a relationship with me?"

Instead of a reasonable explanation, he got a shrug. "Can't we please just…do it? The waiting will drive me crazy."

So this wasn't about her softening toward him; this was about her calling the shots. "Oh, my dear Dani. You can't stand to let someone else have control. Can you?"

"Nate…"

"I'm going to make love to you."

She grabbed his hand and started dragging him toward the porch.

He planted his feet. "But not yet. Not until we have the relationship thing down first."

"You're serious?"

"Dead serious."

Her eyes searched his. "What do you want, Nate? What do you really want?"

"You. In every single way possible. Your mind. Your heart. Everything."

Chapter 13

Dani fiddled with her pretzels, not at all interested in eating. The Ladies sat with her at the lunch table, chuckling at her predicament. "I have no idea why you all think this is so damned funny."

"It *is* funny," Beth replied. "That man knows you too well."

"What's that supposed to mean?"

Jules let out a snort. "Oh, puhleeze. You are Miss Control Freak, and Nate knows it."

"And that's funny because…?"

"Because," Mallory said, "we love that he's not going to let you lead him around by the nose."

"Because," Beth said, "we think he's gonna be very, very good for you."

Jules popped open her soda. "Because it's about time you found a guy who can give you exactly what you need. And I don't mean an orgasm." She laughed before taking a sip.

Not sure whether she should scold her friends or simply stand up, grab her food, and walk out of the lunchroom, Dani just shook her head. "I thought you were my friends."

Beth put her hand over Dani's where it rested on the table. "We are your friends. That's why we're happy for you."

"You're happy for me? Nate turns me down flat and you're *happy* for me?" A few deep breaths didn't help ease her growing anger and frustration.

Mallory nodded. "Admit it, Dani. The guys you've dated have all been a bit…well…a bit accommodating."

"Meaning," Jules said, "that you could easily boss them around, and you were bored with every single one of them after three dates."

"You need a guy like Nate." After dipping her celery in her jar of peanut butter, Beth pointed it at Dani as if to emphasize her point. "Let him lead the dance. You might find out it's nice to have someone else call the shots for once."

Having her friends point out what Dani had tried so hard to ignore only made her angrier. "If I'm that bad, if I'm really that much of a control freak, then why are you all stupid enough to be friends with me?"

"Because you're a wonderful person," Beth replied. "Shoot, Dani, we all have faults."

"Especially where men are concerned," Jules said. "Friends don't let friends make huge mistakes and get in their own way. If all of you hadn't pointed out how stubborn I was being with Connor, I might've missed the best thing that ever happened to me."

Mallory nodded. "Same goes for me and Ben. The three of you did so much to make sure I understood how truly sorry he was for hurting me, and I'm grateful for it every single day."

"Dani," Beth said, her eyes growing misty, "you were the one who brought Robert to me when you knew I needed him most. Now it's our turn to help you and Nate. We're only telling you these things for your sake. Please don't think we're being mean."

"Far from it," Mallory said. "We love you, honey."

Jules nodded. "We really do."

"We want to help you because we see something good happening in your life," Beth added.

Jules tossed Dani a lopsided grin. "And we don't want you to screw things up for yourself like all three of us almost did."

* * *

The Ladies' advice clung to Dani for the remainder of the day. It was difficult to concentrate on teaching the intricacies of *Macbeth* when her thoughts were on Nate.

Her friends were absolutely right. Her need for controlling everything had gotten out of hand, and it had taken Nate to point it out and the Ladies to make sure Dani opened her eyes. Just recognizing how nitpicky she'd gotten about everything— from her house to her life—made her shake her head in disdain. It was a wonder they hadn't all demanded she go to her family doctor and get something to help with her anal-retentive nature.

She stayed late at school to finish grading essays, not in a hurry to face Nate. The biggest problem was that she had no idea how to change things. Her life was in a rut, each day nothing but a parody of the movie *Groundhog Day*. Same damned thing, day in and day out.

Sniffing back tears, she punched the garage door opener, wincing when she saw Nate's car. Not only had she endured her friends forcing her to open her eyes, but also Dani was sure Nate would continue to press his point.

Once she killed the engine, she sat in the car, wondering if there was any way at all to avoid her tenant. She just wasn't up to another round of the "What's Wrong with Dani's Life?" game.

Then her stomach growled. She'd been so upset at lunch, she'd barely eaten. Supper was already late and would be even later since she'd have to cook herself something. After flirting with driving straight to McDonald's, she settled on going inside, searching for something in the freezer, and tossing it in the microwave.

Heavenly aromas filled her nostrils the moment she stepped into the house. Spices mingled with the scent of roasting meat made her mouth water in anticipation. She kicked off her shoes, hung her tote on a hook, and peeked from the mudroom into the kitchen. "Nate?"

"Wait!" He smacked a wooden spoon against a pot, set it aside, and then hurried to her.

"Did you make supper?" she asked, feeling stupid the moment the question slipped out. "Duh. Of course you did. What—"

Nate stopped her with a kiss.

Dani surrendered, letting him hold her close as he lazily stroked her tongue with his. When he pulled back, she smiled up at him.

"Now…wait right here." He hurried back to the kitchen island and picked up a folded piece of black satin. "I've got something for you." He let the material drop, holding tight to an attached ribbon.

It was a blindfold.

Her first thought was that the man had lost his mind. "You're joking, right?"

"Joking? About something this important?" he scoffed. "Not in the least. Tonight you get your first lesson in trust."

Still concerned, she put her hands on her hips and tried to glare him out of the idea. "You really want me to be blind? That seems kinda mean."

He settled his hands on her shoulders, smiling down at her, blue eyes twinkling. "It's not meant to be mean, Dani. It's meant for you to surrender a little of that precious control of yours and learn that you can trust me."

The man was serious. Despite the grin, he was really serious. Panic bubbled inside her. "I'd be blind, Nate. I'll trip and fall and probably break a leg. I mean, I'm super clumsy and—"

Nate's smile dropped to a deep frown. "There's not a single thing about you that's clumsy. You're graceful and strong and you damn well know it. This is about you not trusting me enough to give me this one meal, this one night, to show you that I'd never let you get hurt."

His accusation hit her hard. Added to all the things the Ladies had said at lunch, the conclusion was obvious. Dani didn't trust Nate—at least not yet.

He was offering her a chance to change things. All she had to do was give in.

For once, she listened to her heart and not her head. "Fine." She closed her eyes. "We'll do it your way. So have at it. Blindfold me."

"Really?"

She opened her eyes so she could give him an exasperated glare. "Really. You want me to show I trust you by letting you lead me around like Stevie Wonder—"

His victorious grin was the last thing she saw before she closed her eyes again.

Nate gently put the black material over her eyes and tied the ribbons behind her head. "Too tight?"

"No," she replied, feeling a cross between fear and excitement when she realized the blindfold did an excellent job of blocking out everything. Not even a sliver of light could enter. "Now what?" It was no wonder that her voice quavered.

Her hearing seemed heightened, his shuffling footsteps telling her he'd moved behind her. His arms snaked around her waist and he pressed his front against her back. A moment before his lips brushed the sensitive skin of her neck, she felt his hot breath and inhaled the spicy scent of his cologne.

With a content sigh, she dropped her head to the side.

* * *

Nate hadn't expected her to surrender without a fight, but the resistance she'd given had been token at best. He nuzzled her soft skin as he brushed aside her silky hair and kissed and licked her long neck.

She shivered and let out a mewl.

Damn, she pleased him more than she could know. This wasn't easy for her, to give him the privilege of guiding her through their meal…and what he planned after. He wasn't about to disappoint her when she'd given him her tentative trust.

"Now what?" she asked in a whisper.

"Now, we enjoy dinner."

Moving in front of her, Nate took her hands in his and walked backward to lead her to the barstool he'd pulled out. He'd set their places at the bar, knowing if he fed her on the couch, he'd probably jump her before the meal ended. No, the kitchen was safer. For now.

"Up we go." Hands on her waist, he lifted her.

Dani's hands clutched his biceps, her grip tight enough to

reveal her fear. Yet she didn't let out a squeal, only allowed herself to be plopped onto the seat.

Nate turned her stool so she faced the bar. "Let me get our dinner ready."

She delicately sniffed the air. "Mmmm...it smells wonderful."

"Good. I spent quite a bit of time making some special things for you."

While he assembled their plates, she kept tossing out theories on what he'd prepared. He neither confirmed nor denied her guesses, enjoying her nervous chatter. He set their plates next to his barstool, poured two glasses of wine, and then took his seat.

"I'm gonna make a mess if I try to use a fork," Dani said.

Nate grabbed her wrists only a moment before she would have put her hands in the middle of her food. "No fork, baby. I'm going to feed you."

Her lips dropped to a frown. "I'm not a baby."

"That wasn't what I meant, and you know it."

"Oh, I *know* what you meant. It's you who doesn't get it, Nate. I'm not anyone's 'baby.' I'll never be anyone's 'baby.' Got it?"

This was a battle he was willing to lose, and he couldn't really blame her. The term did seem a bit demeaning now that he thought about it. "You win."

"Thanks for understanding."

"So what endearments am I allowed?" he asked.

She thought it over. "You know...I'm not sure."

"Well, then, no 'baby,' but the rest we'll just play by ear. Let me know if I hit on one you like." He picked up one of the small pieces of the appetizer. "Now open up. I made something unusual to start us off."

It wasn't a surprise when she didn't immediately comply. Dani was never going to be a woman who gave anyone, even someone who loved her, blind obedience. "I'm allergic to—"

"Pineapple. I know. I checked with Beth to be sure I didn't use anything you didn't like or might be allergic to."

She cocked her head. "That was very thoughtful."

He let out an exasperated sigh, one she'd heard often from many people.

She reached out for him. "That came out wrong. I just thought it was a little above and beyond what most men would've done."

His hand grasped hers. "I keep telling you, Dani, I'm not like most men."

Holding tight to him, she put her other hand on his arm, sliding it up to his shoulder and then his neck so she could finally brush her knuckles against his cheek. "Lesson learned."

He kissed her fingers and then put her hands back on her lap. Then he picked up the food again. "Open up, Dani. Trust me, you'll like this."

A few heartbeats passed before she opened her mouth.

Nate put a dainty piece of the appetizer in her mouth. She chewed, an appreciative hum coming from her lips.

"Is that Gorgonzola?" she asked after she'd swallowed.

"You've got a good palate. Here's another bite."

This time, she parted her lips without being asked.

Feeding Dani was so damned erotic. Each time she opened her mouth, Nate had to close his own eyes to block the sensual image. Her lips were so full, so sexy. Every now and then, her tongue would dart out to lick away bits of food from those lips or the corners of her mouth. Even imagining the things she could do to him with those lips and that tongue had his cock hard and aching.

She fawned over the portabella mushroom with the melted Gorgonzola, a dish his stepfather had taught him to prepare.

It was a good thing Mark was a good cook since Nate's mother could start a fire just by boiling water. Nate had taken to the skill, and now he enjoyed coming up with his own creations, some of which he now shared with Dani.

"That's amazing," she said after he fed her the first bite of the entrée. "Portabella mushrooms. Gorgonzola cheese. Filet mignon. You must've spent a month's salary on this dinner."

He'd probably spent more than he should have, but he wasn't about to tell her that. "Ah-ah-ah. You're not supposed to be worrying about anything tonight. Remember? Let me do the worrying for both of us."

His own appetite was forgotten as he focused on pleasing Dani, putting small bites of the food he'd lovingly prepared into her mouth and savoring each of her startled and appreciative expressions.

Dessert almost pushed him over the edge. Nate swiped his finger through the meringue on the coconut cream pie and then said, "Open your mouth, sweetheart."

She cocked an eyebrow. "Sweetheart?"

"You said you weren't anyone's 'baby.' Figured I'd try 'sweetheart' this time."

After a few seconds, she smiled. "That might work."

"Well, then...open up, sweetheart. I have a special treat."

A smile played over her lips before she slowly parted them.

Desire punched him in the gut so hard he let out a harsh breath.

"Are you okay?" Dani asked. "You sound like someone hit you."

"So your hearing's become more acute? Interesting."

"You didn't answer my question. Are you okay?"

"I'm fine. Now here's dessert."

She opened her mouth and let him put his meringue-covered index finger inside. Then her lips closed around it. Her hands rose to grab his wrist, and she started licking his finger like some sweet treat. It didn't take much imagination to picture her savoring his cock in the same manner.

With a seductive smile, she released his wrist. "More, please."

He'd had enough play; it was time to move to the main event before he gave in to his licentious thoughts, ripped off her blindfold, and carried her upstairs.

Without warning, Nate scooped Dani into his arms and carried her to the sofa. "Do you trust me?"

Although she had to think it over, he took no offense. This wasn't easy for her—that much was plain. She'd come so far in such a short time, but he meant to push her a little further.

He set her down and then sat at her side. "Time for the hard part."

Her lips bowed into a pouty frown. "Not sure I like the sound of *that*."

"I promised you, I won't hurt you. Do you trust me? Or…"

She turned to face him, her hands fumbling until she found his arm. "I trust you, Nate."

Taking her hand in his, he lifted it and brushed a kiss across her knuckles. "Then we get to play a little game."

Dani's hand trembled as she pulled back. "What happens in this little game?"

"We learn about each other."

* * *

Shivers ran over her skin, and heat pooled between her thighs, making Dani squirm with desire. How odd that she couldn't see a thing—his handsome face, that delectable dimple, or his charming smile—yet she wanted Nate with a bone-deep need.

The sound of his voice was tattooed on her brain; the scent of his cologne was branded on her heart. In her mind's eye, she could see his deep blue eyes, his blond hair, the lean muscles of his body…

That morning, he'd asked why. She knew damn well what he was asking, but she couldn't find the words to explain something she wasn't sure even she understood.

Why? Why was she ready to start exploring a connection with Nate? Because Nate had opened her eyes. Because the Ladies had opened her eyes. Because she started thinking of him as something other than one of the teachers in her department or her tenant or a younger man.

"For the first reward," he said, his voice deep with what she believed was yearning, "you need to tell me one thing that you've done that no one else knows."

Her heart started slamming in her chest as her brain scrambled for some lie that would make her look good in his eyes. "Um…I…I…"

Nate squeezed her hand. "No thinking about it. Just blurt it out. I want the truth, Dani. Not something you think I want to hear."

"Nate…"

His lips touched hers for a kiss far too brief for her tastes. "You open up to me, and I'll give with equal measure."

Why couldn't she believe him?

This trust stuff was the hardest thing she'd ever done, more difficult than losing her virginity or facing a classroom full of students for the first time. Both of those events seemed like a cake walk compared to having to bare her soul to Nate Ryan, to tell him things she'd never told anyone, even the Ladies.

Then she suddenly understood. She'd worn figurative masks

her whole life, especially in those earlier events, those events that had terrified her. She'd put on a face to show people only what she'd wanted them to see to hide her fear, her vulnerability. Instead of a frightened virgin, she'd revealed only confidence. Rather than show her students that she was intimidated by being a real teacher, she'd shown only a tough-as-nails leader. Now, because she feared Nate and the way her feelings for him were growing, she was still hiding behind the same kind of mask.

And that was why he'd chosen the black silk that now covered her eyes.

"Fine," Dani said, her voice full of conviction. "I sing show tunes in the shower. Every single time."

She could almost see the grin on his face as she enjoyed his warm chuckle.

"I *do*," she insisted. "And I'm absolutely tone-deaf, so I imagine it's unbearable for anyone to hear. I've never told anyone that."

His lips were suddenly on hers, and she quickly pushed aside the initial surprise and enjoyed the kiss. He took his time, leisurely stroking her mouth with his tongue, and when she tried to lean closer, he moved away.

She frowned. "That was my reward?"

"You didn't like it?"

"I didn't say that. I just told you a deep, dark secret, so I expected something…more."

He took her hands in his. "It was a secret, but hardly deep and dark."

"You promised equal measure," she couldn't help but point out. "So now tell me something you've never told anyone."

"Last night, you had me so wound up, I had to masturbate or I'd never have gotten any sleep."

When the man told a secret, he didn't hold back.

"And I thought about you the whole time," Nate added.

Her face felt as if it were on fire. "About me?"

He put her hand against his cheek and then nodded. "You were naked, by the way."

"How could you picture me naked when you've never seen me without clothes?"

"I have a *very* vivid imagination."

The heat spread down her neck, and she had trouble catching her breath.

"Tell me this, Dani," he coaxed. "Have you ever touched yourself while you thought about me?"

She wasn't about to answer *that* question. Shit, it would be easier to just strip off her clothes and stand there in the middle of her great room stark naked. Her body was easy to reveal; her secrets weren't. "Nate…"

In one quick move, she found herself sitting on his lap. He rubbed his chin against her forehead before he rained kisses over her face and down her neck, making her shiver in pleasure. His tongue tickled her collarbone. "Tell me, sweetheart. Did you want me as much as I wanted you?"

"Yes," she hissed.

"And did you touch yourself the way I had to touch myself to ease the ache?"

"Yes." Her dilemma had been every bit as bad as his, and had she not pulled out her trusty vibrator, she'd never have slept a wink.

Telling him hadn't been nearly as bad as she'd feared, but that didn't mean she could speak quite as brazenly in the future.

Or could she?

He nibbled lightly on the sensitive place where her neck met her shoulder. "That wasn't so hard, was it? To tell me the truth should never be hard."

"It *was* hard." Her voice was a whisper as tears stung her eyes.

Nate cupped her face in his hands and kissed her. "It'll get easier. In time. I promise."

Chapter 14

"That sounds so romantic." Beth let out a happy little sigh. "What happened next?"

Dani wasn't sure why she'd waited so long to talk to Beth after Nate had blindfolded her—almost two weeks of pretending everything was status quo through lunches that seemed interminable. When Beth had stopped by her classroom after her last class, Dani had finally found the words to talk to her best friend.

She'd been unnerved in a way that she wasn't sure she'd ever get used to. Nate was demanding a kind of intimacy that she'd never known before. Physical, she could handle. This emotional intimacy would be the death of her.

"Romantic?" Dani shook her head. "Try terrifying."

"It doesn't have to be terrifying," Beth insisted.

"But...but..." Throwing her hands up in frustration, Dani said, "He wants me to share everything."

Beth didn't appear at all fazed. In fact, she seemed hard pressed to suppress a grin. "And that's bad?"

"Bad? Shit, Beth. I don't even know if it's *possible*."

"It's quite possible, I assure you. I share so much with Robert. I think he knows me as well as you do. Maybe even better."

Dani knit her brows, having a difficult time understanding two people being that open with each other. "You don't have *any* secrets?"

"I didn't say that, but there isn't much I hide from him." Then Beth's cheeks grew ruddy. "Maybe there's one important thing…"

"I knew it! So tell me all about it."

Beth shook her head. "Not yet. But soon. I promise. Right after Robert, you'll be the first to know."

After rolling her eyes, Dani let out a sigh. "You can't tell me? Or Robert?"

"Nope."

"Then how in the hell can you expect me to bare my soul to Nate?"

"Do you like him? I mean really like him?"

"I…I think so." That wasn't the truth. Dani did like him. *Really* liked him. If she was going to start being open, perhaps she should begin with her best friend. "Yeah, I like him. Shoot, I might even be falling in love with the guy. And if that isn't stupid, I don't know what is."

Beth cocked her head. "Why would falling for Nate be stupid?"

"Because I'm his boss," Dani replied. "Because I'm a bunch of years older than he is." *And because I'm bound to get my heart broken.*

"Tell me this—how did you feel when he was feeding you?"

"That question is every bit as scary as the ones Nate was asking."

Beth's face lit with a smug smile. "Well, then, answering me will be good practice for dealing with him."

Although the question was frightening, coming up with the

answer was easy. All Dani had to do was work up the courage to say the words aloud.

"C'mon, Dani. What do you have to lose…except a guy who might be your Mr. Right?"

"Wonderful."

"Wonderful? Do you mean wonderful you could lose him?" Beth asked.

"No, I mean having him feed me felt…*wonderful*."

* * *

"Hey." Nate leaned back against the wall next to Dani.

"Hey." She'd grown accustomed to him popping out of his room most passing periods to help her keep an eye on the students as they dug through their lockers or palled around with their friends. Locker bank duty was one of her least favorite parts of teaching, but having Nate there made it bearable. The worst part of being out with the kids during their five free minutes between classes was watching the boyfriends and girlfriends who treated the end of each passing period as though they were parting for the rest of their lives.

"So Jim Reinhardt bullied me into chaperoning the homecoming dance. Wanna go with?" he asked.

"That's probably not a good idea."

"Why?"

"I'd rather play things low-key."

"What's wrong with a couple of fellow teachers chaperoning the dance together?"

Dani shrugged. "Probably nothing." Truth was that dances brought out the romantic in her, and she'd probably drag his ass out on the dance floor just so she could be in his arms.

"Good. Then it's a date. We can grab dinner first." Nate inclined his head at the principal working his way down the hall, dodging the kids and their hefty backpacks. "Wonder what's up?"

Jim stopped in front of them. "Dani, I need to ask a favor."

"Sure."

"I need more chaperones for the homecoming dance. Since you haven't done much this year…I hoped you'd take this one."

How like him to guilt her into something—although she had to admit guilt gave him a weapon to make sure all school activities were supervised. And he was right. She hadn't taken tickets at any sporting events or chaperoned any student events this school year. If she did Jim this favor, he might remember it when evaluations rolled around. "I'd be happy to."

Jim nodded at Nate. "Really enjoyed the class yesterday."

A grin bloomed on Nate's lips. "Thanks, Jim. I appreciate that."

"Keep up the good work." On that, Jim headed back down the hall.

Nate fixed his smile on her. "So about dinner before the dance…?"

She couldn't help but smile in return since Jim had all but sanctioned the two of them going to the dance together. She'd simply have to behave herself while they were there and show any gossips that there was nothing between them worth talking about. "Sounds great."

He pushed away from the wall and went to his classroom, stopping long enough to turn back and say, "And don't forget Friday. We're trying that new Italian place they opened downtown."

Damn if her face didn't flush hot when a couple of students heard him and kept shifting their gazes between her and Nate, smiles plastered on their faces. She pressed her finger to her lips, hoping he'd pick up the hint.

All he did was chuckle.

Chapter 15

Nate pulled Dani's chair back so she could stand. She murmured her thanks, but the smile she'd given him through dinner had vanished.

He held back a frustrated sigh. Everything with this woman was two steps forward, one step back. They'd connected so well that first night. She'd been open and honest, and he knew he'd reached a part of her she'd tried to hide.

After two weeks of letting things between them settle into a comfortable calm, he'd figured they should be comfortable enough to go on a dinner date. He was more than ready to try to push a little harder when they got back home. Throughout the meal, she'd been animated, sharing some stories from school and discussing how they should start dividing up the grocery bill now that they were both eating there so often. He tended to take most of his meals upstairs instead of using his kitchenette.

Dani's demeanor had changed the moment the check arrived. After the waiter set the black folder next to Nate, who'd planned on the meal being his treat, she'd argued, keeping her voice low and practically begging him to go Dutch. He'd stubbornly insisted and had let the waiter whisk away his money before she could try to add her own funds.

That was when she'd done the one-eighty. Now she was sullen and silent, and all he could think was that he'd somehow offended her. But how? Because he'd turned this dinner into a date by paying?

That made no sense.

Nate puzzled over Dani's temperament change the whole walk home. He'd made some plans, another exercise in trust that he hoped would please her as much as the meal she'd been fed while blindfolded and the intimate talk they'd had after. He feared that if he tried to press her tonight, she'd shut down entirely.

Hell, she'd already shut down.

Since they'd eaten in the new restaurant in the old town area, they walked home along one of the paths they liked to run. The October weather had taken a decidedly chilly turn, and he was about to button his jacket when it dawned on him that Dani hadn't worn one.

He doffed his. "Here. Wear my jacket."

She shook her head. "You'll get cold."

"I'm fine." Holding open the coat, he waited for her to comply.

"We're almost home," Dani insisted. "I'm fine."

"C'mon, sweetheart. You can't deprive a guy of the perfect chance to be gallant. Let me show you chivalry isn't dead."

"Thanks." She let him help her into the jacket.

Nate turned her so he could pull it shut and button it. "Looks a lot better on you than it does on me anyway."

The sun had already set, but there was more than enough light along the trail for him to see the confusion on her face. She stared up at him, almost as though she was waiting for him to say something.

He tucked a stray wisp of her long blond hair behind her ear. "Better?"

"Pardon?"

"Did the jacket make things better?"

"Much." Still, she didn't move, only kept her eyes locked with his.

Nate took her hand. "What's bothering you so much?" When she tried to glance away, he gripped her chin to keep her looking at him. "You were great all through the meal. Now you're being so quiet. I want to know why—I want to know what I did wrong."

"I'm sorry, Nate. You didn't do anything wrong. I was just thinking hard on something."

His hand fell away from her face. "I'm not sure I like the sound of that…"

She quickly grabbed his free hand. "No, no. Nothing bad. I promise." After a deep breath, she said, "I had a long talk with Beth today."

He quirked a brow. "About…?"

"About you. About our little dinner a couple weeks ago. About the blindfold."

A smile bloomed on his lips. "You know, I'm really glad to hear that."

"You're not mad?"

That question took him by surprise. "Mad? Why would I be mad?"

"Because I shared our private stuff with Beth."

"No, Dani. I'm not mad at all. I'm actually happy that you have that kind of friend. I know you and Beth are close. Have you talked to Mallory and Jules, too?"

She shook her head. "Beth and I are a lot closer to each other.

We were friends before the Ladies Who Lunch began. Mallory and Jules have the same kind of connection. When the four of us are together, it's wonderful. But Beth is the one I trust most."

Her choice of word could be nothing but an accident. "You *trust* her?"

Edging closer, the tips of her shoes touching his, Dani nodded. "And I...I trust you, too."

The sincerity in her tone made Nate long to take her into his arms, carry her straight home, and make love to her. But it was still too early. Instead, he brushed his lips over hers just to let her know how happy she'd made him. Then he draped an arm over her shoulders and got her moving again.

The faster they got home, the faster they could begin the next round of the game.

*　*　*

Even though they were inside now and she wasn't cold any longer, Dani didn't want to give back the denim jacket. Nate's scent clung to the fabric, and she had to resist the urge to keep burying her nose against the material and sniffing.

She felt as if something inside her had been freed, a rather odd thing considering that free feeling was about to get her tangled up in a romantic relationship. The irony brought a smile to her lips.

The decision had been made—in her heart and in her mind. This man was exactly what she wanted, who she wanted. Yes, there were speed bumps on the horizon, the biggest being how people at school would react. But she wouldn't let those problems stop her from enjoying her time with Nate. They'd just have to do their best to keep their relationship on the down-low, especially doing their best to hide it from the people at Douglas High.

Nate took her hand and led her to the couch, where he pressed on her shoulders to get her to take a seat. "We should talk."

"All right," she replied sweetly.

His eyes widened a moment before his brows knit.

"What's wrong?"

"I can't seem to figure out what's up with you tonight."

"Nothing's up."

The welcome she'd seen glowing in his eyes under the lamplight gave way to irritation. "You're like a chameleon tonight. You're happy, then you're pissed, and now you seem happy again."

"That's because I *am* happy," Dani said with a nod.

After Nate raked his fingers through his hair, he let out a frustrated sigh. "Then I hope you'll tell me exactly what I did to make you that way so damned quick. I'd like to be able to do it again sometime in the future."

She patted the cushion next to her. "C'mere, lover. Have a seat. I'll try to explain."

The same way he'd tried "sweetheart" on for size, she'd struggled to find the right endearment for him before it hit her that she could affectionately call him exactly what she hoped he'd become. Her lover.

He took a seat but still eyed her warily.

She couldn't blame him. From where he was sitting, she probably appeared to be suffering from bipolar disorder. Her moods had been volatile. The easy conversation throughout the meal, the way they could share so many things about their lives at school, and the humor and foibles of them sharing her home had relaxed her. Thanks to Beth's admonitions about sharing, Dani had finally opened up.

And it had felt grand.

Then the waiter had set the check next to Nate, and her guard had snapped right back into place. They'd been on a date, a *real* date, and she hadn't once tried to protect herself from him. In that moment, she'd realized with stark clarity that she not only wanted him to make love to her, but she also wanted him to love her. Period.

More shocking was the reason why it was so damned important that Nate learn to love her—she'd already let the guy wiggle into her heart. Oh, she might not love him yet. But it would be so very, very easy to take him inside her soul and hold tight.

Turning, she cocked her knee so she could lay her leg across the couch and look him in the eye. He copied the gesture, his knee pressing against hers. A cozy scene, one that she found surprisingly comfortable.

Dani began to do something she'd never imagined she could do. She opened up. "I've been thinking…"

Curiosity radiated from him like an aura. "About…?"

"You. Me. *Us*." She offered him a weak smile. "I've come to a decision."

His fingers brushed against her knee in a light caress. "Am I gonna like what you decided?"

"I hope so."

"And do you think that in coming to this decision you might be trying to take back the control you think you lost?"

The question felt like a slap. "I'm not trying to take control, Nate. I'm not."

He sat silently, his fingers still moving over her knee.

She wasn't sure what to say, whether he was teasing her or goading her. The mischievous gleam in his eye told her he hadn't meant the question to be cruel, but she was having a hard time trusting her own judgment.

"Let go, Dani," his warm voice coaxed. "Just let go."

"I am!"

Nate shook his head. "Don't think. Don't decide. Don't—"

Dani tackled him to the sofa, kissing him before he could even finish. He'd wanted her to just let go? Then damn it, she was *really* going to just let go.

Wriggling around, he stretched out on the sofa as her body covered his. She cupped his face in her hands and kissed him with a ferocity that she couldn't command. Everything about him had infected her, and she refused to control her desire any longer.

His growl made her bolder, and she swept her tongue into his mouth. He responded by returning the caress and wrapping his arms around her.

All she wanted was to get closer and closer. Closer still, to crawl inside him and never, ever leave.

* * *

The kiss was hot. Consuming. Nate returned her passion in equal measure, letting her know with his lips, his tongue, his hands, and his body that he wanted her.

Only her.

She pushed back, ending the kiss and rising over him, straddling his hips and staring at him with the most enchanting smile. As she started to take off his jacket, he sat up to help her, stealing another kiss as he opened each button, wanting their connection to never end.

He had a plan.

After Dani eased out of the jacket, she was about to toss it aside when Nate caught it. Moving quickly, he pulled the sleeves forward and tied them around her waist so her arms were pinned against her sides.

She glanced down at the restraint and then at him. "Nate?"

"Shhh." He brushed his mouth over hers. "Let me play."

A saucy smile formed on her lips. "So you like tying women up, do you?"

"I don't know. I've never tried it before." He threw his legs over the sofa and stood up, scooping her into his arms to take her with him. Then he laid her down on the couch.

Her eyes were shining when she looked up at him. "Now have you got me where you want me?"

"Close, but not quite." He sat on the edge of the cushion and framed her face before he settled a gentle kiss on her lips.

When she tried to deepen the kiss, he eased back. "Nate! C'mon. Kiss me."

"In due time. First, you need another lesson in surrendering your control."

"Why does that make it sound like you've got something planned?"

"Because I do."

Her eyes widened. "You mean you planned to tie me up?"

Since he demanded nothing but honesty from her, Nate gave her the same. He reached under the couch and pulled out the necktie he'd left under there when he'd planned out what he could do to give Dani more tutoring. "I did. Planned to use this, but your wearing my jacket only made it easier."

The cadence of her breathing increased. "Does that mean you're finally ready to make love?"

He shrugged, a truthful reply since he wasn't at all sure if he was going to be able to resist her too much longer, especially now that she was so vulnerable. By not telling her exactly how much he wanted to carry her upstairs, he was trying to show her that she could enjoy herself without plotting or planning each little move she made.

"When will you—"

He silenced her question with a kiss. It took three kisses for her to finally stop asking. Only then did he reach for the first button on her blouse.

Fully expecting her to fight what he was doing, he grinned when she simply arched an eyebrow.

He answered the tacit question by leaning in to press his lips against the skin he'd just bared. Damn if his hands weren't shaking when he opened the next button.

She squirmed. "I want to touch you."

After he shook his head, he kissed her soft skin. Inhaling deeply, he breathed in her sexy scent and closed his eyes, savoring the desire that flowed through his veins like molten lava.

"Nate…"

His reply to her plea was to unfasten the next button, revealing the valley between her breasts, which he kissed and then licked.

"You're killing me," she said, her voice becoming a moan when he popped the next button open.

"Am I?" As he smoothed his fingers from her throat down her chest, he raised gooseflesh in his wake.

"Yes." The word ended on a hiss when he grasped both of the open sides of her blouse and jerked them free of the tied jacket, baring her chest to him.

Nate buried his face in the swell of her breasts, trying hard to regain the self-control he almost lost. Seeing her in nothing but a lacy bra hit him harder than he'd thought possible. All he wanted to do was untie the jacket, rip off her shirt, and open the front clasp of her bra. His cock was as hard as rebar, and he feared he wouldn't be able to leave her tonight, that the only end to the evening was with them in bed together.

But was it still too soon? This wasn't about a short-term physical release; it was about getting past all of Dani's defenses so she'd let him into her heart, not just her body.

He needed to get away from her while he still held tight to a thread of sanity. Pressing another kiss against the silky skin between her breasts, he found the strength to pull back. One by one, he buttoned up her blouse, wondering at how ridiculous his life had become. He was dressing the woman he wanted instead of trying to get her out of her clothes. The last thing he did was untie the jacket.

Standing, Nate offered his hand to help Dani up. Unable to stop himself, he gathered her into his arms for one more kiss. When he tried to step back, she clung to him.

"I need to ask you something," she said.

"I really should go."

"Are we still going to the homecoming dance?"

She'd blurted the question out so quickly, he'd had a hard time understanding what she'd said.

"The homecoming dance? Of course."

"You don't have to wear a tux or anything..."

"Good thing since I don't own one. Not even a good suit."

"A dress shirt and tie would be fine." She grabbed the tie he'd dropped on the coffee table and let it dangle from her fingers. "Maybe you could even bring a couple more for after the dance. I'm sure I could find a way to put them to good use."

"You could?" His voice cracked like an adolescent's when she pressed her palm against his chest.

"Absolutely. Have you ever seen my four-poster bed?"

Chapter 16

Nate wasn't sure why he was so damned nervous. They were only going to chaperone a school dance, not elope. Hell, he hadn't been this jumpy when he'd taken Carrie Rooney to the senior prom. Or when he'd lost his virginity to Kat.

It wasn't as though he and Dani had enjoyed many official dates, especially now that they lived in the same house. But their cozy arrangement had been perfect for them to get to know each other. Every meal, every run, every night sitting side by side and grading papers gave them another chance to talk, to share. He spent more time upstairs than down and learned a lot about her, and she'd seemed generally interested in finding out more about him.

One thought kept torturing him, which was probably the root of his anxiety. It kept his heart pounding and his body responding.

Was tonight *the* night?

Perhaps he was jumping the gun because he wanted her so badly. Perhaps he was allowing his cock to take the lead instead of listening to his brain. Or perhaps Nate had reached the level of emotional intimacy that he'd desired and was finally ready to plunge into physical intimacy.

Tonight was *definitely* the night.

"I love dancing," he commented as he helped Dani don her heavy cloak.

She'd opted to wear a deep blue dress, a wraparound that had short sleeves and hugged her curves. The color complemented her pale skin and hair and set off the enchanting blue of her eyes. The cloak she'd pulled from the closet was a surprise. He hadn't known anyone who wore such an old-fashioned garment.

After he draped it over her shoulders, he nuzzled her neck. "Love that perfume, but it's not your usual Angel. What is it?"

She turned to face him, laying her palm against his chest. "Sometimes I'm a Coco Chanel girl."

He covered her hand with his. "Classy."

"You look pretty classy yourself. Love the tie." Picking up the end, she slid her fingers over the silky material. "In fact, I love *all* your ties, especially the ones I see when we're not at school."

Her flirting made him smile, and he stroked her arm, petting her like a cat. "Thanks. Who knows? If things go well at the dance, maybe I'll show you some more of my ties."

He loved how her breath caught, much as his own did when he pictured her on her big bed, naked, arms open and raised in invitation. Or bound to the headboard.

If he kept thinking like that, he was going to be damned uncomfortable the whole night.

"I'd like that. A lot." Dani let out a little sigh before she dropped his tie. "We should probably get going. Meet you there?"

"Do we really have to go in separate cars?" Nate asked. "Seems kinda silly. You know if we're really gonna do this relationship thing—"

"Are we?"

"Are we what?"

"Going to do this relationship thing?"

It was his turn to sigh. Her question was so disappointing, he wanted to grab her and shake her. "What exactly do you think I've been trying to do for all these weeks? Just get you in bed? Damn, but I thought you knew me better than that." He shook his head, a bit disgusted at his burst of anger.

At least she had the good sense to look contrite. "Fine. You drive."

He closed his eyes for a moment, pinching the bridge of his nose and settling his temper. The question and her terse order were just a couple more of Dani's attempts at anticipating everything that might happen so that she could prepare herself.

Opening his eyes, Nate brushed his knuckles against her cheek. "You know so much about me now, probably as much as anyone ever really has. Which means it's time for me to turn your question back on you and ask you this…Now that you know me, the *real* Nate Ryan, do you want to do the relationship thing with me? Do you want to be with me and only me?"

"To be your girlfriend?"

"For want of a better word, yes. Do you want to be my girlfriend?"

"What about school?"

"Dani, you worry too much. But if it's that important to you, we'll keep this between us. No gossip. No 'I'm your boss.' Only you and I—and the Ladies and guys—know. Okay?"

A small smile lit her face as she laid an index finger against her cheek as though giving the question deep thought. "Hmm… let me think about it." The teasing lilt of her voice softened her implication that she might refuse him. "How about I tell you my decision after the dance?"

"You're going to decide based on my dancing skills?"

She shook her head and patted his chest. "I'll let you know when I see you in my bed. Naked."

* * *

Normally, Dani despised chaperoning Douglas High dances.

Although there were codes about the students' clothing—no strapless dresses, no bare midriffs, no miniskirts, and guys had to wear dress shirts and ties—the principal had never set down rules about how the kids danced. The faculty had begged and pleaded, but there wasn't a single written rule about what happened on the dance floor.

Whenever she'd helped keep an eye on things, Dani spent far too much time breaking up couples who were bumping groins. The worst was twerking. At least that's what the kids called it. To her, it looked like simulated sex. The girls would bend forward while the guys pressed their pelvises against the girls' asses.

As she watched Nate separate yet another young couple, she felt ancient. When had she become such a prude, one of those old ladies who fretted over young women not being "ladies"?

Then again, she couldn't remember ever being so blatantly sexual when she'd been that age. There might have been some close dancing, a boy holding her in his arms and perhaps getting a little too busy with his hands, but leaning forward and rubbing her butt against some guy's crotch? In front of the whole world?

Never. She'd had a hell of a lot more self-respect than these girls seemed to have, and it took every ounce of her self-control not to tell them they didn't have to dance like that to get a guy's attention.

Nate was sidetracked by a student asking him something, and she watched his easy manner with the young woman. Dressed in a sky-blue button-down shirt and dark blue trousers with a silver and burgundy striped tie, Nate probably had no idea how appealing he was. The girls at Douglas had taken notice from his first day on the job. Many nurtured crushes, a rather dangerous part of being an attractive male teacher in a high school.

Being his mentor, she'd shared some wisdom, letting him know to avoid any situation where he was alone with a female student. All it took was the *hint* of impropriety, and Nate's career would be over.

Dani wasn't about to let that happen to Nate.

He strode across the gym floor, shaking his head. "The way these kids dance is killing me." He took his place at her side, clasping his hands behind his back and rocking on his feet. "I can't wait 'til this ends."

Her stomach did a little flip-flop, and she leaned closer to rub her shoulder against his. "I'm looking forward to it, too. I'm ready to go home."

When he tried to take her hand in his, she avoided him and shook her head. People would see them, and then the gossip would begin. They might be consenting, unattached adults, but she wasn't sure she wanted to have their names bandied about as people—teachers, students, and parents—speculated on their relationship.

Did you hear Ms. Bradshaw is dating Mr. Ryan?

Mr. Ryan's got the hots for Ms. Bradshaw!

They were holding hands at the homecoming dance!

A slow song mercifully brought Dani's troubled thoughts to an abrupt halt.

Nate squeezed her hand. "Wanna dance?"

"We shouldn't."

"Why?" he asked.

"You promised, Nate. Just us. Only us."

He stole away her worries by dragging her toward the empty hallway that led from the gym to the locker rooms. "One song, sweetheart. Just one. Dance with me here, where it's only us." His hands settled on her waist and he began to sway with her to the notes of the love song.

She put her hands on his shoulders to let him lead her through the dance. It felt so damned good to be there with him, even better to let the world fall away, leaving behind nothing but the two of them.

* * *

Nate held Dani's hand the whole way home, hoping he'd read her mood correctly. The anticipation was exquisite, making him smile and savor the feel of her hand resting in his. He'd been living in her home long enough that it felt so natural to pull alongside her black Civic in the garage. She got out of his car before he could come around to open the door for her.

He did manage to get to the door leading to the kitchen before Dani, so he swung it wide and let her inside. He helped her take off her cloak, and he hung it on one of the mudroom pegs. Since he hadn't worn a coat, he led the way to the kitchen.

Every night before he headed down to his own suite, he stopped in the kitchen to kiss her good night. Then she'd head upstairs as he headed down.

But what about tonight?

Where had all his confidence gone? He was suddenly so rattled, he was amazed his hands weren't shaking. He should be sweeping her into his arms and carrying her up to her bed. She'd let him know in many ways that she was ready for this step.

He let out a little snort. Dani had been ready *weeks* ago. Or at least she thought she was. Nate was the one who'd put on the brakes. He'd been reaching for more than her body.

He wanted her heart.

"What?" she asked, her gaze searching his.

Since she had to be referring to his snort, he just shook his head.

Leaning back against the island, she kicked off her high heels. When she'd had them on, they'd been eye to eye. Now that she had to look up to keep their eye contact, she seemed a bit more vulnerable. And oh so sweet.

Nate gave in to his growing desire and embraced Dani, settling his mouth on hers and kissing her the way he'd dreamed of all evening. He swept his tongue into her mouth, loving how responsive she was, how she rubbed her tongue over his as she reached her arms around his neck and tangled her fingers in his hair. Her soft moans urged him on. Splaying his palms against her back, he slid them down until they covered her shapely butt. Then he pulled her tight against his hard cock.

Damn, he wanted her. Her scent intoxicated him, making his head swim as he kissed her long and deep. She gently tugged at his hair, her way of telling him how much she enjoyed what he was doing to her.

Their ragged breaths mingled when he broke away from the kiss. "Dani…do you want to—"

"Oh yes, I want to."

Her words sent a jolt straight to his groin. With a growl, he picked her up, cradling her against his chest as he rested his forehead against hers. "I want to, too. I bought some condoms."

"Where are they?"

"In my bedroom."

"Well, then"—she gave him the sexiest smile—"why don't we head downstairs? I'm ready to answer your question."

He quirked an eyebrow. "Which question?"

"Whether I'll be your girlfriend or not."

"And?"

She framed his face in her hands and kissed him. A short, no-nonsense kiss. "Yes, Nate. I'll be your girlfriend. Now make love to me."

Chapter 17

Every cell in Dani's body came alive.

Nate had carried her down the stairs into his suite, holding her tight. He acted as if she didn't weigh anything. Not a shock since she'd seen the sleek muscles in his chest and arms. Once he'd passed through his living room and into his bedroom, he'd kicked the door shut behind them. Then he'd put her on her feet, flipped on the small lamp on his nightstand, and started working at removing her dress.

She kept getting in his way as she tried to take off his tie and unbutton his shirt. She wanted to be skin to skin with him, to run her fingertips over his chest, to kiss every inch of him.

Between tugging on each other's clothing and helping with their own, they got undressed. Dani drank in his sleek form, from his blond hair to his sculpted chest, over his rippled abs, and finally taking in his cock. Nestled in a patch of light brown hair, it was long and thick and more than any woman could want. She wrapped her fingers around him and stroked, loving the satin skin and how it covered the hardened flesh beneath.

He closed his eyes and let his head fall back. "That feels so damn good."

She'd never been shy during sex, knowing that only by showing and telling her partner what made her happy could they both be satisfied. So she decided to take ruthless advantage of his temporary blindness. She dropped to her knees, took his erection into her mouth, and reached between his legs to squeeze his soft sac.

Nate muttered something incoherent, spread his legs a little farther apart, and spiked his fingers through her hair.

Dani ran her tongue around the swollen head as she stroked him, enjoying the pleasure she was giving him—enjoying the pleasure touching him gave her.

"Stop," he said, gulping for air. "Please."

Looking up at him, she laid her cheek against his muscular thigh and smiled. "Are you sure? I mean, do you *really* want me to stop?"

He nodded, gripping her upper arms and helping her to her feet.

"I won't even ask if you liked it." She put her arms around his neck, pressing her breasts against his chest. "Because I know you did."

"Smart lady." He held her close, teasing her with nibbling kisses until she couldn't wait a moment longer.

She kissed him with all the passion he inspired, tickling his lips until he opened them so she could drive her tongue into his mouth. As their tongues exchanged caress after caress, she rubbed herself against his cock.

Breaking their kiss, Nate jerked back the quilt and then swept Dani into his arms. He set her in the middle of his bed. His eyes raked her from head to toe, setting her heart to pounding. "I feel like I've waited a lifetime to see you like this."

"The view from here's pretty good, too." She returned his perusal, taking in the handsome man who was about to become her lover.

He opened the drawer of his nightstand and pulled out a small box. After opening it, he plucked a condom loose and threw the box aside.

"Let me." She held out her hand.

After he handed her the silver packet, he knelt on the mattress next to her. The package was a pain to open, so she finally used her teeth, tossing the wrapper toward the nightstand and then unrolling the condom over his erection.

Nate stretched out at her side before rolling her to her back and running his tongue over her neck, licking and nibbling his way down her chest. His tongue swirled around one of her nipples, forcing Dani to let out a moan. Then he took the hard nub into his mouth and suckled.

Heat ripped through her, zinging from her breast to her core. He teased and taunted one nipple before switching to the other and continuing his exquisite torture. This time, when he drew her nipple deep into his mouth, his hand moved between her thighs.

She opened up to him, tunneling her fingers through his hair and arching into him. His fingers delved between her folds before one sank inside her, making her tug hard enough on his hair she wouldn't have been at all surprised if she'd yanked out a few strands. An added second finger had her bucking off the bed in rhythm with his thrusts.

Kissing his way back up her body, he settled his mouth on hers just as his clever fingers found her sensitive nub and started to rub. She dug her heels into the mattress, raising her hips and wanting nothing more than for him to be deep inside her.

"Slow down, sweetheart," he whispered in her ear. "We've got all night."

"I want you now, lover. *Please.*"

* * *

Dani's ragged plea swept away what fragile self-control Nate had held. He rose over her, roughly separating her thighs with his knee and settling against her core. Still, he didn't lunge inside. He cradled her face in his hands and kissed her. "You're so beautiful."

"Nate…"

"I mean it, Dani. You're beautiful and I want you more than I've ever wanted another woman."

Tears brimmed her eyes. "Oh, Nate…I understand now."

"Understand?"

"I know why you wanted to wait, why you wanted us to get to know each other first. It makes this better…*so* much better." She opened her thighs wider, rubbing against him. "Make love to me."

Everything in his senses was Dani—the taste of her lips, the light in her eyes, the heat of her body. He thrust inside her. She let out a gasp, so he stilled, worried that he'd hurt her.

Then she wrapped her legs around his hips and caught his bottom lip between her teeth. He kissed her, lost to all but giving her pleasure and finding his own. He pushed into her tight heat, again and again. Just when he feared he'd beat her to the finish line, she caught and held her breath. A moment later, she cried out as her body clenched around him.

Nate surrendered, letting the orgasm race through his body and mind as he drove into Dani one last time, feeling as though he couldn't get as close as he wanted to be. He whispered her name over and over, still pushing into her in small strokes before he collapsed in sated exhaustion, using his trembling arms to keep from letting his weight rest entirely on her.

Slowly coming back to earth, he reluctantly left her body. After a quick trip to the bathroom, he slipped into bed beside her and flipped off the light. Hauling her into his arms, he loved how she snuggled up against him, pillowing her head on his shoulder.

"Was it worth all the time you invested in getting to know me? Was it everything you'd hoped?" Dani whispered.

The worry in her voice touched him deeply. Giving her a squeeze, he smiled in the dark. "And more. How about for you?"

"It was great, but"—she kissed his chest—"we'll just have to keep practicing until we get it *perfect*."

* * *

Nate woke up with a smile on his face, hungry for Dani. But when he rolled to his side to take her into his arms and kiss her awake, he found nothing but cold sheets.

His first thought was that she was in the bathroom. The door was shut, but there wasn't any light peeking out from under the bottom. Nor were there any sounds.

She'd left.

Throwing his legs over the side, he ran his fingers through his mussed hair and glanced at the clock. Five minutes before they usually went for their Sunday morning run. He scrambled to find something to wear, hoping she would be waiting for him out front—hoping that she hadn't run away because she was upset about something.

Last night had been the best sex of his life, but women could get a little…*weird* afterward. While she had been very vocal about enjoying herself, he couldn't help but worry that something he'd said or done had made her go.

Grabbing a hoodie from a hook on his way through the mudroom, he breathed a sigh of relief when he found her stretching in her typical spot on the driveway.

He jerked on the hoodie. Instead of asking her why she hadn't stayed in his bed, he made chitchat. "Kinda chilly this morning."

Dani gifted him with a smile. "Yep. Autumn is definitely here."

Thankfully, there was nothing awkward in the exchange. "What made you decide to run this morning?"

Subtle one, jerk. Why not come out and ask why she was gone when you woke up?

They were still the same people they were before last night. Or at least he hoped so. That had been his goal—that they'd know each other well enough that sex wouldn't change things.

She shrugged. "You were snoring like a chainsaw, and I was wide awake. Besides, I'm a creature of habit."

"That you are, sweetheart." When he lunged forward to stretch, a yawn made his whole body shake. He hadn't slept well, unaccustomed to having someone else in his bed. Dani was a restless sleeper, her constant movement something he'd have to get used to if they'd be sleeping together often.

As though reading his mind, she stepped closer, mimicking his lunge. "Last night was great. Sorry if I kept you up after, though. I've been told I flip and flop a lot."

He thought about lying to her. "Just a little." Damn if he didn't yawn again.

"A helluva lot more than that. Beth won't even share a hotel room with me anymore. None of the Ladies will. Of course, that always means I have privacy on our trips."

"You were fine, Dani. But I am a little punchy."

"I'm tired, too." She stood and yawned as well. "I'm not sure if I'm up for a run this morning or not."

Since Dani was an animal when it came to long runs, Nate frowned. "Something wrong?"

"Nope," she replied sweetly. Then she moved closer and took his hand. "I was just thinking…Maybe we could try a little different kind of workout this morning. An indoor workout."

Arching an eyebrow, he waited for her to explain.

"I thought we'd go up to my room, get hot and sweaty, and then share a shower. Might be a nice change of pace."

As if he needed to be asked twice. He took her hand and dragged her back to the house.

They worked their way upstairs, discarding pieces of clothing along the way. By the time they reached her bedroom, he was down to his briefs while she fumbled her way out of her tight jog bra.

He'd seen the pink ribbon tattoo under her breast last night. He moved to her and traced it gently, then looked up. "Ink?"

"Beth, Jules, and I all got one to show support for Mallory a while back."

Just one more reminder of the caring woman Dani truly was. Nate bent his head and briefly pressed his lips against the ribbon. "It's beautiful," he murmured.

A thought sobered him. "Shit. I need to run downstairs real quick and grab a condom."

She grasped his arm when he tried to go. "Before you do that, maybe we should have a quick talk about…things."

"Things?"

"You don't need a condom. I'm on the pill."

His heart skipped at the thought of enjoying Dani's body without a condom between him and her wet heat, a pleasure he'd never known before. "I got tested for you."

"You did?"

He nodded. "When I figured...when I *hoped*...things would get serious between us, I went to get tested. I wanted to be able to tell you that I was clean. Got a great report card, too." He winked at her.

"After my last...um...Anyway, I had a test, too. Aced mine as well." She put his hand on her breast.

Nate's cock twitched in response.

"I'm fine with no condom if you are," Dani whispered.

He answered her by swooping down to draw her nipple between his teeth, loving how she arched into him and held his head. After lavishing one breast with his attention, he shifted to the other, trying to be just as thorough. A soft purr rose from her chest.

She'd been so daring last night, and he was ready to return the favor. That, and he had such an overwhelming need to know *all* of her. Lifting her by the waist, he walked to the bed and set her down. Then he fell to his knees and roughly forced her thighs apart before burying his face against her core.

* * *

Dani let out a throaty moan and held on to Nate's hair to keep herself grounded. The sensations he sent ripping through her—his tongue sliding between her folds, tickling her sensitive nub, delving into her—were almost more than she could bear. She drew her knees up, not even trying to stop the feral sounds spilling from her lips.

This pleasure was one she'd seldom been able to enjoy. The men she'd slept with had acted as though gifting her with this kind of intimate kiss was costing them dearly. Not Nate. No, he loved her so thoroughly she quickly found herself rising to a crescendo. Everything inside her tightened into a knot that was ready to unravel.

"C'mere, Nate. Please…" She tugged hard on his hair. "I want you."

He stopped long enough to say, "No. Like this." Then he became more intense, more insistent as he sucked gently on her bundle of nerves.

Dani gave him what he wanted, letting the waves of pleasure wash over her.

Nate kissed his way up her body, running his tongue around her navel and laving each nipple.

When she could finally draw a decent breath, she sat up on her elbows, her face close to his as he leaned over her. "That was amazing."

"You're amazing." After a quick kiss, he took her hand and helped her to her feet.

Her legs trembled as she whipped back the quilt. "My turn to have fun. On your back, mister."

"Anything the lady wants." He crawled to the center of the mattress and flopped on his back. "What next?"

Crawling toward him, she smiled. "Now I'm going to make love to you." She wrapped her fingers around his cock and stroked him.

His head fell back against the pillows. "That sounds like a wonderful plan."

She loved his teasing and how easily they'd become comfortable with each other. He'd been right in insisting they develop the relationship first. She would never have felt so free with a man she didn't know as well as she knew Nate.

"Thank you," Dani said before she gave him a slow, lazy kiss. When she finally pulled back to look into his eyes, he had a bemused expression on his face. "What are you thanking me for?"

"For caring enough about me to insist we wait to do this." After she straddled his hips, she eased herself down on his erection until she'd taken him inside her.

"You're wel—" His word turned into a growl when she squeezed her inner muscles tight. He settled his hands on her hips and thrust deeply, setting a fast and rather rough pace.

She caught his rhythm, loving how quickly her body responded to the feel of him deep inside her. It wasn't long before she found herself again on the precipice of release, but she wanted him there with her.

Capturing his lips, she thrust her tongue into his mouth. When he squeezed her hips and groaned into her mouth, she let the feel of his hot seed spilling into her sweep her into another overwhelming orgasm.

Sated and happy, Dani made a quick trip to the bathroom and returned to the bed to wait while Nate made his own foray. When he crawled back into bed, she pulled the sheet over them and snuggled up against his side.

He brushed a kiss over her forehead. "I'm not sure there are any words to describe how great that was."

She rubbed her cheek against his shoulder. "Ditto."

"That was a helluva lot more fun than a run."

"I guess we'll have to make it a new Sunday habit."

"Fine with me." He let out a yawn. "Fantastic sex followed

by a nap. When we wake up, I'll take you to Yia Yia's Pancake House."

"Sounds like a plan." Dani decided to follow his lead and be as honest with him as he always was with her. "I'd like you to start staying up here now. With me—that is, if you can stand me being a whirling dervish in bed."

He chuckled. "Was that supposed to sound dirty?"

She made a fist and gently tapped his chin. "I'm being serious. I've got this king-size bed, and if we're going to be doing *this*—"

"Making love?"

"Yeah. Then you might as well move upstairs. With me."

"Are you sure you're ready for that?" he asked.

"The only time you head to the basement is to sleep, right?"

"Right."

"Then let's make it official and really move in together."

He thought it over longer than she'd expected. "I want to, sweetheart. But are you sure? Jules is waiting to start a search for a fixer-upper for me." He shrugged. "I kinda put that on hold since I like your basement so much."

"Then I'll save her some work."

"You've got to be sure," he insisted. "I mean…now we each at least have a place to retreat for privacy."

"We still will."

"*I* will, since I'll still have the basement. But if we share this bedroom…"

She leaned up on one elbow. "I don't mind. We practically live together anyway. This really isn't that big a change. Unless you don't want to."

"I want to…if I can have a bathroom drawer?"

"You can have your own vanity. There are two, after all. And there's plenty of room in the closet."

Nate cupped her neck and pressed his lips to hers. "If you're sure this is what you want…"

Dani nodded.

"Then I'll move a few things up later. After a good nap."

"But remember the cardinal rule."

"I know. No one can know. Only us."

Chapter 18

Dani shoved her empty containers into her thermal lunch bag. "Anyone have any big plans for the second week of fall break?"

Beth shook her head. "I'll need every minute of that time to recover from our Chicago trip."

"This year will be epic," Mallory said. "Four of us, three days, two musicals, and a crap-ton of shopping."

"And sheer exhaustion since I have to share a room with Dani." Beth softened the rebuke with a wink.

"Sorry," Dani couldn't help but say. Since they'd decided to stay downtown for this year's installment of their annual trip to the Windy City, the hotel costs were much higher than if they'd stayed in the suburbs like they usually did. Beth had reluctantly agreed to share a room with Dani. "I'll *try* to behave."

"I was teasing," Beth said, picking up the remnants of her lunch. "There are two beds instead of us sharing a king. I'll be fine. Besides, I'm really looking forward to this trip. You know how much I love *Wicked*." She sealed her plastic bag full of crackers.

"Will this be the fifth or sixth time we've seen it?" Jules asked, wadding her fast-food bag into a ball and shooting it at the trash like a basketball. It banked off the wall and sank into the basket. "Swish."

"The sixth for me," Dani replied before knitting her brows at Beth. "Just crackers and peanut butter?" Since that was all Beth had eaten at lunch this week, Dani was worried her friend was trying yet another fad diet.

Beth just shrugged. "It's all I had here, and I keep forgetting my lunch. Emma's still such a handful in the mornings. I'm lucky to get her dropped off at day care and make it here on time."

"If you're like me," Jules said, "your lunch is probably still sitting on the kitchen island. Mornings with kids can be such a joy."

"Amen," Beth said. "I might not have plans for the second week, but do any of you?"

"Ben and I are going to spend a couple of nights in Nashville," Mallory said. "Indiana, not Tennessee."

Jules smiled. "Connor and I did that last year."

"Which is why I'm going this year." Mallory dropped her silverware into her lunch container. "You raved about all the little shops and how beautiful the leaves were this time of year. I need to see it all for myself."

"Is Amber going?" Dani asked.

Mallory shook her head. "She's heading to stay with her mother."

"I thought she hated Theresa."

"They've come to a sort of truce," Mallory explained. "I think Amber can stand a couple of days. So how about you, Jules?"

"Connor and I are taking the twins to Holiday World while it's still fairly warm, at least jacket weather. Maybe we'll get extra lucky and Indian summer will roll around while we're there." Jules settled her startling green eyes on Dani. "And how about you?"

Although Dani had mentioned to Beth that she might go on a mini-vacation with Nate, plans had changed. "Nate's taking me to stay with his mom and stepdad for a couple of days."

"Good thing you already know his mom. Shouldn't be a big deal to meet her husband." Jules's tone was reassuring, which meant she'd picked up on Dani's anxiety.

While Dani felt as if she and Nate were on solid ground in their relationship, she also worried about how Jackie, Mark, and Patrick were going to react when he finally told them that she and Nate were an official couple. She knew exactly how close he was to his family, and their reactions to his living in the basement suite hadn't been good.

How would Jackie feel when she found out Nate had moved upstairs and was sleeping with his landlady—his older landlady, who also happened to be his boss?

Exactly as they'd promised each other, they had kept their relationship low-key and private. The Ladies and their men knew, but not too many other people. Oh, they might speculate. Douglas High ran on gossip, and Dani feared being the latest grease for those gears. They'd been very careful not to show too much affection in public, especially at school, which sometimes made her day difficult.

There were so many times she wanted to take his hand, to give him a quick kiss, or to see that sexy smile. She wanted to shout to the whole world that he was hers, to tell the young women on the faculty making goo-goo eyes at him that he was taken. The barely leashed jealousy was hard for Dani to admit, even to herself, because she knew exactly what it meant.

She was falling in love with him.

His patience in teaching her that their relationship was every bit as important as sex had kept her moving swiftly down the path to handing him her heart. Each day, he showed her that she mattered to him in a way no one ever had—except for the Ladies. They were sisters in Dani's heart.

But Nate? Could he become her partner, her mate, the better half of her?

Since when had she started being so damned sappy?

"Dani?"

Beth's concerned tone was sobering. "Sorry. A little lost in thought."

"You're nervous about spending time with Nate's family."

So like Beth to state the fact rather than pretend to ask. "Yeah, I am."

"Just be yourself," Beth advised. "They'll love you just as much as Nate does."

There was that word again. *Love.* Seemed to be hanging over her head like a storm cloud.

Dani thought about denying it, figuring if he hadn't said he loved her, he obviously didn't feel it. But his actions showed otherwise. The way he worried as much about her pleasure as he did his own. The way he helped around the house without being asked. The way he always touched her whenever they were together—a quick kiss as he passed her in the kitchen or a shoulder rub after they ran together.

Could he really love her?

"Beth's right," Mallory said right before the tone ending lunch sounded. "Just be yourself. You're a wonderful person."

Jules hefted the strap of her heavy tote over her shoulder. "You've got a killer sense of humor. I'm sure they'll love you."

"See you," Dani said, hanging behind, hoping for a quick moment alone with Beth.

Jules and Mallory left the lunchroom, talking to each other and not even looking back.

"What's wrong?" Beth asked.

"You know me too well," Dani said, a bit frustrated that she sounded so pitiful.

"Tell me. We've only got a few minutes, and I need to pee." Her sweet smile belied her strict tone.

"Afraid I'll need more than a few minutes," Dani replied. "We'll have tons of time to talk in Chicago." She needed to sit down and think. Hard. She needed to decide what she should do now that she'd admitted how she felt about Nate.

"Are you sure?" Despite the sincerity in Beth's voice, she quickly checked her watch.

"I'm sure. Let's head to class."

* * *

"Thanks for coming down, Dani," Jim Reinhardt said. "I won't keep you long." He inclined his head at the door as he sat down behind his desk. "Could you please close the door?"

Dani's heart skipped a beat. In her years at Douglas, there had been only one time she'd been summoned to a meeting in the principal's office and asked to shut the door—and that had been bad news.

With a hand that trembled slightly, she pulled the door closed and took a seat across the desk from her boss, hoping he wouldn't notice how nervous she felt.

"First, I wanted to give you a 'that-a-girl.' You've done a great job with the English department. The kids were more than ready for state testing, and I sure hope the numbers reflect the effort you and your teachers put into preparing."

"Thanks."

"I also think the *Hunger Games* project went over well."

"I do, too."

He blew a long breath out his nose. "Any concerns with Nate Ryan?"

"I beg your pardon?"

"I've observed him a couple times. I think he's great on content knowledge."

"Oh, I totally agree. I think his having a bachelor's in English—especially with his emphasis on literature—gives him more of a handle on content than we'd typically get with a newbie." Dani folded her hands in her lap. "So why do I hear a 'but' in your statement?"

Jim leaned back in his chair. "Just a small one. I worry about discipline."

Scrambling to figure out what he was alluding to, she said, "Whenever I've been in his classes, I don't see any problems."

"You don't think he's a little too…personal with the students?"

"In what way?"

"This is secondhand, mind you, since I wasn't able to get to the homecoming dance, but I was told he danced with some of the students—especially the female students."

Mary Henry, no doubt. She'd been bitching rather loudly to someone in the teacher workroom about how younger teachers needed to stop being so friendly with students, that it was totally inappropriate. The moment Dani had walked into the room, Mary had shut her mouth.

Time to set the record straight. "I was there, and yes, he danced with students. Girls and guys. But there was nothing inappropriate. In fact, he taught them some new dances so they'd stop with that ridiculous grinding and twerking."

Jim winced. "You mean when they act like they're having sex instead of dancing?"

"Exactly. Nate showed them some line dances and a little bit of disco."

"I'm amazed he's old enough to even know about disco."

"Jim, everyone knows about disco."

At least she made him laugh. "Point taken."

Hoping that was the end of the discussion, Dani half stood.

"Hang on a minute," he said. "Please."

She sat back down.

"Let me get right to the point... There aren't any rules about teachers dating other teachers."

Her whole face flushed hot, but she held her tongue. Better to let Jim show his cards first before giving him a verbal reaction. No doubt he'd already seen her blush.

"A parent called me this morning with a concern. About you. And Nate."

"A parent?"

Jim nodded.

"A concern?"

"Perhaps that's the wrong word. She wasn't concerned. I suppose I'm the one who's concerned."

Dani folded her hands and interlaced her fingers to try to appear calm. This was what she'd feared all along. People knew about her and Nate. Sure, there wasn't a "rule" about teachers dating. But department heads dating their department members?

"There's absolutely no reason to be concerned," she said.

"Were you dancing with Nate?"

She nodded. "I did some of the line dances with him and the kids."

He shook his head. "The parent was talking about slower dancing. She thought it might be an inappropriate display of affection in front of the kids. That's all."

"We weren't slow dancing in front of the kids."

"Evidently, she was there to take pictures of her son and saw you two slip outside the gym."

"Are you saying she followed us?"

His nod made her stomach lurch. "Without giving you her name, let's just say she's one of those parents who thinks everything in the world is her business. So, yes, she followed you and saw you dancing and said you two were a bit too... close."

Small towns. So judgmental. So unforgiving. "What exactly do you want from me, Jim?"

"Easy there, Dani. This isn't something you need to get upset about. What you do in your personal life is your own business. Yours and Nate's. All I ask is that you and Nate keep your focus on the students whenever you're chaperoning an event."

Afraid that she'd lose her temper if she stayed in his office too much longer, Dani asked, "We will. May I go?"

"Dani... this isn't a big thing..."

"Thanks, Jim. I'll be sure and let Nate know what you expect from us."

* * *

Dani let Nate take her suitcase at the top of the stairs. She followed him as he headed downstairs and out to the garage.

He shoved her suitcase into the trunk of her car before slamming the lid. "I'm amazed everything fit. We're only going for a week. You didn't need to pack the kitchen sink."

"I just want to be prepared," she said.

After taking her hand, he rubbed his thumb over her palm. "I know you're nervous…"

"A little."

"I'm really sorry that you didn't get to go to Chicago."

So was Dani. She'd been so disappointed when the call came. "Beth couldn't help getting sick. I just hope she gets to feeling better soon. I still wonder if I should stay to help her. Poor thing can't stop throwing up."

"It's up to you, but Robert swears she's going to be fine. You sure don't want to catch that kind of stomach bug." He tugged on her hand, pulling her into his embrace. "We'll have a great time in Indiana. There's no reason to get this worked up about my mom."

A week. A whole *week* with Nate's mom and stepdad. Once the Ladies' Chicago excursion had been canceled, he'd suggested they stay a lot longer than their planned three days. Now Dani was wondering if she should have agreed so readily.

"I want her to like me," she said.

Nate rubbed his chin against her temple. "She will. No doubt at all. Once she gets to know you, she'll realize how special you are. And you'll learn to like her, too."

"Let me check things one more time and grab my purse. Then we can get on the road. Thanks for taking my car."

"Not a tough choice," he said with a grin. "Yours isn't nearly as likely as my beater is to leave us sitting on the side of the highway, waiting for a tow truck. Are you going to let me drive your car, or do I resign myself to shotgun?"

"Drive my baby?" Dani stepped back and blew a raspberry. "No way, José."

"Shotgun it is. At least I can catch a nap part of the trip."

Although she took another fifteen minutes to give the house one more go-through, she made up the lost time and then some by speeding most of the way to Indiana.

Nate's parents had a condo in Indianapolis, which wasn't far from Patrick's house. No doubt she and Nate would visit there as well, but the plans had called for the two of them to bunk with Jackie and Mark. Nate's stepsister Carly was supposed to be there later in the week—another person Dani would have to try to win over.

As she pulled along the curb and parked the car, she had a thought that made her stomach twist into a painful knot. "Exactly how much does your mom know about us? You did tell her we were dating, right?"

Looking a bit sleepy, Nate shook his head. "I haven't told her much of anything yet. Figured we'd surprise her and tell her about us in person. She'll be thrilled, I'm sure."

"Then what reason did you give her for me coming with you?"

"I told her we were coming for a teacher conference."

Her eyes wide, she had no idea what to say. She'd taken for granted that he'd smoothed the path by letting Jackie know about them being a couple and about the new living arrangements. Why wouldn't he have told her that Dani was his girlfriend—his roommate?

Her disappointment and apprehension were her own fault. She'd had a stupid fantasy, born from her favorite movie, *How to Lose a Guy in 10 Days*, that they'd be welcomed into Jackie and Mark's home, and Dani and Nate would play card games with them and grow closer to each other when his family embraced her with open arms. She'd even pictured him taking her for a ride on a motorcycle he'd happen to own exactly like Matthew

McConaughey in the movie. And then there was that hot sex scene in the shower...

Instead of a romantic comedy, Dani faced a potential disaster.

"You're thinking awfully hard over there," Nate said. "I probably should've told her, but"—he shrugged—"it's really no big thing."

"To you, maybe."

"Why are you so worried?"

She'd never seen a reason to share her thoughts about Jackie with him. But now that the two women were about to come face-to-face, now that Nate was going to let his mom know he'd attached himself to his boss, a woman eight years older, Dani needed to tell him about the tension the last time she was with Jackie. "Remember the day you moved in?"

He nodded.

"Your mom came in and had a cup of coffee with me."

"So?"

"She seemed kind of...angry about you moving into my place."

He cocked his head. "Why would she be angry? I was renting your basement, and it was a huge step up from that horrible room I had."

"I know, but she acted upset about the move."

"Are you sure? Mom is sometimes a bit intense. She was probably just being her crazy self. I love her to death, but she honestly takes some getting used to." Nate let out a light chuckle. "Ask Mark. He'll have a million stories about Mom's volatile emotions. Besides, my guess is that she was just tired from the long drive so early in the morning. Mornings are definitely *not* her thing."

His words were comforting, but Dani couldn't quell her

anxiety as he got their luggage out of the trunk. Ever the gentleman, Nate carried her suitcase and his duffel to the front door. When she reached for the doorbell, he shook his head. "You're family now. Just go on in."

Damn if her hands weren't trembling as she opened the front door. She held it open as Nate headed inside, and then she shut it behind them.

The town house was amazing. The two-story foyer made the place seem huge. The enormous chandelier was made of crystal and dark wrought iron. She'd seen one in the lighting store Robert used and had considered it for her own foyer before settling on a brushed nickel finish with frosted glass. The walls were painted a warm beige, and the travertine floor tiles were an inviting mixture of beige, walnut, and gray. The pleasant scent of roasting meat wafted through the air.

Jackie Brennan obviously had excellent taste, but after hearing Nate's stories about her lacking any kind of cooking skills, Dani wondered about that heavenly smell.

"Mom?" Nate's voice echoed in the cavernous foyer. "We're here!"

"Nate?" a feminine voice called from down the hall.

He set their luggage by the bottom of the staircase, took Dani's hand, and led her down the hallway into the enormous kitchen. When he stopped suddenly, she ran right into him as he stared at the young woman drying her hands on a blue towel.

Peeking past him, Dani gaped. The twentysomething woman was nothing short of beautiful. Her long, dark hair fell in thick waves around her slender shoulders. A heart-shaped face was dominated by brown doe eyes. Her slender figure had to be a perfect size 4, and she was dressed in skinny jeans and a pink long-sleeved blouse.

"You must be Carly," Dani said, extending her hand. "Nate's told me a lot about you."

The brunette set the towel on the counter and gave Dani a cool, rather smug smile. "Carly won't be here for a couple of days. I'm Kat."

Chapter 19

The moment Nate saw Kat standing in his mother's kitchen, he'd wanted to grab Dani, toss her over his shoulder, and run right back to Illinois.

The look on Dani's face—the horrified expression that was immediately replaced by the mask of calm it had taken Nate forever to breach—had felt like a stab to the chest. Every bit of progress he'd made to win her heart might have been lost.

The thought chilled him to the bone.

While Dani just stood there with her fake unemotional smile, Kat hurried to him, wrapped her arms around his waist, and rose on tiptoes to brush her mouth over his. "I missed you so much."

Although his arms remained at his sides, Nate caught the narrowing of Dani's eyes. A good sign since it meant she was jealous of Kat laying hands on him. He finally found his voice. "What are you doing here, Kat?"

The type of sensuous smile she gave as she kept her arms around him would have had a profound effect on him a long time ago. Now it only irritated him that Kat was being so brazenly affectionate. Not only did he want to spare Dani any more pain at seeing his former fiancée throwing herself at him, but he also wanted to give Kat a shake and remind her that she'd walked away from him, that what had ever existed between them was dead and buried.

"I'm home for good," she announced.

"I beg your pardon?" The last he'd heard, she'd been in London with plans to backpack her way through Europe with some guy named Norm.

"I'm home for good," she repeated. "Jackie helped me get a job as a school aide while I finish school." Kat let out a little chuckle. "I'm just about done with my paralegal certification."

Although he had no intention of having a friendly conversation with Kat, he needed to know what the hell was going on, and he needed to know right now. There was a reason she was here today, and he couldn't stop thinking his mother had something to do with it.

Jackie had always been so supportive of Nate's relationship with Kat, and when they'd split, she hadn't even tried to hide her disappointment. Could this be her attempt to throw them back into each other's paths?

All he could think to ask was, "Why are you here?"

"I live here."

"You *what*?"

Instead of answering, Kat turned her dark eyes on Dani as she thankfully stepped back so he didn't have to push her away. "Since Nate's obviously in shock at seeing me again, he's forgotten his manners." She held out her hand. "I'm Kat Brennan."

Dani shook her hand. "Danielle Bradshaw." Her voice was as monotone as a computer simulation.

"You're Nate's boss. Jackie said Nate was bringing you to some education conference." Her gaze shifted back to him. "Where exactly is that conference being held, honey? Funny thing...I couldn't find anything online about a conference for teachers anywhere in Indy."

How in the hell could he have found himself in this ridiculous predicament?

By lying to his mom. If he'd been open and honest with her about his relationship with Dani, especially about them living together, he wouldn't be facing this awkward conversation with Kat, nor would he have to have a similar awkward conversation with his mother.

No way around it—he'd been a chickenshit. Nate had put off telling Jackie about Dani because he knew how she'd likely react. It wasn't that she disliked Dani; it was that she couldn't get past her being his boss and a few years older, silly notions she'd repeated in almost every one of their conversations. Kat's words only emphasized that point.

Utter nonsense, but he'd learned from experience that once his mom had her stubborn mind set against something—or someone—she needed to be confronted, told why she was wrong, and then buried in evidence before she would be convinced to change her opinion.

Dani had been acting even more reticent since Friday, as though something had happened. But in her typical fashion, she hadn't said a word. Since he couldn't do anything about her change of attitude, he decided to focus on what he could do.

It was time to straighten things out. "Where's Mom?" he asked.

"Right behind you," Jackie said before poking him in the back. "Welcome home, Nate."

Nate embraced her and waited until she'd greeted Dani with a polite aloofness. "Mom, can we sit and talk?" he asked.

"Oh my. That sounds ominous."

Dani moved closer to Nate. "I'm sorry to be a bother, but I'm getting a really bad headache all of a sudden. Is there someplace quiet I can go to and lie down for a little bit?"

Jackie was the one to answer. "Of course. The basement suite's ready for you." She tossed Dani a lopsided smile. "Figured you'd like to see things from Nate's point of view. Plus you'll have tons of privacy."

"Thank you," was Dani's flat reply.

"Downstairs. It's the second door on the right," Jackie said. "If you see a washer and dryer, you've got the wrong room."

As Dani went to the stairs, Nate followed. "Are you okay?"

"Fine. Just getting a splitting headache."

"Can I get you anything? Aspirin? Tylenol?"

She shook her head.

Damn if she didn't move her hand out of his reach when he tried to take it so he could give her a reassuring squeeze. Then she left him to face the music.

Thankfully, his mother didn't speak again until Dani was well out of earshot. "Call me paranoid, but something's wrong here. Nate, I really expected you to be a helluva lot happier to see that Kat has finally come home."

"Happy?" Kat pouted her lip. "More like catatonic..."

"Look, let's go sit down and talk. Okay?" he asked.

His mom nodded and went to plop on the sofa. He wasn't at all surprised that Kat followed and took the seat right next to Jackie.

Inwardly, he shrugged at her audacity. It was pure Kat, so he figured he might as well get this over and done with, with both women at the same time.

Sitting on the coffee table to face them, Nate took a deep

breath and blew it out as he leaned forward to rest his forearms on his thighs. "I need to tell you about Dani."

"She looked kinda sick," Kat said. "She got really pale all of a sudden. Is she ill?"

Catty as always. "No, she's not sick. She's...upset."

"Upset?" Jackie knit her brows. "Over what? Did you have a fight or something? Is she kicking you out of her basement?" She gave him a curt nod as though she accepted that idea as the truth. "We'll start looking around for a house for you to rent and—"

"Stop, Mom. I'm not searching anymore. Maybe later, but not right now. Look, I know you didn't like the idea of me living with Dani, but—"

"I'm fine with you renting her basement," Jackie snapped. "I told you that. I shouldn't have made such a fuss. She's a nice lady. I was just afraid it would be a problem since she's your department head and a little older. Figured she might not like a twentysomething kid in her house."

"Are you ever going to let that shit go?" This was going to be more difficult if she couldn't open her mind and start looking at Dani as a beautiful woman instead of his boss and some sort of desperate cougar. "She's a department head, not my *boss*." He sarcastically punctuated the word with air quotes. "And I'm twenty-four—twenty-five next month—and not exactly a kid anymore."

"I didn't mean that like it sounded."

Since his mom's tone was contrite, he let some of his anger slip away. "Dani's only a handful of years older than me. You really don't need to keep bringing it up."

Kat frowned. "Why would her age matter to either of you? She's just Nate's landlady."

Nate shook his head. Kat had opened the door, so he stepped right through. "Dani's my girlfriend."

Both women gave him the weirdest looks. Jackie's expression was a cross between shocked and upset. Kat's was pure pissed.

He didn't care about either of their reactions. Dani meant the world to him, and he wasn't going to let his mother or his ex hurt her any more than they already had. "We started dating and we're serious about making things between us work. We live together now."

"Oh, Nate…" Jackie shook her head.

Her disappointed frown sent his temper soaring again. "What exactly is your problem with Dani?"

"It's not *her* so much…" Letting out a sigh, she raked her fingers through her short hair.

It had never dawned on him how many of her mannerisms he'd adopted. "Then what exactly is it, Mom? Hell, I thought you'd be playing matchmaker since she's so great. What made you set your mind against her when you don't even know her?"

Folding her arms under her breasts, she glared at him. "I wasn't set against her."

"Bullshit."

Kat was still scowling, that same glare she'd always given him when he hadn't allowed her to have her way. Funny how when he'd been so besotted with her he hadn't noticed some of her more annoying traits. "I can't believe you'd do this to me, Nate. It's just plain cruel to throw her in my face when I came home to be with you."

"To be with me?" He shook his head, not even wanting to know exactly what motivated her to suddenly want to resurrect the dead relationship. "We were over a long time ago, Kat. And I didn't bring Dani here to throw her in your face. I didn't even know you were going to be here!"

"Let me guess," she continued in a snide tone. "There is no stupid conference. You brought her here to surprise your mom with your new toy." She let out a snort. "Like some cat dragging home a dead mouse for its owner."

Probably seeing his temper start to boil over, Jackie stepped in. "That was uncalled for, Kat. You don't have to be mean about it." She looked to Nate. "So she's your girlfriend now?"

He nodded.

"Can't say I'm surprised."

"What's that supposed to mean?"

"I could see the sparks, and you...well, you were clearly taken with her. So I'll try to make her feel more welcome. I'm sorry she walked into...all this." Jackie stood up. "Let me make Dani some tea. You can take it down and let her know she's more than welcome here." As she headed into the kitchen, she called over her shoulder, "Since you like her, I'll refrain from cooking anything except tea."

At least he could chuckle now. Until he saw Kat sitting on the sofa, her eyes angry. "Kat—"

She held up a hand. "Don't say a fucking word."

"Hey, now," Jackie scolded. "Watch the language."

While the admonition was hilarious coming from a woman who talked like a sailor, Nate let it go. "We should talk."

"No, we shouldn't." Kat jumped to her feet. "I'm heading up to my room. I've got homework."

Nate didn't try to stop her. The hurt in her voice surprised him and made guilt wash over him. Despite feeling as though he owed her some kind of explanation or excuse, he actually didn't. Any commitment he'd made to her had ended when she'd walked away, and she'd seemed to do it with an ease that indicated she'd never truly loved him the way he'd loved her.

Seeing her now, he could finally put any residual hurt to rest. He cared for her, but he didn't love her. Not anymore, and with the intensity of his feelings for Dani, he had to wonder if he ever truly had.

But he'd misjudged Kat's feelings. A woman couldn't fake that kind of heartache. While he was here, he'd have to find some time to sit down and talk with her so any wounds remaining from their relationship could finally heal.

Now it was time to soothe Dani. He went to his mom and helped her put together a small tray with hot tea and graham crackers. Then he carried it downstairs. At the bedroom door, he kicked it softly in lieu of knocking. "Dani? Are you asleep?"

"Come on in."

She was lying on her side on top of the blue quilt, her back to him. The only light came through the slim basement window.

"I brought you some tea and Tylenol."

Rolling toward him, she wiped her hand across her eyes as though she'd been crying.

His stomach clenched. "I'm sorry about all the stupidity upstairs."

"It's not your fault."

He sat on the bed by her legs and set the tray down where she could reach it. When she sat up and propped the pillows behind her, he lifted the tray long enough for her to finish and then put it over her lap. "Drink some tea. Should help you feel a little better." He picked up the bottle of pills and spilled two on his palm. "Take a couple of Tylenol, sweetheart."

"Thanks," she murmured as she obeyed, tossing them into her mouth and then taking a drink of the small glass of water he'd added to the tray. After she poured a couple of pink sweetener packets into the tea, she sipped for a while as they sat in the quiet. "Did you know Kat was going to be here?" she finally asked.

Nate rubbed his hand up and down her shin. "Not a clue. The last Mom told me about her was that she was in England."

"Wonder how long she's been back." Dani nibbled on one of the crackers.

"I honestly don't give a shit how long she's been here or how long she plans to stay. You're the one I care about."

* * *

Dani could hear the emotion in his voice, the sincerity in his words. She just needed to force herself to believe him.

Seeing the beautiful woman Nate had loved, the one he'd been engaged to, the one he'd almost shared a child with, had been a shock she'd had no time to prepare for. Even worse, to watch as Kat threw herself at him and kissed him had been gut-wrenching.

Overwhelmed by jealousy and worried that Nate had dragged her here as some sort of weird way to try to win Kat back, Dani did what she did best where emotions were involved.

She retreated.

It had seemed the best tack, and she hadn't been lying when she'd told them she had a headache. Her head pounded in rhythm with her wounded heart. She'd allowed some tears of disappointment to fall, and crying, even if only for a minute or two, had helped ease the hurt of both her head and her heart.

Only a woman in love could have been so devastated by a friendly kiss of greeting, and she simply didn't want to accept that she'd fallen in love with Nate Ryan.

Once she could push aside the jealousy, she'd started to see things as they truly were. Nate hadn't been at all happy to see Kat. Although she'd hugged him, he hadn't hugged her back. Nor had he kissed her. There had been no welcome in his words, only the same confusion Dani had felt.

"I'm sorry I ran away." She held the warm cup in her hands before sipping more tea.

"You didn't run away. You had a headache."

She nodded. "Car rides get to me sometimes."

"Car rides and unexpected surprises—*bad* surprises. So how about a good surprise?"

"Hmm?" she hummed as she took another drink. "A good surprise?"

"Yep. Turns out my mom likes you."

Dani didn't mean to snort. It just slipped out.

"I mean it," Nate insisted. "She does, and I can prove it."

"How?"

His dimples were going to be the death of her. "She promised not to cook for you."

Chapter 20

Nate had chosen the restaurant, but Dani didn't really care. She wasn't particularly hungry, so it really didn't matter where they went. To have to sit across the table from Kat and Jackie would be difficult regardless of the locale.

A week. How was Dani supposed to survive a week with Nate's ex hanging around, probably trying her best to seduce him? And then there was his mother. He might have tried to convince Dani that Jackie liked her, but doubt remained. For the time being, she put on a confident façade and tried not to let anyone know exactly how flustered she was.

All she truly wanted was to go home, but there wasn't a chance she would run. She would never let Kat or Jackie know exactly how much they rattled her. She was already angry at herself for her cowardly retreat. The victorious look in Kat's eyes when Nate had led Dani from the basement had been more than enough to put starch in her spine.

"So is Nate going to be as good a teacher as his mom?" Mark asked.

Meeting Jackie's husband had been a pleasant surprise. Mark

Brennan was handsome enough to be a model, the gray peppering his dark hair only adding to his appeal, and he was kind and welcoming. Having expected him to be in Kat's corner for her obvious attempts to snag Nate back, Dani was pleased that Mark accepted her with open arms.

Dani favored him with a smile, and not one of the fake ones she had to give Kat or Jackie. "From the way you phrased the question, I'll assume Jackie was a terrific teacher."

"You betcha I was," Jackie replied.

Mark simply nodded.

"Then, yes. Nate is going to be every bit as good. The kids adore him, and from all the times I've observed his class, I can tell he really knows his stuff."

Nate's hand settled on her thigh, where he gave her a pat. "Thanks."

"Just telling it how it is," she said. "English is such a tough subject to teach. Most of the kids come to class thinking it'll be boring."

With a shake of his head, Nate said, "Silly kids. With all the great books out there to read? Boring my ass."

Dani nodded. "I know, right?"

"Biology was easier," Jackie admitted. "The students got to get their hands dirty. Dissections. Labs. Experiments."

Mark draped his arm over Jackie's shoulders, something Nate also had the habit of doing that Dani enjoyed. "That and every single one of them thought you walked on water."

"Hardly," Jackie said with a scoff.

Kat had been a bit sullen through the meal, probably sulking at how comfortable Mark seemed to be with Dani. She jumped into the conversation. "So do all the girls flirt with Nate? I imagine with his good looks—"

"They do," Dani replied as sweetly as she could manage. "He's just humble enough not to see it."

"Nate, be careful." Jackie's brows gathered in concern. "Don't ever be alone with any of the girls."

He nodded. "Dani already gave me that talk. Helps that her room is right across the hall." His hand moved over her leg, tickling a little closer to the juncture of her thighs with each rub. Thankfully, his actions were concealed by the long green tablecloth. "She seems to have a sixth sense as to when I need her."

The heat in the restaurant shot up, or at least Dani's internal temperature did. The way Nate had so openly showed her how much she meant to him every time Kat was around had helped Dani find her confidence to stand firm against the little digs Kat kept throwing her way.

"Must be weird," Kat said. "Having all those young girls making eyes at you."

"I honestly don't see it," he replied.

"You never did realize your own appeal." Kat batted her eyes at him.

Nate appeared unfazed, which made Dani smile. "Dani was the teacher of the year for the whole corporation last year," he said. "Quite an honor, and she was one of the finalists for Illinois teacher of the year."

Her face flushing warm at the compliment, she winked at him. "It was just my turn. After all, Mallory won a couple of years back. Jules was teacher of the year her fifth year at Douglas. And Beth has won that title twice."

"So it's the Ladies Who Lunch for the win." He punctuated the teasing by giving her a pinch on the butt, which only made her face warmer.

Bad thing about being so fair skinned was that blushes were like flashing neon lights.

Kat cocked her head. "Are you okay, Dani? Having a hot flash or something?"

How old does she think I am? Dani needed some payback, which made her bolder than she probably should've been. "Nah. Just blushing since Nate's over here pinching—"

"Hey," he scolded. "That's private."

From the scowl on Kat's face, she'd figured out exactly what was happening. "How long have you been a teacher?" she asked. "Nineteen years? Twenty? Longer?"

Ah, finally. The slam about the difference in their ages. Dani let it roll right off her back. "Long enough to know the ropes."

"Put the claws away, my wee Kat." The stern frown Mark threw at his daughter was enough to almost make Dani bust out in a grateful giggle. Then he directed his attention to Dani. "What did Nate mean by the Ladies Who Lunch?"

Dani gave him the story of how the Ladies had been born that cold day in Chicago so many years ago. "The name just stuck. Everyone calls us that now, although Jules isn't teaching anymore. She's selling real estate with her husband. But Mallory, Beth, and I are still in the trenches. Probably always will be."

"Don't let Jackie get you alone." After Mark playfully jostled his wife with his elbow, he added, "She'll give you her lecture on why you and Nate should be getting out of education, like you're on the *Titanic* and it's going down, down, down." He held his nose and puffed out his cheeks, as if going underwater.

Jackie punched him on the upper arm. "I won't *lecture* them. I'll simply give them some good advice and the benefit of my hard-earned wisdom."

"I understand totally why you'd think education is a bad

career," Dani said. "It's pretty crazy right now. I guess I like working with the kids so much, I put up with the crap and try to minimize it."

"Can I ask you something?" Kat had folded her arms under her breasts and leaned back in her chair, shooting daggers at Dani with her dark eyes. "Doesn't it bother you that you're so much older than Nate? I mean, you live in such a small town. Don't people gossip about you having a younger boyfriend?"

"Kat…" Mark growled.

"No, it's okay," Dani said. "I don't mind answering." She leveled her best don't-fuck-with-me smile at Kat. "I'm really not that much older than Nate. Not quite…what?" She turned to Nate to include him, even though she knew exactly how much older she was. "Eight years?"

"Seven and change, sweetheart. You could be my very own cougar if you were older. But alas"—he picked up her hand and kissed the back of her knuckles—"we're just a regular couple."

"So you can see," Dani continued, "the age thing really isn't an issue."

Kat let out a snort.

The waiter came over to see if anyone wanted dessert. The pasta had more than filled Dani's stomach, and all she wanted was to go home and relax. Unfortunately, she'd be going to the Brennans' home, and she couldn't even look forward to snuggling up against Nate when it came time to go to bed. When he'd told his family that he'd moved upstairs with her, he hadn't asked if the Brennans minded his sharing a room with her now. The basement was Dani's for the week, but Nate was taking one of the upstairs bedrooms.

No one was in the mood for something sweet, so the waiter was leaving the black folder on the table right when Dani's phone rang.

She'd wanted to get the check, but Mark reached for it first. Since her phone continued to ring, she wasn't able to argue with him. She fished her phone out of her pocket, ready to silence the ringer and let it go to voice mail. Then she caught the name of the caller.

Robert.

A rush of adrenaline sent her heart slamming against her chest. There was no reason for him to be calling unless… "Beth." She offered the group a sheepish apology. "I'm sorry, but I really need to take this." As she rose to stride toward the entrance so she could step outside the restaurant, she answered the call. "Robert. What's wrong?"

"I'm sorry to bother you, Dani. Beth's in the hospital."

Shoving open the door, Dani stepped out into the quiet night air. "What happened?" A million horrifying scenarios ran through her head. A car accident. A mugging. Beth's stomach bug was really appendicitis.

"She couldn't stop throwing up. Well, not throwing up so much as heaving. There can't be a thing left in her stomach. I finally insisted we go to the ER because she was so damned dehydrated that her lips were cracking and bleeding. They've got her on IV fluids and are keeping her at least a day or two."

"That's a hell of a stomach bug. I'll get home as soon as I can." If Nate wasn't ready to leave his family, she'd just drive back by herself. Maybe he could get a rental car, or once Beth was better, Dani could come back and get him.

"That would be great. She's really worried about Emma. We dropped her off with Jules, but…"

"I know, I know. Jules already has her hands full with the twins since her manny has fall break off."

Nate came outside to stand next to her and took her hand. "Everything okay?"

Dani grasped his hand and squeezed, hoping he'd realize she couldn't answer him yet. "I'll call Jules and let her know I'll be there as fast as I can drive. I can get Emma and take her to your place—if that's okay? Figured it would be easier if she had her own stuff."

"That would be great," Robert said, his voice full of relief. "You've got the garage door code, right?"

"Yep."

"I want to stay here with Beth."

"I understand. I'll text as soon as I have a rental car for Nate."

"He won't come home with you?" Robert asked.

"Not really sure," she replied. "I haven't asked him yet, but he might want to stay with his family."

"Well, drive carefully. I need to get back to Beth."

Nate jumped as soon as she pulled the phone away from her ear. "What's wrong?"

"Beth's in the hospital."

"What happened?"

"The stomach thing was a lot worse than she thought," Dani replied. "They need me to come back and take care of Emma." Instead of putting him on the spot, she asked, "Think you can get a rental car for the ride home?" She pulled up Google on her phone. "Maybe you can go with me now since we passed the Indy airport on the drive in. Then you could get a rental—"

"Put that phone away," he insisted. "We'll go to Mom's house and grab our stuff, then get right on the road." He checked his watch. "We should be there before midnight."

"You don't have to leave, Nate. I'll pay for the rental."

"Don't be silly." He held the door open. "I know you're worried about Beth, and I can give you some help with Emma." He took her hand and led her back to the table. "Mom, Mark, I'm really sorry, but we have to cut our visit short."

Dani couldn't stop a smug smile at the notion he'd deliberately excluded Kat from his apology.

"What happened?" Jackie's gaze kept shifting between her son and Dani, who tried hard not to see accusation in her eyes.

"My best friend's in the hospital." Dani took her jacket from the back of her chair and then plucked the black folder, hoping that it still held the check. "Please let me pick up the tab for tonight."

"Too late," Mark replied as she opened the folder. "Took care of it while you were outside."

The final receipt showed his credit card payment. He'd left a generous tip, so she couldn't even offer to pitch in for that. "Thank you." She set the folder back down. Figuring she needed to give Nate one more chance to change his mind, she took his hand. "I know you were looking forward to visiting your family. I can help you get a rental car before I drive back to Cloverleaf. It's not a problem. The airport's on the way home anyway, and—"

"Nope. We're both going." Turning to his mom, he said, "I'm sorry. I really am, but Beth and Robert are my friends, too. Dani's going to stay with their daughter, Emma. She's barely a toddler and Dani will need my help."

Jackie didn't even try to hide her disappointment. "Maybe you can come back in a day or two?"

"Maybe," Nate replied before looking to Dani.

If Beth was in the hospital, she was in bad shape. The woman avoided doctors as though going to their office was a sure way to turn a simple problem into a life-or-death situation. Allowing herself to be admitted meant it would take days for her to recover, and Dani planned to be there for her, Robert, and Emma.

But she sure didn't want Jackie blaming her for Nate leaving.

"I really think you should stay. I doubt I'll be able to come back, but there's no reason for you to go."

Jackie opened her mouth, but Mark's hand quickly covered it. "We understand." He frowned at his wife until she sighed against his palm. "You two need to be there for your friends. I hope Beth gets well soon."

Kat stood. "Nate, may I speak to you in private for a moment?"

The look he gave her was the same one he offered students when he was about to send them to the office.

Dani intervened. "Go on." She nudged his ribs. Not only was she dying of curiosity for Kat to finally show her cards, but she also didn't want to come across as the jealous girlfriend.

Hesitating, he stared down at Dani.

She nudged him again, a little harder. "Go on. The faster you talk to her, the faster we can get going."

"Well, since you're finally agreeing that I'm going, too, I'll give in. This time." Motioning to Kat, he led her toward the entrance, probably to go outside where it was quiet for their little chat.

* * *

Nate would rather have been doing anything else in the world than talking to Kat. A flu shot. A punch to the face. An IRS audit. All would've been preferable. But then again, it was time to get her to stop her attacks on his girlfriend.

Damn, he was proud of Dani. She'd stood her ground, no matter how snarky Kat got. At least Mark had called his daughter out for being so rude, but had Dani not been asked to come back to Cloverleaf, that disrespect would no doubt have continued. Then Nate would've had to intervene as well. And he wouldn't have been half as nice as Mark had been.

"What do you want, Kat?" Nate asked as soon as they were away from the people waiting at the entrance. He made no effort to hide his annoyance with her. If she was going to be impolite, two could play at that game.

Clasping her hands in front of her, she let her head hang. "I'm sorry about today. I'm ashamed of myself."

Having been burned by her false apologies on far too many occasions, he wasn't about to let her off the hook. "For what?"

"For being such a bitch to Dani."

"Got that right." He raked his fingers through his hair. "You know, I just don't understand your motivation. We broke up a long time ago. Who I date isn't your concern."

Her head snapped up. "But that's what I want to talk to you about."

"What?"

Taking a step closer, she put her hand on his arm. "I made a big mistake. I realize that now." She shrugged. "Shit, I've made *a lot* of big mistakes. Losing you was the worst, though."

While his ego loved that she'd finally appreciated exactly what she'd thrown away by leaving him, her words didn't move him—at least not much. There would always be a part of him that loved Kat. But he wasn't in love with her anymore.

No, he was in love with Dani.

Admitting it to himself was easy. The feeling had been blooming inside him almost from the moment he met her. So different from the instant love he'd had for Kat. The way he'd chased her around seemed so damned juvenile now. To compare that feeling to the affection he held for Dani was just…wrong.

Everything about the two women was different, so it shouldn't have been such a surprise that his love for each of them was different as well. Kat—dark, petite, and so open about everything she thought and felt. His desire for her had been like a bottle rocket. Hot, bright, and every bit as fast dying as it had been in developing. Dani—light, tall, and secretive about what was in her heart and in her mind. She was passion and goodness and everything he wanted for his future and for the future mother of his children.

Nate suddenly wanted to find Dani and tell her that he loved her. There was no doubt in his mind that he'd have to find the balls to say it first. Knowing her as well as he did—and loving her as much as he did—he knew she'd never admit that she loved him.

If she did…

Oh, she *did*—but did she realize it yet? And if she knew, would she ever admit it?

Kat rubbed his arm, and the hurt was there for him to see in her eyes and hear in her voice. "Nate, can't you stay? Please? I want some time with you. I want us to see if there's still something between us, something worth saving. Stay with me. Let Dani go take care of her friend and give me a chance to explain everything."

The best thing to do would be to pretend she hadn't ever said the words, but it was more difficult than he thought it should be. To discuss the past with her would be akin to telling her there was a sliver of hope. He'd learned the hard way that she had a habit of hearing things she wanted to hear instead of what was actually said. "I need to head home with Dani."

"Please, Nate." Her brown eyes searched his, and he recognized that look—the one that she'd used on him so often to try to sway him. "I need you to forgive me. Please."

"I forgave you a long time ago, Kat."

"Then stay. Please. Let me have the time I need to explain."

"Sorry, Kat. I need to be with Dani."

Her eyes filled with tears. "After all we've meant to each other? After all we've been through? You won't even give me a chance to explain?"

"There's nothing to explain. We're history, have been for a long time. Dani's my life now. I love her."

He hadn't known Dani was there until he heard her gasp. He whirled to find her standing by his mom and Mark, her expression one of stark surprise.

Although Nate hadn't meant to tell her like this, he was relieved the cat was out of the proverbial bag. "Hi, sweetheart. Guess you heard everything we were saying, right?"

"Just the last bit," Mark replied. "Let me see if I can recall it word for word… 'Dani's my life now. I love her.' Pretty close?"

Jackie looked every bit as surprised as Dani, and for once, she held her tongue.

"Damn near perfect," Nate said with a grin.

Chapter 21

Nate looked up when he heard his bedroom door latch click. Kat leaned back against the closed door, her face, for once, unreadable.

He rolled up his extra pair of jeans and shoved them into his duffel. "What do you want, Kat?"

"I just wanted a minute alone with you so we could talk."

"About what?"

"Us."

A heavy sigh slipped from his lips. From the moment she'd told him she wanted him back, he'd known they'd have to hash things out if only to make sure she understood that anything between them was in the past. "There isn't an 'us,' Kat."

"There could be—if you wanted to give it another try."

Zipping up his bag, Nate shook his head. Then he turned to face her. "I don't. I'm with Dani now."

Kat pushed away from the door and took a few steps closer. "I've missed you, Nate." Another step. Then another, until she was close enough to touch him if she chose to. "I've missed you so much."

"Kat…"

The familiar scent of her perfume wafted toward him, and a moment of melancholy over what might have been stunned him. A long time ago, he'd believed this beautiful woman had represented his future. They'd be married and share a child—then later, more children. They'd be a family.

His most painful childhood memory was of hearing his father tell him that he was leaving his mother and that he was marrying a woman only a few years older than his own sons. Nate had fantasized that he could create a perfect family of his own, one where he'd be the perfect husband and father—one where he wouldn't abandon his wife and kids like David Ryan had.

But that dream had slowly died when Kat had changed so drastically after the miscarriage.

Her arms went around his waist. "Kiss me."

"Kat…"

"One kiss. Just one. Then I'll know if you don't love me anymore."

Maybe a kiss would bring an end to all this nonsense. "Fine. See for yourself…"

"Oh, I will." On tiptoes, she pressed her lips to his.

For that moment, he remembered her as she was. Young. Beautiful. He'd been head over heels for her. Kissing her seemed… familiar. Comforting.

Then the moment ended, and he stepped back. Even though now she was so much more like the Kat he'd fallen in love with, and he'd always have feelings for her, he'd left her in his past.

His plans for Dani were so very different. They were real. They weren't some young guy's way to soothe the pain of losing his father to a new family.

"I knew it," Kat declared, a note of triumph in her voice. "I knew you still wanted me."

He shook his head. "Not at all, Kat."

Turning on her heel, a wicked smile on her face, she left the room.

"Good riddance," he mumbled to himself.

* * *

Dani finished packing the few things she'd pulled out of her bag since she'd arrived. Just as she was zipping it up, the sound of the bedroom door closing drew her attention.

Kat leaned back against the closed door. Instead of the stereotypical spurned ex-fiancée frown, she had unshed tears in her eyes. "I just had a long talk with Nate."

Since Dani had wondered why he wasn't tossing stuff back into his own duffel, she shouldn't have been surprised that Kat had cornered him. Nate was a great guy. She wouldn't give him up without a fight. Kat was only doing the same thing—holding on to the man she loved. The difference was that Dani hadn't stolen him away; their relationship had been over for a long time.

"This won't work, you know," Kat said.

"And what exactly do you think won't work?" Dani asked, playing coy in hopes of sparking the woman's obvious hot temper. If Kat got angry, she wouldn't guard her words, which might give Dani something that would help in the fight to keep Nate. Women played dirty, especially when battling over a guy. The more ammunition, the better her chances of winning.

The brunette pushed herself away from the door. "Can we stop playing games?"

So Kat's thoughts ran along a similar vein. "I hadn't realized that was what we were doing…"

Kat's snort was in sharp contrast to her beautiful face. "You and I both know damn well that's *exactly* what we're doing—playing a game."

"And Nate's the prize?"

All of Kat's cockiness vanished. "Nate's not some prize. He's my whole life. I need him. I want to make a family with him."

While she didn't want to be snarky in the face of what seemed to be Kat's real pain, Dani couldn't help but state the obvious. "*You* left *him*. If he's your whole life, why would you do something like that?"

"Because I was young and stupid."

"And you suddenly realized that the moment Nate said he loved me?"

Kat shook her head. "I've known since I came home from Europe. I just haven't had the chance to talk to him until now."

"So he doesn't have a phone or e-mail? Face it, people aren't so hard to get in touch with nowadays."

Narrowing her eyes, Kat said, "You don't have to be a bitch about this."

"You're trying to steal my guy." Dani kept her voice low and controlled, hiding the emotions tumbling through her. "Damn right I'm going to be a bitch about it."

They stood there in stilted silence until Dani couldn't take another moment. "Kat, I have no idea what you want me to say. If you think I'm just going to walk away—"

"No, I know you wouldn't do that. Nate's too great a guy to give up that easily." Kat gave a delicate sniff as though fighting tears.

A knock on the closed door made Kat jump.

"Dani?" Jackie called through the door. "Anything I can do to help you get ready?"

"This isn't over," Kat hissed before jerking open the door. She tossed Jackie a fake smile and disappeared down the hallway.

Jackie's brows gathered as she watched her stepdaughter walk away. Then she let out a heavy sigh and shook her head. "I saw her come up here, and I figured you might want someone to bail you out."

"I can hold my own."

Jackie smiled. "I kinda thought you could."

When she didn't move out of the doorway, Dani assumed it was time for the second family confrontation about Nate's announcement that he lived with her. "Did you want to talk to me?"

"I shouldn't," Jackie admitted. "If I were smart, I'd just walk away and mind my own business." Her eyes met Dani's. "Evidently I'm not very smart, because I really want to talk to you."

This conversation had to rank among the most uncomfortable of Dani's life. "Well, since I need to be getting back to Cloverleaf to help my friend, let's talk."

Strolling to the bed, Jackie sat and then patted the space beside her. "Come. Sit."

If this woman was going to be a part of her life, Dani needed to get along with her. For Nate's sake. It wasn't as if anything Jackie could say would be as bad as the challenge Kat had tossed at her feet.

Dani sat next to Jackie. "What did you want to talk about?"

"Kat."

Having figured Jackie was here to caution about moving in too quickly, the topic stopped Dani cold. "What?"

"I want to talk about Kat," Jackie replied. "I wasn't exactly eavesdropping…but I heard quite a bit of what she said to you."

Trying to give Jackie the benefit of the doubt, Dani had to admit if she'd been close enough to hear the kind of exchange that had happened between her and Kat, she'd also have stayed to hear as much as she could. "So what exactly did you want to say?"

"Kat's a little spoiled." Jackie leaned close enough to bump her shoulder against Dani's in a friendly way. "Please don't tell my husband I said that. Don't get me wrong, he's a good dad. It's just that his first wife died when the girls were adolescents. He always gave Kat and Carly just about anything they wanted—Kat more so than Carly. Probably because Kat looks so damned much like her mother."

Unsure as to what to say, all Dani did was nod. Being spoiled might be part of the reason Kat was adamant that she'd get Nate back.

"What's flying through your head?" Jackie asked. "I mean, Kat threw the gauntlet at your feet and all…"

"I know."

"What you probably need to know is that Nate won't go back to her."

Dani let her eyes find Jackie's. "You're sure of that?"

"Absolutely. And if you knew Nate better, you'd be every bit as sure." Jackie's mouth dropped to a frown. "I think that's what's bothering me most—the fact that you two haven't known each other all that long."

Only three months. "We're not exactly kids. We know our own minds."

"How old are you, Dani?"

So Jackie had finally found the temerity to ask. "I'm thirty-two—almost eight years older, like Nate said back at the restaurant."

"You're right, then. You're not a kid. But Nate…?" Jackie let the thought hang in the air, implying that her son was too young to make this kind of choice.

"He's more mature at twenty-four than most thirtysomething guys I've known."

Jackie nodded. "He had to grow up pretty fast when his dad left me. And then there was the miscarriage. Did he—"

"Yes, he told me about that."

Jackie cocked her head. "It's kind of ironic that he was the one who started thinking like an adult and Kat was the one who retreated back to hedonistic childhood. When I was a teacher, most teenaged parents were the opposite."

"I know what you mean," Dani admitted. "The girls always take the responsibility and grow up. The guys try to find a way to escape."

Jackie let out a rueful laugh. "Like a wolf chewing off his own foot to get out of a trap." She sobered quickly. "I'm not sure exactly what I'm trying to say."

The talk hadn't been at all what Dani expected, so she wasn't sure what to say, either. "If you think I'm going to roll over and play dead just because Kat said—"

"No, no," Jackie insisted. "From what I've seen, you're far too much like me to ever let that happen." They shared a smile. "I guess I just wanted you to know that Kat is all talk. She always has grand ideas and thinks everything will fall into place easily since that's what Mark allowed her to think after her mother died. But when it comes time for Kat to step up to the plate and actually do something that requires effort to achieve a goal?" She shook her head. "She's all talk."

"Thanks." Feeling awkward, Dani let the silence hang between them.

"You should get going." Jackie got to her feet. "You've got a long trip to get back to help your friend."

Staring up at Nate's mom, Dani said, "Thanks, Jackie."

She smiled down at Dani. "For what? For talking your ear off and not really saying anything?"

"You said a lot more than you realize."

And I think you're on my side now…

Chapter 22

Nate pulled Dani's car into the garage in the wee small hours of the morning. Not only had she trusted him with her precious car, but she'd also been comfortable enough to fall asleep on the drive home.

He sat there for a moment, looking at her, wondering what he'd done to deserve a woman that beautiful. And her beauty was more than skin deep. Here she was, hurrying back to help a friend. That was so very Dani. Then there was the compassion she gave her students, mixed with exactly the right amount of motherly sternness. How could he not love her?

One day, when she admitted that she loved him, too, he'd have to go ring shopping.

Marriage. He was thinking about marriage, and not in the same way he had with Kat. This time, it was because he wanted to marry her, not because he felt as if he had to. Had Kat not found herself pregnant, marriage would never have been brought up. Not for years.

So why the change? Why even think about jumping into the choppy wedding waters?

Because of Dani and all she inspired in him.

Dani stirred before Nate had to nudge her awake. With sleepy eyes, she turned her head to smile at him. "Hey."

"Hey. We're home."

"Hmmm. Yeah."

Nate stroked her cheek, loving how she tilted her head to get more of his touch. "Want me to carry you upstairs?"

"No, thanks." After another drowsy smile, she popped open her seat belt and then got out of the car.

He followed her, hitting the garage door closer before joining her in the kitchen.

She put her purse aside and kicked off her shoes. "We should get some sleep. I want to get to the hospital early."

"It was nice of Jules to keep Emma for tonight."

With a nod, Dani took his hand and started leading him toward the stairs. "Better to let her sleep since she was already down for the night."

While she might have sleep on her mind, Nate's thoughts were focused solely on making love to her as a way to seal his declaration of love. He needed to make it real, to feel the connection they shared.

Once they were in the bedroom, she yawned again, making his hopes plummet. She was clearly too tired to do anything except go right back to sleep. A big disappointment since he'd had an interesting idea of what he'd wanted to do to her, *with* her—another way to help her learn to trust. So far she'd been an outstanding student. He had no doubt she'd love this lesson every bit as much as he would.

Some other time, perhaps. When she wasn't exhausted.

Dani whipped her shirt over her head and then shoved it in the wicker hamper. Facing him boldly, she peeled down her tight jeans, kicking them and her socks aside. She stood before him in a white lace bra and purple panties.

His cock had already begun to harden at the mere thought of making love to her. One glimpse of her body now made it rigid as a board. "Shit, I want you, Dani."

Her sexy smile stole his breath away. "Then come get me."

"You're not too tired?"

"Not tired at all. I did sleep most of the way home, remember?"

"Well, then…" Scooping her into his arms, he kissed her soundly before setting her on the bed. "I'd like to try something… different."

She eyed him warily. "Different? As in kinky different?"

"A little," he admitted. "It's about trust."

"Isn't everything with you about trust?"

Since Nate wasn't sure if Dani was teasing or not, he wasn't sure what to say. Had he taken his need for her to trust him too far, turning into a control freak himself as a result? Had he pushed too far too soon to try to get the woman he loved to open up to him completely?

"Different, huh? Sounds like fun," she purred. "What did you have in mind?"

"I'll show instead of tell."

Scrambling across the bed, she tried to follow him into the huge master closet. She ran into his chest.

"Stay here, Dani."

With a pouty lip, she nodded.

He dropped his clothes on the floor of the closet before looking around until he found what he wanted.

"Nate?" she called as he grabbed the items.

"Coming!" Then he chuckled when he realized the double entendre. "Not right away, though." He came out of the closet naked, holding a couple of neckties and a folded blue bandana. "It's time to put that fantastic bed to use."

He moved behind her, placing the bandana over her eyes. "I want you to trust me," he whispered in her ear as he tied the cloth tightly and rubbed his erection against her backside. "Completely. Can you do that, Dani? Trust me completely?"

He stepped around her before he brushed his lips across hers, forcing a quick gasp since she couldn't have expected his touch.

Nate took her wrists in one hand and bound them with a silky tie.

"Should I be afraid?" Dani asked in a soft whisper.

"Never. Remember that I love you. Now, follow me." A tug on the ties, and she slowly walked until she collided with his chest. "You can stop now," he said with another chuckle.

He let her bound hands drop and she reached forward, trying to touch his face. A quick jerk of the ties pulled her arms down. "You can only do what I tell you." He kept his voice authoritative.

She nodded.

Encircling her waist, Nate lifted, letting her toes scuff the floor. He walked her backward until the bed pressed against the backs of her thighs. "Sit."

Dani let her bottom rest on the sheets. "I want you."

"Patience, sweetheart."

"All right."

He knew exactly how difficult this was for her. The woman had to hate not being able to see, not being able to control even a moment of this experience, and she was probably dying to know how he would punish her if she didn't obey his commands. The only true punishment he could give would be to leave her alone, but that would punish him as well. Everything inside him was screaming to take her. *Now.* And how he'd be able to let the rest of this scenario play out, he wasn't sure. The anticipation alone was killing him.

This had to be special—*more* than special—and he'd hate himself if he didn't make her enjoy this more than any other time they'd come together. No, tonight was unique.

He sensed an enormous change in her. For the first time since they'd been together, Dani wanted *him* to lead, wanted *him* to run the show. Perhaps she'd finally realized that in letting someone else call the shots, she still won. Now all he needed to do was keep enough self-control to give her as much pleasure as her trust was giving him.

"Lie back," Nate whispered, his voice ragged with desire.

"Okay." Dani scooted back to lie on the mattress close to her usual spot.

Pulling the tie, he lifted her arms until he could bind her to one of the headboard spindles. Then he popped the front clasp on her bra. "So beautiful." He laved each nipple, loving how they hardened in invitation. Then he traced her pink ribbon tattoo with his tongue. With trembling hands, he dragged her panties down her legs and tossed them aside. "Spread your legs."

He savored her quick breaths and the smile widening on her lips when his fingers separated her folds. She was already so wet. Without a hint of warning, Nate sank a finger deep inside her and stroked the walls of her tight sheath.

"Oh, shit." Dani dropped her head back before her teeth tugged on her bottom lip hard enough he was amazed she didn't draw blood.

"You can speak, sweetheart. Just don't ask questions."

"Thank you."

"Such a good girl," he said with a chuckle. A second finger joined the first, and he tortured her with them until she started undulating her hips. Then he stopped and jerked his hand away. "That was your reward for good behavior."

"Nate…" she pleaded.

"You please me; I please you."

He kissed his way down her flat stomach, tickling her navel with his tongue, and then rubbed the stubble on his cheek against her inner thighs.

"Nate!"

He buried his face between her thighs, loving her with his mouth, his tongue. Her back arched, and he promptly stopped his attentions. Her pouty sigh made him smile.

"I love you," he said as he kissed his way back to her breasts. "I do. I love you." A reverent kiss to each breast before he settled beside her. His mouth touched hers. She turned her head and parted her lips when his tongue teased the seam.

Although she didn't return the words, he was a patient man. She loved him. Somehow he knew that in his heart.

The words would come. In time.

Nate kissed her long and deep, coaxing her tongue into his mouth where he gently sucked. Damn, he loved kissing her. An appreciative sigh slipped from her when he pulled away. Then he slipped his fingers between her legs, stroking her until he found the sensitive nub he sought.

"Oh!" Her back arched as she drew her knees up.

"Relax, sweetheart. Just let it happen."

"But—" She bit back whatever she was going to say, planted her heels against the mattress, and started moving her hips again.

Sensing her imminent orgasm, he became more enthusiastic, sucking first on one breast before drawing the other nipple deep into his mouth as he rubbed her and then slid a finger deep inside her tight heat.

When she came, she shouted, "I love you, Nate!"

Peace settled on him as he waited for her breathing to slow and her body to settle. "Did you like that?" he whispered in her ear as he placed a palm against her belly.

"Yes."

Nate moved between her thighs, his hard cock pushing against her core. "I wanted this to last longer, but, God, Dani. I need to be inside you."

* * *

Was Nate asking for permission? After everything Dani had allowed him to do, he shouldn't need her permission to take that last step.

"Sweetheart?"

The pleading in his voice brought tears to her eyes. She'd bared her soul to him by offering him her total trust and by admitting her love. Now he was baring his, showing that despite his wild side and this wonderful night they were sharing, the man was still a gentleman at heart. "Now, Nate. Please."

One hard thrust, and he planted himself deep inside her at the same time his mouth claimed hers again. Although she often closed her eyes when they made love, now all she wanted to do was look into his eyes to see if the love reflected there was as deep, as fathomless, as the love she felt for him at that moment.

The blindfold was jerked away, and his face loomed over hers in the dim light from the open door of the closet. He pulled back until he almost left her body, then thrust inside her again. "I love you so much."

"I love you, too." She arched her hips to take him deeper. His groan hit her hard, and suddenly he started moving, fast and furious, slamming into her again and again as she matched his rhythm.

Nate reached for the tie binding her hands, gave it a good tug, and suddenly her wrists were free. She would have shouted her thanks, but she was too busy being ravished and enjoying every damn minute of it. Her hands roamed his back, his backside, his shoulders.

Dani wrapped her legs around his hips just before her orgasm took hold. Her core contracted as she breathed his name, clutching at his shoulders the same way her body clutched at his cock. His back was sure to be marked with fingernail trails. A few frantic thrusts and he cried out, bathing her in his heat. For a few moments, all she could do was cling to him, waiting for the storm to pass. He collapsed on top of her, his head buried beside hers on the pillow.

"Damn, Dani. I think you killed me."

She chuckled as she ran her hand lazily up and down his spine, too content to budge. Every muscle in her body felt totally relaxed, and if Nate hadn't moved, she could have easily fallen asleep in that position. But he broke their connection, rolling onto his side. He took her into his arms.

She fell asleep listening to him whisper his love in her ear.

Chapter 23

Beth looked like hell. Not that Dani would ever tell her that, but her best friend was as pale as she'd ever seen anyone, and her eyes sported dark half-moons as though she hadn't slept in days. She offered a wan smile when Dani walked into the hospital room.

"Hi," Dani whispered, trying not to disturb Robert. He was asleep on one of the hospital's chair-beds, snoring loud enough to wake the dead. She would've given Beth a kiss on the cheek if she weren't lying on a hospital bed with a bad case of a stomach bug. Instead, she patted Beth's blanketed feet. "How weird is it to be on the pediatric unit?"

"A bit surreal, but it evidently couldn't be helped. The hospital is jam-packed right now, according to my nurses." Beth pointed to a rather creepy clown painted on the far wall, which put it directly in her line of vision. "That scary thing makes it hard to sleep."

A tray of barely touched breakfast food sat on the bed table. "Stomach still a mess?" Dani asked as she nodded at the tray.

"Yeah. But getting better. I was able to keep some oatmeal down this morning. See the big white IV bag?"

Dani nodded.

"My doctor called it a 'calorie milkshake.' It's a nutritional supplement."

That meant Beth's case was so much worse than Dani had believed. "They're feeding you through IV? For the stomach flu? Good Lord, Beth…"

"It's not the stomach flu." Beth patted the bed beside her. "Come here. Sit with me."

While Dani wanted to go to her, to wrap Beth in her arms and rock her sick friend, she hesitated. The last thing she needed was to wind up in the hospital herself or to give Emma the illness she'd thus far luckily escaped. Jules was supposed to have her ready for Dani and Nate to pick up sometime after their pancake breakfast.

But why wasn't Robert sick? "So it's not the stomach flu?" Dani asked.

"Nope. And I'm not contagious. Promise." Another pat on the white blanket.

"Should I leave you two alone?" Nate stood just to the side of the half-drawn curtain. He'd slid his hands into his front pockets, looking terribly uncomfortable. "I don't want to intrude."

"Why don't you wake up Robert and take him to the cafeteria?" Beth suggested. "He'll want some coffee for sure, and he could probably stand to stretch his muscles." She frowned at her sleeping husband. "That thing can't be very comfortable."

Robert was such a great guy. He'd accepted Emma as his own child, loving her every bit as much as any true father. Her mother, Beth's sister Tiffany, had died while serving in Afghanistan.

He'd stayed at Beth's side through this illness. Dani couldn't help but compare him to Nate, and she was sure he would be sleeping in the same uncomfortable chair should she ever wind up in the hospital.

Nate jostled Robert. Although Robert gladly followed Nate's

suggestion that they go get coffee, he didn't appear to be fully awake, yawning and stumbling after Nate like a zombie searching for fresh brains.

Sitting next to Beth, Dani offered her a weak smile, wanting to show support and strength but full of anxiety for her best friend's welfare. In her typical overanalyzing manner, she started worrying about the horrible things that could be assailing Beth. Appendicitis. Ulcers. Cancer.

No, no, no. Beth was her best friend. She couldn't have something that might take her away from Dani.

But Mallory had battled cancer. No one was immune from the insidious disease. Not even a pure soul like Beth Ashford.

Dear God, I need her. Please let her be well.

Shaking her head to fight back the tears brimming in her eyes, Dani focused on being strong for Beth. "So what's wrong? An ulcer or something?"

"I'm pregnant."

Those two words shouldn't have come as such a shock, but Dani could only gape at Beth. Sure, the Ashfords had been trying to have a baby for a while—since not long after they'd adopted Emma.

Emma coming into Beth's life had already changed their friendship, giving Beth less freedom and different priorities. Since Dani had no intention of having children of her own, she had trouble mustering up enthusiasm for things like strollers or car seats or cute little ruffled dresses. Sure, she was Emma's "Aunt Dandy" and loved her with all her heart, but to have the responsibility of a child twenty-four/seven wasn't at all what Dani wanted for herself.

"Why are you here if you're only pregnant?"

"My morning sickness is horrible," Beth replied. "First of all, that's the worst name ever. Morning sickness?" She snorted. "Try all darn day sickness. I threw up so much I got really dehydrated. I mean…I wanted to lose a little weight, but geesh. Down ten pounds in a week." Her fragile smile was pure Beth. "Be careful what you wish for."

"I'm so sorry." Dani wrapped an arm around Beth's shoulders.

"It's called hyperemesis gravidarum."

Dani nodded. "I read about that in the news, some royal princess had the same problem, right?"

Beth echoed Dani's nod. "Hence the calorie milkshake. I really can't take strong meds to stop the nausea or vomiting 'cause they might hurt the baby." She frowned. "You don't seem very happy for me."

So like Beth to be attuned to what Dani was thinking and feeling. "I'm sorry. I really am happy for you and Robert. I'm just worried about you. You're in the hospital, after all."

"I should be able to go home later today or tomorrow."

Dani withdrew her arm and stood, not because she wanted to distance herself but because the stupid bedrail was digging into her thigh. "I'll keep an eye on Emma until you do. I can stay after you get home if you need me to. You're not going to be up for doing much until this stops."

"I just might take you up on that offer." Beth's gaze shifted to the door. "Robert's exhausted. He's such a good daddy. A good husband, too. I don't know what I'd do without him."

Seeing that statement as the perfect segue, Dani smiled. "Nate told me he loves me."

After doing nothing but gaping and blinking for a few long moments, Beth let a slow smile bloom on her pale face. "I'm impressed."

Of all the reactions Dani had expected from her friend, this wasn't one of them. "Impressed?"

"He's a guy who knows what he wants and goes for it. He's got balls."

"Beth!"

"Well, he does. Give me the details!"

At least telling the story of his spontaneous declaration helped Dani stop worrying about Beth. "Kat came to see me before we left. She wants him back."

"Too bad, so sad," Beth said. "Nate won't go back to her."

"You sound like his mom."

"Did you two get along? I know you were worried she doesn't like you... Although I have no idea why you think that. Everyone likes you."

"I love that you think that, no matter how wrong you are," Dani said. "I'm well aware of exactly how annoying I can be."

"We all have our faults."

The memory of her talk with Jackie made Dani grin. "Jackie heard Kat's threat."

Beth knit her brows. "Threat? You didn't say she threatened you." Her eyes swept Dani from head to toe. "Is she as tall as you?" Her worried expression shifted to a smile. "I'll bet you can take her."

"That's enough of that, Rocky. It wasn't a physical threat. And, yes, I think I could take her." She winked at Beth.

"Then what kind of threat— Oh, you mean to steal Nate, right?"

Dani nodded.

"You can still take her, Dani."

Wishing she was as confident as Beth sounded, Dani paced at the foot of the bed, too restless to sit still. "I sure hope so."

"I mean it. You love him, don't you? Not that you'd admit it..."

"I did," Dani said proudly.

"You did?"

Dani nodded.

"Way to go! He'd never turn away from that. Ever."

"Yeah, well...Kat was his first love." Although Nate might not appreciate her sharing his past, Dani needed to talk to Beth and to show her exactly why Kat might still stand a chance. Then her reassurances would hold a lot more weight. "They got engaged because Kat was pregnant. She told me he was devastated when they lost the baby."

"That's sad, but—"

"No but," Dani insisted. "She wants to have another baby with him."

"There's only one way she can do that, and I have a feeling you're not going to let him sleep with her." With a lopsided smile, Beth added, "Maybe you could suggest she go to a sperm bank and make a withdrawal?"

Dani stopped and whirled to face Beth. "It's not funny, damn it."

"Dani, you've got nothing to worry about."

"You know how I feel about having kids of my own. Will he still want me if he knows I won't give him a child?"

Before Beth could say anything, the door opened. Robert came in, holding a foam coffee cup. Nate was right behind, carrying his typical water bottle. The guy drank enough water every day to fill a kiddie pool.

He took one look at Dani and frowned. "What's wrong?"

Before Dani could answer, Beth fumbled for the pink emesis basin and started gagging.

Robert set his cup on her bed table and started rubbing her back. "I'm here, B. Breathe in through your nose and out through your mouth like the nurse said."

Already angry at herself and feeling horribly selfish, Dani almost burst into tears at watching Beth struggle. She wanted to blurt out an apology for having taken up so much of her time when she clearly should have been resting. "Can I do anything to help?"

Beth had stopped heaving and was taking deep breaths.

Robert shook his head. "The doctor said she might get over this soon—around the end of the first trimester."

Wasn't the first trimester three months? How long had Beth been pregnant? "How far along is she?"

"Eleven weeks," he replied.

A warm hand settled on her shoulder. "We should go. Jules is expecting us to get Emma," Nate said, his voice soft.

Although all Dani wanted to do was crawl into the bed and hold Beth until she felt better, there really wasn't anything she could do to ease her suffering. Except watch Emma. "Please call if there's anything I can do."

Beth gave her a curt nod, still looking a bit green around the gills.

"Just take care of our girl," Robert said. "It helps knowing that Emma's in good hands."

Good hands? Dani was more comfortable handling hundreds of teenagers at a time than one toddler.

* * *

Nate fished his phone out of his pocket when his text message tone sounded.

Kat. Again.

i just want to talk will drive 2 meet you if you want

She'd said more than enough when he'd been in Indiana.

There wasn't any reason for them to meet. In typical Kat fashion, she'd decided she wanted something and was going to move heaven and earth to get it. And what she wanted was him to come back to her.

"Everything okay?" Dani asked, keeping her eyes on the road.

"Just my mom checking in." Lying didn't come easy. Nate had always made it a point never to fib, since sorting lies from truth was just too difficult. Better to keep things simple by using honesty.

But this lie was for Dani. If she had any inkling that Kat was putting on the full-court press, trying to win him back, she'd be upset. With Beth being sick—and pregnant—and Emma needing Dani's total attention, he wasn't about to burden her with Kat's machinations.

You're a liar, Nathaniel. You love the attention.

His stupid conscience had the right of it.

He texted Kat back.

Enough. Leave me be.

Her response was quick and concise.

never i love you

Sure, he was flattered that Kat was pursuing him so doggedly. What man wouldn't love hearing that the woman who'd dumped him now regretted it?

He'd betrayed Dani.

Betrayed? With one kiss?

Not really. In fact, the kiss had driven one point home quite clearly—he loved Dani with every piece of his heart. Kat's kiss had been familiar, but it hadn't been enjoyable. It hadn't sent a flood of need running through him the same way a simple smile from Dani could set him on fire.

Some people might dismiss the fact that he got hard just looking at Dani as lust. But Nate loved Dani. Period. Kat might try to win him back, but she had no chance in the world of succeeding. His task now was to try to shield Dani from anything Kat might do that could upset her while trying to convince Kat to leave him alone.

Hence the lie.

They pulled up along the curb by what everyone now called the Wilson Building. Dani killed the engine, got out of the car, and led Nate to the entrance of the Wilsons' upstairs home. She pushed the intercom button.

"Dani?" Jules's voice called over the speaker.

"We're here."

A loud buzz sounded, and Dani pulled the door open. They climbed to the second floor and met Jules, who waited in the doorway, holding Emma against her hip.

Emma started bouncing as she kicked her legs and clapped her hands. "Aunt Dandy!"

"Hi, munchkin." Dani took her from Jules's arms. "Ready to go home?"

"*Matka* and *Bobber* at home?" Emma asked in toddler English.

Nate arched an eyebrow. "Matka? Bobber?"

"Matka is Beth. It's 'mother' in some language," Dani replied.

"Polish, I think," Jules said, following them into the foyer and closing the door behind her.

"And Bobber is how Emma says Robert's name." She kissed Emma's cheek. "Thought you were calling him Daddy now."

Emma shrugged; then she slapped her hands on either side of Dani's face and gave her a sloppy kiss.

"How you doin', munchkin?" Dani asked. "Did you like playing with the boys?"

"Wanna go home," Emma announced. "Carter's mean."

"Mean?" Dani shifted her gaze to Jules.

"He took her doll and hid it," Jules replied. "Then Craig tried to dress it in his Batman outfit."

"Where's your doll now?" Dani asked Emma. "Do you need me to go talk to the twins?"

"My backpack." Emma shook her head, probably in response to Dani wanting to verbally berate Carter and Craig. "Wanna go home now." She turned her enormous blue eyes on Nate.

Since he wasn't sure if Emma remembered him from the cookouts he'd attended, he figured he should introduce himself again. "I'm Nate, Emma."

She let out a heavy sigh and laid her head against Dani's shoulder. "I know that."

"Connor?" Jules yelled.

"Yeah?" his reply came from down the hallway.

"Can you please go put Emma's car seat in Dani's car?"

A few moments later, Connor marched down the corridor, carrying a gray car seat. "Sure thing, Red." He held out his hand to Dani. "The keys to your chariot, m'lady?"

She took her keys out of her jacket pocket and laid them on his palm.

After Dani was accosted by the Wilson twins, giving them hugs and kisses even as she scolded them to be nicer to Emma, she was finally able to leave. Connor showed Nate how to buckle Emma into the seat; then he waved good-bye as they pulled away.

"Did Robert give you the key?" Nate asked. Since it would be easier to take care of Emma at her home, they were heading to the Ashfords' place.

"I can use the code on the garage door." Dani glanced in her rearview mirror. "Ready to go home, munchkin?"

"Yay!" came the reply from the backseat. "Home!"

Chapter 24

Dani was exhausted. She picked up the last of Emma's toys and set them in the large, wooden toy box Robert had hand carved for his daughter. He'd probably set about making another one for his new child.

The Ashford family was going to add a new member.

Now that she'd had time to think, Dani was genuinely happy for Beth and Robert, and she found herself sharing her friends' delight at having a baby on the way.

After a last quick check on Emma, who was sleeping comfortably in her toddler-sized bed, Dani headed to the spare bedroom, the one they'd occupy until Beth came home.

Nate was already in bed, dressed only in boxers and a T-shirt with his back propped against the headboard. He was grading papers while reruns of *The Simpsons* played quietly on the flatscreen TV. "She's finally asleep?"

Dani nodded. "Robert said it's up to us to take her to day care tomorrow or not."

"I'm fine with your choice," Nate said. "Almost done with the research papers, so I'm caught up. For now. We've got tons of time left on fall break. Wanna take her to the zoo?"

"Brookfield?"

"Sounds good."

"That's a little bit of a drive…"

"Then we could just stay home. Emma's got more toys than most stores stock." His smile always hit her like a warm caress.

Crawling into bed beside him, Dani wanted him. Now. But being as they were in the Ashfords' home, she wasn't sure if it would be proper.

Nate set the papers aside, dropped his red pen on top of the stack, and then gave her another dimpled smile. "You're really good with her."

"Thanks."

"I mean it. Most people have trouble being patient with kids, especially two-year-olds who have questions about absolutely everything."

"Emma's pretty smart."

"I noticed. She asks some awesome questions. Can't believe she's only two."

Dani stretched out on her side of the bed; then she ran her fingers over his ribs. Still afraid of what the future would bring for them, she needed him to make love to her, to show her that here and now he still wanted her, still belonged to her.

They needed to have a serious talk. His declaration of love had finally settled in her mind, and with that acceptance came panic. They knew so little about each other. If they didn't discuss a long list of things that affected their future, their relationship would be doomed before it ever began.

Finances. She had a nice nest egg set aside for retirement because she had an eight-year head start on him. In another seven years, her mortgage would be paid off. Then she could really start squirreling away the savings. What were Nate's plans for his money? Would they pool their resources or keep separate accounts? Did he even have a savings account or an IRA?

Career goals. Dani held a master's degree in educational administration. She was biding her time until the next principal in the Cloverleaf school system retired or moved on so she could start pressing the superintendent to promote her. She even kept an eye on other districts within driving range to keep all her options open. Did Nate also want to be an administrator one day? Was he even thinking beyond surviving his first year as a teacher? And what happened if she became a principal in the school system where Nate taught? Hell, what if he had the same aspirations? She'd never known a couple who were administrators in the same school corporation. It simply wasn't done.

And family. She had no intention of changing her mind about having children. Once she'd made that choice, she'd felt as though a heavy weight had been lifted from her shoulders. So committed to her decision that she'd considered having her tubes tied, she couldn't help but fret that Nate would regret marrying her since it would mean the end of any chance of him being a father.

He blanketed her body with his, kissing her and helping her to scatter her worries. For now. Easing back as he held his weight up on his elbows, he looked into her eyes. "I want you."

"I want you, too." Dani pressed her palms against his backside. "I don't want to wake up Emma."

"She's sleeping like a drunk after a bender," he replied before kissing her again. "Besides, Robert and Beth obviously make love with Emma in the house. Parents have to adapt, but they find a way. In fact, I'm *sure* of it." His devilish grin made her smile in return. "After all, they made a baby."

She ground her hips up against his hard cock. "Then make love to me."

"Gladly."

When Nate kissed her, Dani could forget everything. All the fear for their future was lost to his kiss, to his touch. He stroked the inside of her mouth with his tongue before rubbing it against hers. She loved how he growled deep in his chest.

Flipping off of her, he stood and whipped his shirt over his head and then wiggled out of his boxers. His erection was too tantalizing to ignore, forcing Dani to her hands and knees so she could move closer. She wrapped her fingers around his penis and licked the crown before she swallowed his length as far as she could.

Nate slid his fingers into her hair, holding her right where she wanted to be. He ever so lightly moved his hips in rhythm with her taking him deeply into her mouth. Then she eased back as her lips and teeth caressed the silky flesh that covered his thick cock. Content to love him that way until he came, she let out a mewl of disappointment when he pulled away.

"I didn't want to stop," Dani said.

"I want to be inside you when I come." Nate crawled past her and then flopped on his back. "I want you on top. Fuck me, sweetheart."

His words and gruff tone sent heat straight to her core. Quickly shedding her nightshirt and panties, she straddled his hips. His hands settled on her waist before sliding up to cup a breast in each hand. He pinched her hardening nipples before leaning forward and taking one into his mouth and suckling.

She dug her fingernails into his shoulder as she arched her back. A moan of pleasure fell from her lips before she bit her bottom one, not wanting Emma to wake and disturb their interlude. Thankfully, the monitor remained quiet.

Nate shifted to her other breast, the roughness of his unshaven face adding to the sensations he sent racing over her body. This wasn't going to be one of their lingering sessions. No, as desperate as Dani was to feel him deep inside of her, and the way he seemed to be every bit as frantic, this would be fast and rough. Exactly the way she liked it.

He held his cock up as she rose over him, rubbing it between her folds before he plunged inside of her. A moan of pure ecstasy rose from deep in his throat, a similar sound coming from her. Every time they were intimate, she couldn't help but believe they were meant to be together. Despite all the obstacles, despite the struggle they faced to make a future together, here they were entirely compatible. Here, they were true mates.

Cupping her neck, Nate pulled her down, kissing her as she flattened her breasts against his lightly furred chest. The cadence he set sped up and she didn't resist the tightening in her body that signaled she was close to release. Squeezing him strongly, she let the coil contract, every nerve, every muscle preparing for climax.

He came first, clenching his fingers into her hips as he chanted her name with each thrust of his hips. Dani was a moment behind him, the heat of his essence bathing her insides, forcing her own orgasm.

* * *

Nate turned off the light after they'd both cleaned up and crawled back into bed. His mind and body were content. Each new day he spent with Dani only convinced him more that they belonged to each other.

Dani snuggled up against him, hauling the blanket over them. "That was wonderful."

He kissed her forehead. "Damn right. But then again, isn't it always?"

She rubbed her cheek against his shoulder. "I sure think it is."

"I mean it, Dani. Every single time we make love, it just gets better."

Before she could say anything, his phone vibrated, skittering across the nightstand. He snatched it up and let out an exasperated sigh. Another text from Kat. At least Dani couldn't see the screen since he held it in the hand of the arm he had wrapped around her. A quick couple of touches yielded Kat's latest appeal.

good night love you

All the flattery that had first accompanied her quest to win him back had become pure frustration. If she didn't let up, Nate would have to either keep lying to Dani or tell her about the kiss. For all her strength and fortitude, deep down Dani was insecure where their relationship was concerned. He'd worked so damned hard to earn her trust. He wasn't about to shatter that precious trust simply because Kat had thrown herself at him.

Women were funny about some things. He'd learned that lesson the hard way—by watching his mother struggle in her relationship with Mark. After a couple of great dates, Mark hadn't called for several days. Each hour that passed without hearing from him made Jackie more restless and forced her anger higher. A guy would've just picked up the phone and called to say, "What's up? Haven't heard from you in a while." Instead, she'd put herself through hell, refusing to break down and contact him first. Turned out Mark was conflicted, feeling like he was betraying his dead wife by falling for Jackie so quickly. One call would have fixed the problem, or at the very least prevented a ton of worry.

So why couldn't Nate open his mouth and tell Dani about Kat?

Because she would be distraught, and the weeks of helping

Dani realize that he could be reliable would be washed away in one great wave.

His conscience niggled at him.

You kissed her back. You loved the attention.

Plus the day Kat had walked away, Nate had sworn that he'd always be there for her if she changed her mind. He'd been so young, so naïve, and so convinced his first love would be his only love.

Dani taught him otherwise simply by being the wonderful, loving person she was. What he felt for Kat was easily eclipsed by the strength of his love for Dani.

Before he could pop off a quick text, saying the same thing he'd already told Kat every time she'd reached out to him—that he wanted her to leave him alone—Emma's voice filtered through the monitor. "I wanna drink."

When Dani started to stir, Nate patted her shoulder. "Stay in bed. I'll get her this time." He pulled his arm from under her, dropped his phone on the nightstand, and winked. "You can get her if she wakes up at three in the morning."

"Who texted?" she asked as she grabbed his abandoned pillow and hugged it to her chest.

"Just my mom."

"Something wrong?"

"Nope. She's been checking in a lot lately. Probably miffed we didn't stay very long." He shrugged, trying to appear nonchalant even though lying was so against his nature.

He headed to get Emma a drink of water.

* * *

Dani stared at the phone, trying to talk herself out of picking it up and reading the text, knowing she was fighting a losing battle.

Nate was lying. She had no doubt about it. Did he realize that he tugged on his right ear whenever he fibbed? Not that he did it often, but even when he lied about something as simple as whether she looked good with bed head, he gave that earlobe a pull.

That, and ever since they returned from Indiana, he was fielding a slew of text messages. His phone sounded every hour or so. Sometimes more frequently. He always said it was his mother. Or Mark. Or his brother, Patrick.

So why didn't she believe him?

That damned right ear.

Through the monitor, she heard him whispering to Emma, probably patting her back to help her get back to sleep. Angry at herself for being suspicious, Dani picked up his phone. It wasn't locked. Quickly checking his text messages, she found what she'd feared the most. A string of texts from Kat that stretched the length of the screen no matter how far she scrolled. Words of love. Promises for the future. Pledges to bear his children.

Before Dani could find the courage to read any of Nate's replies, she heard him bid Emma good night and start back toward the spare bedroom.

Frantic about being caught snooping, Dani set his phone back on his nightstand and lay back on the mattress. Her heart was hammering and her mind was whirling. What was she supposed to do now?

If she confronted Nate, she'd have to admit to two sins—invading his privacy and not having faith in him. Somehow she felt the latter would be a greater crime than the former. Trust was everything to him, and he'd spent all their time together helping her learn to depend on him, to believe in him. To love him.

And then what had he done? He'd turned around and lied to her.

He crawled back into bed, but this time, Dani didn't roll into his arms. She kept her back to him, hugging herself and fighting a cross between fierce anger and abject sorrow. If she faced Nate, she'd either shout at him or start weeping all over him. Neither would be helpful, so she held tight to her emotions and tried to find some calm in the storm. Only then could she figure out what to do.

She'd trusted him. With her heart.

Had she made the biggest mistake of her life?

Chapter 25

Beth was released from the hospital the next day, and Dani was relieved. Not only because Beth felt better, but also because caring for Emma wasn't easy. Plus, a whole week of fall break remained for Dani and Nate to enjoy.

He clicked away on his laptop. Sitting on the couch, he'd propped his feet on the coffee table, looking very relaxed. While he cruised the Internet, Dani watched a television show about renovating old houses and found herself grateful to Robert for building her such a beautiful new home.

"We could still do the zoo," he said. "Even without Emma. We could drive up to Chicago tomorrow and spend the whole day. Maybe even stay in a hotel and hit a couple of museums the day after."

"I figured you might want to go back to Indiana to see your family." Although the last thing in the world she wanted to do was deal with Kat Brennan again, Dani wouldn't disappoint Nate. Their visit had been so short. He deserved a chance to return for a few more days.

He shook his head. "I saw my mom and Mark. I'm good."

"We were supposed to have dinner with your brother and his wife." His *pregnant* wife.

Damn, but she and Nate needed to talk. She just couldn't manage to broach the topic of children. She loved him too much to lose him, but no matter how much she tried to convince herself he loved her, too, she couldn't stop believing he'd leave if he knew she had no intention of having kids.

No. She needed to do this. For him. For herself.

After a deep, steadying breath, she dove right in. "Nate, I need to tell you something."

Before he could say anything, his phone chimed yet another text. Kat again, no doubt.

That woman was another topic Dani should address. But if she said anything about Kat, it would show him that she'd been snooping. The texts she'd read from Kat were bound to come up. Trust was everything to Nate. He'd have a hard time forgiving her for invading his privacy.

"Shit." He set his phone aside and closed his laptop, a pained frown on his face.

Dani immediately responded to the hurt in his eyes. "What's wrong?"

"My grandpa—Papa Delgado—had a stroke." Nate had spoken often of his love for his mother's father and about how close he'd always been to the man.

"I'm so sorry. What can I do to help?"

He shook his head. "Nothing. I need to talk to Mom and see what's happening." He laid the computer on the table and picked up his phone. After he dialed, he started pacing. The man seemed to have an inability to stand still whenever he had a lengthy phone conversation. "Mom? Fill me in."

Although Dani could only hear one side of the conversation, she grew more and more worried by the minute. The old man was clearly in danger. Jackie seemed to be pressing Nate to go to Orlando to be with him, but he was resisting.

"My car would never make it," he said, tossing Dani a look of helplessness.

All she wanted to do was make this right for him. She was about to suggest he take her car—and perhaps her, too—when he started talking about airlines and where he could fly out of to get to Florida.

Nate put up token resistance, but whatever his mom said convinced him to accept. "Thanks, Mom. See you when I get there." After he ended the call, he took Dani's hand. "I'm meeting Mom at the airport in Indy; then we're taking a late flight to Orlando. She and Mark were supposed to go to Rome next week, but she cashed in those tickets so we could see Grandpa. I need to throw a few things in a bag and get going."

"I could drive you," she offered.

He shook his head. "I appreciate that, sweetheart, but I have no idea how long I'll be down there. I'll leave my POS in the long-term parking lot. Saves you a trip to come fetch me when I get back." A glance at the wall calendar. "At least this happened during fall break."

"This has been a really shitty break," she grumbled.

"It sure has." He kissed her forehead.

"Hopefully your grandpa will get well quickly." She squeezed his hand.

After a nod, he eased his hand back. "I don't have any banked personal days yet. Not 'til next pay period. I won't be able to stay past Sunday."

"If you have to stay longer, call Jim Reinhardt. He's great

about family stuff, especially emergencies. So is our superintendent. They'll find a way for you to be with your grandfather."

He shrugged. "I guess I'll cross that bridge when I come to it."

Dani brushed a kiss over his mouth. "One step at a time. Let's hope it turns out to be nothing big." Her curiosity was killing her. "It's just you and your mom going to Orlando?"

"Yeah. Patrick can't leave, not when the baby's so close."

"Mark?"

Nate shook his head.

Since Jackie's father was no relation to Kat, Dani had no reason to ask about her. She did anyway. "Kat making the trip?"

"What?"

Trailing her fingers over the island countertop, she tried to sound nonchalant. "Just wondered if Kat was going, too."

"Why would she?"

To be with you. "I didn't think she would."

Nate cocked his head and stared at her. "Dani, are you jealous of Kat?"

Fuck, yeah. "Should I be?"

He gathered her into his arms. "No. Not in the least. Kat is ancient history."

Then why the text messages declaring her undying love? And why are you lying to me if Kat doesn't mean anything to you?

If only Dani could have read some of Nate's replies...Perhaps then the jealousy could be easily put to rest. But having no idea what Nate said to Kat was killing her. "Ancient history, huh?"

Nate kissed her, a lingering and very loving kiss. "I'm in love with *you.* Remember that. Okay?"

Dani gave him a curt nod.

He nudged her chin up so she was looking into his handsome

eyes. "I mean it, Dani. There's absolutely no reason for you to worry about Kat. I. Love. You. I want to be with *you*."

Instead of replying, she kissed him, hoping she could get a grip on her distrust before she ruined things between them.

* * *

Nate purposefully tried to ignore Kat, even though she was sitting right across the airplane's tiny aisle. No matter how many times she attempted to draw him into a conversation or throw him a flirtatious bat of her eyes, he focused on the solitaire game on his phone.

She tried yet again. "I think it would be great if we could go out tomorrow morning and take a sunrise walk on the beach."

He put a red eight over a black nine and counted to ten.

"You know how much I love seafood." She sounded damned cheerful for a woman who was traveling to a hospital to see a stricken man. "We can check out some of the local restaurants. I can look for some good nightclubs, too. That would be so much fun."

Thankfully, his mother finally intervened—the same way she'd been running interference since he'd met her at the airport. He'd been riding up the escalator to head to the airline's check-in, and as he neared the top, there was his mom with an apologetic frown.

And Kat standing at her side.

Nate's first instinct had been to jump over the rail to the descending escalator, hightail it back to his car, and drive straight back to Cloverleaf. The only thing that kept him moving toward her was his need to see his grandfather. If Dani ever found out Kat was going on this trip, she'd *never* believe he hadn't planned for his ex to tag along, especially after she'd asked point-blank about just that. With the way her thoughts worked overtime, Dani was liable to think he'd lied about the stroke to arrange a secret vacation with Kat.

He'd eventually have to tell her that Kat went to Orlando with him and his mother. But not now. Not until he got home and could look her in the eye as he pleaded his innocence. Dani was a woman who needed to see to believe, so once he was with her again, he would explain how Kat had invited herself and that he'd had no idea Kat was heading to Orlando until he arrived at the airport.

But would Dani have faith in him? It boiled down to one thing—had she truly learned to trust him?

"Kat…enough. Okay?" Jackie, who was sitting in the window seat, leaned over Nate and smacked Kat's armrest. "We talked about this before we left. Once we get there, we'll be spending our time at the hospital with Grandpa or helping out Grandma. There won't be time to go to the beach or to some fancy restaurant. Resign yourself to hospital cafeteria food and, for the love of God, suck it up."

Kat pouted her lip. "A couple of hours won't make a difference."

Nate put a red queen over a black king and let his mother handle the princess.

Jackie shook her head. "We're there for my parents, not for us. And most definitely not for *you*."

Thankfully, Kat simply frowned, shoved in her earbuds, and started fiddling with her phone.

"I'm sorry." Jackie patted his arm and spoke in a soft voice. "I shouldn't have let Mark book the tickets. I was so busy packing and getting things ready. Kat told him that since she was on break from school I'd asked her to come along to help. I wasn't there to correct that ridiculous notion."

He put his hand over his mother's. "You already explained three times. I know it wasn't your fault. You'd think Mark would know better."

In all the time he'd known Kat, she'd never been remotely nurturing. Not once. Not even when they lost the baby. Sure, she'd wanted to be pampered and coddled after the miscarriage, but when Nate mentioned his lost child, she'd all but ordered him to "get over it."

Although he valued life, especially helpless infants in their mothers' wombs, he admitted to himself that he'd felt the loss of his baby. Yet the pregnancy was over before he'd even had the chance to get too accustomed to the idea of being a father.

Jackie shook her head. "He's still kinda blind where his daughters are concerned."

"Just Kat. Carly isn't like her at all."

"Even Carly has her moments. Mark sees them both through some kind of filter that softens what they truly are. And Kat has gotten a lot worse since…well, since you two broke up. I imagine he'll always think they're near to perfect." She grinned. "Exactly like me with my boys."

She had him there. Jackie had always been willing to forgive anything Nate or Patrick had done if they offered her a contrite expression and a muttered apology, even if it was a halfhearted one.

After they landed, they headed toward the baggage area to wait for their luggage. Jackie was talking on the phone to her mom while Nate grabbed their stuff off the large conveyer, not at all surprised Kat was standing next to his mother instead of helping.

Jackie ended the call right as he dropped her bag next to her. "Thanks, Nate." She extended the handle on her rolling suitcase. "Ready to head to the hospital?"

"I'm too tired." Kat frowned when Nate slung the strap of her vinyl bag over her shoulder, probably angry he was refusing to carry it. "Can't we just go to the hotel, drop off our stuff, and get some supper?"

"I'm going to the hospital," Jackie said firmly. "You two can go wherever you please. You're both adults."

"I'm going to the hospital, too," Nate said. "Kat can do whatever the hell she wants. I want to see Grandpa."

Kat hiked the strap higher up on her shoulder. "I'm heading to the hotel."

Would it be cruel to say he was relieved?

Fishing around in her purse, Jackie pulled out a folded piece of paper. "Here's the info about the hotel reservation." Then she turned worried eyes to Nate. "I…um…forgot to tell you. We were only able to get one room."

"*One* room?" Damn. He'd be trapped there with Kat. Sure, his mom could run interference, but Kat would be in the same room. All the time. "Mom…" He groaned and rubbed his hand over his face.

"I'm sorry. I really am. It's their busiest season, almost as bad as spring break. Lots of families here for school breaks. Mark said we were lucky to even get a double."

She was worried enough about her father. Nate's disappointment would only add to her burden. "It's fine. I'm sure they can bring in a rollaway for me."

"No. It's a suite, so Kat and I will take the beds. There's a fold-out couch in the living space if you don't mind that."

"Works for me," he said.

"Great," Jackie said. "Then let's go hail a couple of cabs."

While they waited, Nate fished his phone charger out of his bag. When they got to the hospital, maybe he could find a plug and charge his phone. The thing was dead from playing too many games as a way to escape any kind of conversation with Kat. "Can you put this in your purse, Mom? Then Kat can take my bag back to the hotel."

Jackie nodded, took the charger, and shoved it in her purse.

"You want me to haul your stuff?" Kat sighed but nodded. "Anything to help, honey."

Instead of triggering her temper by rebuking her right then and there, he tried being polite. "Please. I'd appreciate it."

A cab pulled along the curb, and Nate helped the driver throw the luggage in the trunk. He slammed the lid as the cabbie crawled back into the driver's seat.

As the cab drove away, Jackie signaled for another. They got into the backseat, and with a shaky voice, she asked the cabbie to take them to the hospital, where her father's life hung in the balance.

Nate took her hand. "Grandpa Delgado is a tough old bird. He'll get through this."

She drew her lips into a grim line. "He's eighty-three years old. We have to remember that. Bouncing back isn't easy at that age." She let out a little snort. "Hell, it's not easy at thirty-eighteen, either."

"You look pretty healthy to me." He jostled her with his elbow.

As the bright streetlights on the busy interstate passed by, she stared out the window, seemingly at nothing. "Let's pray we get there in time."

Chapter 26

Nate had to smile at his mother when he heard Grandpa Delgado's scolding voice echoing down the long corridor. "I wanna go back to sleep. Leave me be, young lady."

The ICU had been quiet, most of the patients asleep, since it was after midnight. The glass doors were closed on each room with the exception of one farther down the hall, the one where Grandpa was admonishing whoever was in his cubicle.

Jackie smiled back as she quickened her steps. "He sounds great considering he just had a stroke." When she reached the end of the hall, her eyes rapidly scanned the name on the whiteboard before she swept into the room. "Hi, Dad. You sound like you're feeling better."

Nate was a step behind, his grin growing when he saw his grandfather giving the poor nurse one of his penetrating frowns. "Hi, Grandpa. You had us worried. Glad to hear you're being grouchy with the staff. Means you're doing well."

"Definitely grouchy." The nurse winked as she finished checking his vitals, which was probably why he'd been complaining. She smiled at Jackie and Nate. "I'm Carrie."

"I'm Jackie. His daughter."

"He told me you were coming." Carrie shifted her gaze to Nate.

"I'm his grandson. Nate."

She nodded. "He's doing fine. The TPA did its job very well, and he's lucky his wife brought him straight to the hospital. If things keep improving, we're hoping to transfer him to a regular room tomorrow morning." On that, she went to the small computer station just outside the room, pulling the sliding glass door closed behind her.

"Spying on me all damn day," Grandpa grumbled, pointing at the window of the computer station that helped the nurse keep an eye on the room.

Carrie smiled back at him.

"This is the intensive care unit, Dad," Jackie said, moving to his bedside. She kissed his forehead. "They have to watch their patients closely."

"Don't need intensive care." He looked to Nate. "You gonna get fired for leaving work?"

Grandpa Delgado. Blunt as always. "It's a school break, Grandpa. I'm not going to get fired. I wanted to see how you were doing." Nate would've given him a hug had the poor man not been hooked up to so many wires and tubes. "So how are you?"

"Doin' fine," Grandpa replied. "Gave me somethin' when I got here that busted up the clot...or whatever the hell it was making me talk wrong. Got better right after."

Whatever the TPA the nurse mentioned was, Nate sent up a thankful prayer that it had kept his grandfather from having a catastrophic stroke. "You sure sound fine to me, Grandpa. Wanna go get a beer?" he teased.

"Told you, doin' fine. Doubt the nurses would let me have a

cold Bud. Sounds good right now, though. Would help me sleep. Those young girls keep coming in to check my blood pressure and such. Always wakin' me up."

Jackie set her purse on the empty chair. "Where's Mom?"

"Sent your mother home to get some sleep."

After searching for an empty plug in the darkened room, Nate found plenty, but they were all red, and he wasn't sure if that meant they were reserved for special equipment. So he gave up on recharging his phone. Once he got back to the hotel, he could catch up on any messages or calls. Besides, it was so late, the nurses and other ICU patients probably wouldn't appreciate him doing a lot of talking.

"I'm going to chat with the nurse for a minute," Jackie said before letting herself out of the room.

Grandpa fixed his wise dark eyes, so much like his daughter's, on Nate. "Heard you went and got yourself a new lady."

The news had traveled fast in the Delgado clan. As usual. "I did. Her name is Dani…um…*Danielle*. She's a teacher at my new school."

"Picked better this time, I hope."

"Much better."

In his typical fashion, Grandpa spoke his mind. "Kat might be a nice girl, but too flighty. Not like her daddy at all."

"No, she's not."

"This Danielle solid? Smart? You need a smart woman, Nathaniel."

"She's smart. Probably smarter than me."

Grandpa nodded. "Good. Good. Don't let her get away, then. Not like your stepdaddy near to let my Jacqueline get away. Gotta close the deal before she changes her mind, if you know what I mean."

Since Nate hadn't been there for the rocky courtship between his mom and Mark—that, and he'd been busy trying to keep his own relationship with Kat from floundering—Nate wasn't exactly sure what his grandfather was talking about. "He almost let her get away?"

Another nod. "She was ready to cut him loose when he didn't call her for a couple of weeks. Dragged his feet too long, gave her too much time to think."

"Oh, you mean after their first dates, right?"

"Yep. Was wrestlin' his conscience, thinkin' he was being disrespectful to his dead wife or some other nonsense. Gave my Jacqueline time to worry, and you know my girl. Can worry up a storm." He laid his hand over Nate's where it rested on the bedrail. "Take my advice, Nathaniel. Don't give your girl time to think too hard. Gets smart women like your mother into mischief. And I imagine she's a lot like Jacqueline."

The advice had set Nate's stomach plummeting to his feet. The man was right; Dani was exactly like his mother. She overanalyzed absolutely everything.

But what could he do to, as his grandfather said, *close the deal*? "It's not like I can ask her to marry me, Grandpa."

"Why the hell not?" Grandpa Delgado flashed Nate a wicked grin. "That's what I did with your grandma. Swept her off her feet and dragged her to a justice of the peace. It was all over and done with before she could do anythin' about it. I'm thinkin' you should make history repeat itself before you lose her."

* * *

Tired of worrying, Dani plucked her cell phone off the nightstand. It was silly to agonize so much, but no matter how hard she tried to get to sleep, she couldn't stop fretting about Nate and all the hurt he might be going through.

He hadn't texted when he got to Orlando, but she didn't want to be the needy girlfriend who kept him on a short leash. He'd check in when he could. Her fervent wish was that his grandfather was doing very well and that Nate had simply been too busy being with his family to let her know he'd had a safe flight and that things hadn't been nearly as dire as they'd feared.

The jealousy over Kat niggled at Dani's confidence. Kat had obviously known exactly how much Dani would worry when she'd said she was going to try to win Nate back. But that didn't make this worry over what Nate was doing Kat's fault. All Dani had to do was trust him to call her when he could and push aside the negative thoughts Kat had planted. The problem was that Kat had found fertile ground in Dani's insecurity about Nate, and once Kat had promised to move heaven and earth to reclaim him, Dani allowed her fear to rule her thoughts and her actions.

Holding tight to her phone, she argued with herself. She shouldn't call the hotel where Nate would be staying. It was almost two in the morning. He was probably exhausted from the trip and seeing his grandfather and was sound asleep by now. After such a long, draining day, he needed his rest not to be disturbed by his unhinged girlfriend.

But she needed to hear his voice.

She called, the whole time reassuring herself that he'd understand. He loved her. He'd know she wanted to talk to him before she could sleep.

"Orlando's Family Resort," a cheerful male voice answered. "May I help you?"

"Could you please ring me through to Nate Ryan's room?"

The click of keys being hit filtered through the earpiece. "I'm afraid there's no Nate Ryan currently registered here."

"Oh…um…is there a Jackie Brennan? That's his mom. He might be sharing a room with her."

"That might be likely, ma'am," the man said. "We're full up tonight. Let me check." More clicks. "There is a Jackie Brennan registered with two guests."

"Two guests? So she and Nate are sharing a room?"

"No, ma'am. I mean, yes, ma'am, but there are three total guests registered in that suite. Ms. Brennan and two more."

Her heart started pounding so hard, Dani could barely hear from the echo in her ears. "Three? There are *three* people in the room?"

"Yes, ma'am."

Refusing to let her imagination run amok, Dani guessed Mark had traveled with them. Nate had said he wasn't going, but he must have changed his mind and decided to be there for Jackie. "Please connect me to that room."

"I'm sorry, but our policy is that we don't ring through to rooms after ten. I can take a message or connect you to voice mail for those guests."

She'd already left at least five messages on Nate's voice mail and a slew of texts. "I really need to talk to him now."

"I'm sorry, ma'am. If you leave a voice mail, there's a red light on the room's phone that will illuminate. If they're awake, the guests are likely to see it right away. Then perhaps they'll call you back."

"Fine," Dani snapped. Then she was immediately contrite. None of this was the poor receptionist's fault. "I'm sorry. I'm just worried."

"Would you like the room's voice mail?"

"Yes, please."

"Thank you for your patience, ma'am. Wait for the tone, then leave your message."

The beep was so quick she didn't even have time to figure out exactly what she wanted to say. "Um…hi. Nate, it's Dani. I'm sorry to bug you. I was just…worried. Hope your grandpa is doing okay. Please let me know you got to Orlando safely and if there's anything I can do. I could try to catch a flight down there tomorrow." She almost hung up before she added, "Hope you and your mom and Mark find time to get some rest. Good night."

Dani put her phone on the nightstand and punched her pillow, angry that she'd given in to the immature need to call. Nate would never believe she trusted him if she spent so much time checking up on what he was doing whenever he left her alone. She lay down, hoping she could finally get some sleep. At least they'd arrived in one piece since they'd claimed their hotel room.

Her thoughts had just begun to scatter into the void of sleep when her phone rang. Although she didn't recognize the number, the area code was the same as the hotel. She answered, wondering if Nate's older-than-dirt cell phone had finally given up the ghost and forced him to use the motel's phone. "Nate?"

"No, it's Kat."

"Kat?"

Son of a fucking bitch.

Dani's stomach flipped, and she hoped she could make it through this awkward conversation before she had to sprint to the bathroom to throw up. "What are you doing there?"

"Nate asked me to come. He's really worried about his grandpa."

"Let me talk to him," Dani demanded, trying hard to hold tight to her rising temper.

"He's still at the hospital with his mom." Kat's voice dripped with fake concern. "I hope they got to see the poor man before... well, you know. Can I give him a message?" She had to be loving this, probably reveling in the hurt she knew she'd inflicted when she'd called Dani back.

"So you listened to *his* voice mail message?" Dani couldn't keep the sneer out of her voice. "And then you figured you would be the person who should call me back?"

"You don't need to sound so bitchy. I was just trying to be nice. Nate might not even be back here tonight, and I thought you'd be worried. I would've been. I mean, he's your boyfriend and he hasn't even found a moment to text you to let you know what was happening. That seemed a bit... cruel to me."

Cruel? Kat knew damn well that Nate might have a valid reason for not calling or texting. The cruelty was her going to Orlando with him and having the audacity to return Dani's call.

"Why are you *really* there, Kat? Nate is with me now. Why can't you leave him alone?"

"You know why. I love him. He loves me, too."

"So you're gonna keep throwing yourself at a guy who doesn't want you?"

"He sure acted like he wanted me when he kissed me. I'll bet he didn't tell you that, did he?"

Swallowing her hurt to try to keep what little pride she still had intact, Dani chose her words carefully. "Please tell him to call me when he can and that I'm praying for his grandfather." She ended the call before Kat had a chance to inflict any new wounds.

Despite the urge to throw her cell against the wall to watch it break into a thousand pieces, she set it down. Destroying her phone might help vent her anger, but it wouldn't fix a damn thing. Kat was doing exactly what she'd promised: she was driving a wedge between Dani and Nate.

Had he really kissed Kat?

No. Dani didn't believe it. Nate was all about honesty. He would have told her.

Wouldn't he?

If Dani trusted Nate, none of this would be bothering her. None of it. She should let Kat's machinations roll right off her back, comforted by the thought that Nate would never betray her.

She wanted to call Beth and cry on her shoulder, but there was no way she'd wake her up this late. After breakfast, she'd get herself together, drive over to the Ashfords', and see if Beth could talk Dani out of confronting Nate over Kat being in Orlando.

And over the kiss he'd kept secret from her.

Maybe her best friend could talk some sense—and some trust—into her.

Chapter 27

Y ou *what?*" Nate couldn't stop shouting at Kat, but he didn't give a fat fucking wildebeest whether he woke up everyone in the whole hotel. He was too angry to think about anything except the damage Kat had inflicted on his relationship with Dani. "Why? Why in the hell would you do that?"

"Kat…" Jackie shook her head. "Even for you, that was low."

Folding her arms under her breasts, Kat frowned at her step-mother. "What's *that* supposed to mean?"

"You know I love you," Jackie said. "But over the years, I've seen you pull some dirty tricks to get what you want. Don't you shake your head at me, young lady. You know damn well you're the queen of subterfuge."

"I'm not *that* bad."

"Yes, you are. And I know exactly what you're trying to do to Nate and Dani," Jackie replied. "I heard the little 'talk' you had with her back in Indianapolis, and I think it's time for you to put on your big girl panties and grow the hell up."

"What talk?" Nate shifted his gaze from his ex to his mother.

Jackie inclined her head at Kat. "She tried to scare Dani off so she'd have a clear path to you. I set Dani straight, though. Told her you and Kat were old news."

"We're *not* old news!" Now Kat was shouting, too. "I love you, Nate. I'm just doing what's necessary to be with the man I love, the man I want to make a family with. All's fair in love and war."

None of this argument even mattered to Nate, nor did he care about the noise. He was getting ready to stomp out. If Kat got kicked out to sleep on the streets, it would be nothing but pure karma. He narrowed his eyes at her. "You can really be a bitch when you want to be."

Her mouth formed a shocked O before she started shaking her finger at him. "Don't you dare call me a bitch, Nathaniel Ryan!"

"Then quit acting like one," Jackie said before lying down on the rumpled bed. "You're such a great girl, and you can be so nice and so caring when you want to be. But you're tormenting people I love, and that I can't allow. Why can't you move on?"

"I'm fighting for the man I love," Kat insisted. "You'd do the same."

"No, I wouldn't," Jackie said. "No matter how much I love Mark, if he didn't love me anymore, I'd never do something underhanded to get him back. Hell, my pride wouldn't allow it. If he didn't want me, I wouldn't beg, nor would I try to sabotage a relationship that clearly made him happy."

"I have pride."

"Could've fooled me. All I see is a pretty young woman who's chasing after a man who doesn't want her."

Kat shook her head. "I can make him want me again. You'll see."

No way Nate would let that misunderstanding persist. "You think submarining Dani will make me want you again?"

She nodded.

"You know what, Kat?"

She cocked a dark eyebrow.

"If there were a plague that wiped out billions of people and the only humans left to repopulate the planet were you and me, I *still* wouldn't have anything to do with you. Got it?" He shoved the last of the stuff he'd just unpacked back into his duffel.

"Where are you going, Nate?" Jackie asked.

"The airport. I'm catching the first flight back to Indy."

"No, you're not," his mother ordered before softening her tone. "Stay. Please. You're exhausted. Get some sleep. I just now texted Mark to get you a ticket ASAP. He'll let us know when he's got a flight booked."

"I'll go home, too," Kat said.

Jackie shook her head. "You came here to help, so help you will. We're going to Mom and Dad's place tomorrow to clean the whole condo and catch up on all their laundry. Then we can go visit Dad at the hospital before we hit the grocery to get the stuff we need to cook and freeze a bunch of meals for them."

Although he should feel bad for leaving Grandpa Delgado, now that he knew his grandfather was out of danger, all Nate wanted to do was get back to Dani. He needed to talk to her, to explain why Kat had ended up in Orlando, but he wasn't going to call at four in the morning. As light a sleeper as Dani was, even a text would wake her. She'd obviously been up most of the night, and she needed her rest. An hour and a half from now, she'd probably be awake, getting ready to run.

Jabbing a finger at Kat, who was now pouting like a pro, he shouted one more time. "Stay out of my life, Kat. I mean it. Stay the hell away from me, and stay the hell away from Dani."

"But, Nate"—she reached out to him—"you know I love you."

"Love?" He snorted. "You love one person. *You*. If you really ever loved me, you'd want me to be happy. You don't love, Kat. You try to own. And I'm done." He flopped onto one of the beds, crossed his arms over his chest, and closed his eyes.

Dani will understand. He kept telling himself that, hoping it would be true. His phone was charging, and he wanted so much to talk to her, to try to soothe away any hurt Kat's selfishness had inflicted. His fervent hope was that Kat's shenanigans hadn't shattered Dani's fragile trust.

Grandpa Delgado's advice swam in Nate's head, making him think he should act boldly, especially in light of Kat trying to destroy his relationship. Once he talked to Dani and assured her everything was fine, he'd reach out to Robert and the guys and make some serious plans.

Maybe a surprise engagement and quick wedding were exactly what he and Dani needed.

* * *

Seven miles. Seven whole miles, and Dani's body still felt as tight as a knot.

Nate had called right after she woke up, and he'd given her a very logical explanation for everything that had happened—from his not calling all the way to Kat being such a manipulative bitch. He'd ended the call professing his love and asking her to forgive him.

What was there to forgive? He hadn't done anything wrong. He'd been every bit as much Kat's victim as Dani was.

Then why did she still hurt so damned much?

Walking to cool down, Dani habitually reached for her smartphone before realizing she'd purposefully left it behind. She had no desire to rehash any of what had happened the last few days if Nate called again. Besides, he'd be on a flight back this afternoon. They could talk more in person.

Would Beth be awake yet?

Probably not. Nor would Jules. Not this early unless she had a client appointment. Dani and Mallory were the early birds of the Ladies.

Mallory. Perhaps Mallory would like a breakfast invitation. Dani sure as hell needed someone to talk to. She'd done so little sharing with the Ladies about her relationship with Nate, and that had been a mistake. The Ladies were her support group, the people who loved her and understood her life even better than her family. Even better than Nate.

She didn't even kick off her shoes when she went inside, heading straight for her phone. There were two missed texts from Nate.

Hope you had a nice run.

Flight is scheduled to leave at 3. Will let you know if it's late.

She texted back a quick response.

Run was good. See you soon.

Then she called Mallory.

A shower and an hour later, Dani sat with her at Yia Yia's Pancake House.

The waitress filled their coffee cups and took their orders. Once she'd left them in peace, Dani opened up. "Kat went to Orlando with Nate and his mom."

Mallory rolled her eyes. "Why doesn't that surprise me? I take it Nate didn't know until he got to the airport."

"That's what he told me."

"Why would he lie?"

"I didn't say he did," Dani insisted.

"You implied it," Mallory retorted.

"I most certainly did not."

Mallory nodded. "By saying that's what he told you instead of that's what happened, you're hinting that he might not be telling the truth. Don't you trust him, Dani?"

"I do. I really do…"

"There's an unspoken *but* at the end of that sentence." After spilling a couple of packets of sugar in her coffee, Mallory stirred the drink as she stared at Dani. "What has you so worried? Nate obviously didn't want Kat on the trip, right?"

Dani nodded.

"Then why all this angst? He loves you."

So he says. "I know. I just…Kat's not gonna go away."

"She will. Eventually. She'll move on. And Nate probably read her the riot act for going uninvited."

"He said he did once he figured out she'd called me."

Mallory set her spoon down harder than necessary. "She called you?"

"I left a message at his hotel since he wasn't answering his phone and asked him to call me."

"Did the hospital make him turn off the ringer or something?" Mallory asked.

With a shake of her head, Dani replied, "His battery died. He wasn't sure what plugs were safe to use at the hospital, so he couldn't charge it until he got back to the hotel."

"So she called you back, probably to let you know about her scheming and implying Nate asked her to go with him."

"Exactly." Dani sipped her coffee before finally asking the question that was gnawing at her. "Is there anything I can do to get Kat to just…disappear?"

Mallory shook her head. "Women like that are pit bulls, especially women after a man who's resisting. They don't give up."

Dani let out a heavy sigh. "Great. Just great."

"But what you *can* do is not let her bother you. Look, Dani, I understand what you're going through. Remember Ben and me? We had trust problems, too. At least *I* did. I know how hard it is to open up to someone, to make yourself vulnerable. But that's love. It's not easy, and you leave yourself without defenses. If you truly love Nate, then you've got to learn to trust him."

"I do. I just—"

"There's no 'just,' Dani. You either trust him or you don't. And until you decide that, Kat isn't the biggest problem in your relationship. Promise me one thing, okay?"

"Promise you what?"

"I jumped to all kinds of conclusions about Ben before he had a chance to explain. At least give Nate that same chance. Let him convince you that Kat doesn't mean anything to him anymore. And remember, he said he loves *you*."

Dani bowed her head. "That's because he doesn't know."

Mallory's brows knit. "Doesn't know what?"

"That I don't want to have kids."

That statement left Mallory temporarily speechless. Slow minutes passed and the waitress brought their food. Although it smelled delicious, Dani's appetite had fled. She picked at her eggs while Mallory buttered her toast.

"You two really haven't known each other long, have you?" Mallory finally asked.

"Since August. Almost four months."

"It was a rhetorical question, but do you see my point?"

"I know," Dani replied. "We barely know each other."

"You two need to sit down and have a long talk about a lot of things."

"Easier said than done. What if he wants a family?"

"Then isn't it better to know now than five years down the road?"

* * *

Nate kept an eye on the boarding gate while he waited to talk to Robert. Although he'd spoken with Dani again when he hit the airport, she sounded so distant and said something about the two of them sitting down to have a chat when he got home. That sounded too ominous for Nate's peace of mind.

His mind was whirling with ideas of ways to show Dani exactly how much he loved her. A surprise wedding would be difficult but not impossible. A quick Google search told him that both he and Dani needed to be there in person to obtain an Illinois marriage license. Vegas was out of the question simply from a financial standpoint. So now his ideas centered on Indiana, a state that allowed same-day marriages. Then during the surprise engagement party, he'd get her to set the date.

Maybe then he'd quit worrying.

While he wanted to scream at Kat for all her ridiculous plots and plans, he knew this crisis wasn't all her fault. Had he truly helped Dani learn to trust him, she would never have bought into Kat's lies. He only hoped their "chat" wouldn't be Dani trying to find a way to break up with him.

He couldn't lose her, not now that he knew she was the love of his life.

His phone vibrated, so Nate plucked it out of his pocket. "Hey, Robert. Thanks for calling me back."

"What's up?"

"I need you and the guys to help me plan a party."

"A party?" Robert's voice held a smile. "And what exactly will we be celebrating?"

"My engagement to Dani. I want it to be a surprise, okay? Make sure the Ladies know that."

"Seriously?"

The incredulity in Robert's voice made Nate breathe an exasperated sigh. "Seriously. I want to sweep her off her feet, to give her such a romantic moment that she'll remember it the rest of her life."

"Nate, are you sure?"

"More than sure."

"You're not afraid it'll all blow up in your face?"

Nate dragged his fingers through his hair. "There's only one thing I'm afraid of—losing Dani."

"If you're sure…"

"I can't lose her, Robert. I *can't*."

"All righty, then," Robert said. "I'll give the guys a call, and we'll get the ball rolling."

Chapter 28

"Dani! I'm home!"

Nate dropped his duffel in the mudroom and hurried into the kitchen. No matter how many times Dani told him she didn't blame him for Kat's attempt to sabotage their relationship, he needed to see her with his own eyes and to hold her again. Instead of his girlfriend, he found a note propped against a scented candle.

Had she left strictly to avoid him? She'd known he was on his way. After making the mistake of staying out of touch on the trip down to Orlando, he'd overcompensated. He'd texted her when he got to the airport, when he'd boarded the plane, when the plane had landed, even after he got to his car in the long-term parking back forty and from the rest area when he stopped to take a leak.

Why would she go and leave nothing but a note behind?

He plucked the paper from its perch and read her precise, feminine cursive.

I'm happy you're back. I have a special surprise for you upstairs.

Her words hit him straight in the groin, which was probably what she'd intended.

Nate jerked off his jacket and kicked off his shoes. Then he took the stairs two at a time. He didn't skid to a stop until he was inside the master bedroom and got a good look at the seductive scene that had been set.

The curtains had been drawn, the bed was turned down, and several burning candles littered the dresser and chest of drawers. Leaning back on pillows propped against the headboard, Dani wore a black lace teddy that revealed a lot more than it hid. She set aside her e-reader, rose to a kneel, and gave him a smile that made his already stiffening cock swell even further. "I'm glad you're home."

He said something, but the words had to be incoherent. His brain just wouldn't function, and he'd lapsed into a primitive sexual need he had no desire to even try to fight.

Plucking a clip from her hair, she shook her head to let the long tresses fall around her shoulders in a blanket of sunshine.

Somehow, he got undressed. There was no memory of taking off his clothes, but he didn't waste time worrying about how. Instead, he got onto the bed and knelt in front of her, his erection bobbing with each movement, pointing right at her.

A purr rose from Dani's throat as she wrapped her fingers around him and stroked. Her mouth found his, her lips touching him as light as a whisper. Once. Twice.

Nate couldn't take the teasing. He brushed her hand away, embraced her, and kissed her deeply, sliding his tongue over hers and loving how she moaned against his lips. His hands caressed her back, settling against her backside and pulling her hips hard against his.

She wouldn't let him run the show, not this time. Her hand slipped between them, and she grabbed his cock again, rubbing her thumb against the crown. Then she cupped his neck and pulled him back into a wild kiss.

He tangled his fingers in her long hair, loving the feel of the silky strands sliding over his skin. Somewhere in his scattered thoughts, he wondered why she chose to greet him this way. Despite her reassurances she wasn't angry, he'd feared a cold reception. Instead, Dani acted as though she were starved for him. Heaven knew he was every bit as hungry for her.

"Lie down, lover," she ordered before releasing him.

She wanted to be on top? "Fine." He dropped to his back.

But she didn't move to straddle his hips. Instead, she took his cock in her hand and licked him from tip to root and back again.

Nate let out a hiss, fisting his hands in the sheets when she took him deep into her hot, moist mouth. After several deep breaths, he regained some fragile self-control and rose up on his elbows to watch her, loving the image of her licking and sucking him. A couple of times she had to brush her hair back, so he lifted the heavy mass aside, not only to help her, but also to get a more tantalizing view.

"I don't know how much of this I can take," he admitted.

Dani released him and sat back on her heels. "Well, then… since I want you to make love to me, I think that's what you should do. Now."

"Yes, ma'am. Anything the lady wants." He held his cock. "Wanna be on top?"

She shook her head. "Nope."

"Fine, I'll be on top."

When she shook her head this time, a saucy smile bloomed on her face. "Nope."

Already near fever-pitch, Nate couldn't wait much longer to be inside her. "Then what exactly do you want, sweetheart? Name it."

Instead of replying, she maneuvered around until her back

was to him. As he watched in surprise, she got on all fours and wiggled her sweet ass. "From behind, lover."

Only by closing his eyes and taking a few more deep breaths could he find enough strength to keep from coming right then and there. The view was exquisite. The pale globes of her shapely behind were barely covered in black lace. Before he could ask if he should undress her, she spread her thighs a little wider to reveal that the teddy had a rather convenient opening, exposing all of her to his gaze.

Nate moved behind her, smoothing his hands over her derriere and up her back. Lost in passion, he rubbed his cock between her folds before plunging deep inside her. He twisted her long hair around his fist, pulled her head back, and kissed her with all the love inside him.

Dani let out a gasp that he captured with another kiss. He let go of her hair, slid his hands around, and cupped her breasts. The nipples were tight pebbles straining against the teddy. He pinched them as he moved inside her, thrusting deep, again and again.

The feel of her tight heat overwhelmed him. His body was demanding release. Nate rose, holding tightly to her hips as he tried to postpone his own climax long enough for Dani to join him.

* * *

Sex with Nate had always been good. But this time? The way he pulled her hair and slammed into her again and again made the sensual heat inside Dani flare to an inferno.

She dug her fingers into the sheets, holding on for dear life as her body tensed, tightening as he pushed her higher and higher until her orgasm rocked her body, making her drop her forehead against the mattress as waves of pleasure consumed her.

Nate let out a low moan before he thrust into her one more time and then collapsed. His weight sent her falling forward, and she found herself flat on her stomach with his chest against her back and his legs tangled with hers.

There weren't any words to express what he'd made her feel. Dani wanted to believe the connection was so intense because they loved each other.

But sometimes loving wasn't enough.

She'd wanted him so desperately because she feared the talk they were bound to have now, the one that would probably change the course of their relationship. That was the reason she wanted to welcome Nate the way she had. She couldn't open up and tell him all the things she really needed to without having a physical connection first, a way to drop all her guards and let him in.

He rolled to his side, and Dani lifted herself up on her elbows, happy to see the contentment on his smiling face.

"You have my permission to greet me like that every single time I leave home," he said.

She giggled before she started to get up.

Nate stopped her by grabbing her arm. "Where are you going?"

"I'm just getting dressed."

"Why? Figured we could snuggle for a bit."

Most men would be thrilled she hadn't wanted to cuddle and be held close after a romp in bed. But not Nate. His smile had vanished, and he looked pretty damned irritated that she hadn't draped herself over him like a blanket.

"I think we should talk instead."

"We can talk naked."

"That would be…uncomfortable."

He furrowed his brow. "Can't say I like the tone of that."

Crawling off the bed, she took off the teddy and picked up the clothes she'd folded and left on the chair when she'd dressed for seduction. Although she wasn't normally shy about being naked in front of him, at that moment she felt far too exposed. Too vulnerable. It was as though once the sexual storm had passed, all of her guards, all of her defenses against emotional intimacy, snapped firmly back into place.

Dani jerked on her clothes as Nate reluctantly got up and put on his briefs and jeans. Then he sat on the mattress and patted the spot beside him.

She sat down and let him take her hand in his.

"What exactly should we talk about?" he asked.

A chuckle bubbled out of her. "So much…I don't even know where to begin."

"If it's about Kat—"

"No," she replied. "And yes."

"What's that supposed to mean?" His defensive tone grated on her, especially when he was the one at fault. He'd been the one to lie, the one to shatter her trust.

Their first fight was brewing, and she had to wonder if it was long overdue. They'd skated through their romance, moving forward with far too much speed and far too little introspection. "It's not just about her; it's about you not telling me she was going."

"I already explained all that, Dani. I didn't know she'd wangled her way into getting a ticket to Florida."

"But you didn't call me from the airport to let me know. Instead, you let her be the one to have the upper hand and feel like she was putting something over on me."

He let out a sigh that sounded rather guilty. "I should've called.

I know. I just…I needed to see Grandpa, and…" He shrugged. "I guess I was afraid if I told you Kat was going that you'd tell me not to go."

Dani tried to hold tight to her temper, but if he kept saying stupid things like that, she wasn't going to succeed. "Why on earth would you think that? I knew you wanted to see your grandfather. I wouldn't have even considered bossing you around like some dictator. So Kat went along—uninvited and unwanted? Big fucking deal. I could live with that. It's that you didn't even tell me, which means I was blindsided by that bi— um…woman."

"You weren't jealous of her?"

"Jealous?" *Yes.* "More like irritated."

"You would've let me go?" Nate sounded so damned surprised that Dani wanted to punch him on the arm. Hard. "Even knowing she was going, too, you wouldn't have asked me to stay home?"

She stared at him, mouth agape for a moment. "Have I ever been that kind of clingy girlfriend before, Nate?"

"Well, no…"

The anger made her eyes narrow. "There better not be a *but* coming."

"No *but*. You're right. I should've called. Okay?"

"Why didn't you tell me she kissed you?"

"Why didn't you tell me she'd threatened you that she was trying to get me back?" he countered.

"You're not Socrates. Don't answer a question with a question." Dani pulled her hand back, trying to ignore Nate's responding frown. "You didn't tell me she kissed you because you kissed her back."

He raked his fingers through his hair. "For shit's sake…I didn't kiss her back."

"Nate…"

"I mean it. I'll admit I was flattered. Who wouldn't love to have an ex suddenly realize she'd fucked up when she left you? But there was zero spark, Dani. Zero."

"Then why have you been texting her?" The question was out before she could stop herself. Now he'd know what a snoop she'd been, and she'd look like exactly what he assumed she was—a ridiculously jealous girlfriend.

"First of all, *she* was texting *me*. Not vice versa. Second, why did you think it was okay to read my texts? Because that's the only way you could possibly know she'd been texting me."

As much as she hated to admit it, he was right. That didn't give him permission, however, to shout at her. "It wasn't okay. I was just…worried. You saw Kat and then all of a sudden you're getting a bazillion texts a day, every day. I knew they were from her."

"So you didn't violate my privacy?"

"You're with me now. You shouldn't be texting an old girlfriend."

Nate arched a blond eyebrow. "Oh, so you're blaming the victim now instead of admitting what you did? I didn't ask her to text me. I told her to leave me alone."

"You could've blocked the number."

He thought that over for a moment. "You're right. That's what I should've done."

The tension between them was thicker than London fog, and Dani figured if she was in for a penny she might as well be in for the whole fucking pound. Better to get everything out in the open. Nate was, after all, obsessed with trust. "I don't want to have kids, Nate."

He sat there and blinked as though he didn't even recognize her. "Where did *that* come from?"

"I've been meaning to talk to you about it for a long time," she replied. "I just...I just couldn't work up the guts to tell you."

"Why now?"

"It's all I've been able to think about since we were in Indiana. You and Kat lost a baby. How did that make you feel?"

Nate took her hand, and although she considered pulling it away, she had to admit she needed his comfort. "Empty."

"Pardon?"

"When Kat lost the baby, I felt empty."

"You're gonna have to explain that, Nate."

After rubbing his free hand over his face, he said, "I didn't want the baby, not when we found out she was pregnant. I was scared it would ruin my life, that I'd have to quit school and end up working at some McDonald's just to keep the kid in diapers. But then the idea of being a dad settled on me, and I remembered how great my own dad was when I was little. I started thinking about how I could teach my son to play catch or swing a bat. Or jog."

Every word felt like a fresh knife buried in her heart. This man wanted to be a father. The reverent tone of his voice said even more than his words.

Dani closed her eyes against the stinging tears. She normally loved being right, something the Ladies always teased her about. Perfect Dani who knows everything. This time being right was going to break her heart.

Nate squeezed her hand again. "Then all of a sudden, it ended. Just like that. I didn't know what to feel except empty. Make sense?"

She nodded, unable to look at him. If she saw the sadness on his face that she'd heard in his voice, she'd start sobbing.

"Dani, none of this has anything to do with us."

"It has *everything* to do with us," she insisted. Hopping to her feet, she started pacing, a nervous habit she had no control over, especially when she was this upset. Nate wanted to be a father. Maybe not now, but in the future for sure. And if Dani held him to this relationship, she'd be denying that one thing she could never give him. "I don't want children, Nate."

Instead of saying anything, he sat there on the bed and watched her move back and forth across the open area of their bedroom.

"This wasn't a decision I made capriciously," she continued. "I thought about it long and hard. I'm not meant to be a mother. It's not in my nature. You saw me with Emma. I love that little girl every bit as much as I love Jules and Connor's boys, but taking care of them day in and day out would send me straight to the looney bin."

"You were good with Emma," Nate said.

"Just because I can care for kids doesn't mean I want one for myself. I have plans for my future. I'm paying almost all my extra money on this house so I can get out of debt. Then I want to travel while I'm still young enough to enjoy it. I want to go to Europe and Alaska and Australia and—"

"I want to travel, too, but that doesn't mean we can't have children."

"I'm not dragging bottles and diapers and car seats everywhere. I'm not worrying about how my kid behaves in fancy restaurants. I'm not leaving places I want to explore early because it's boring to a child." Dani tried to bite back the millions of words that now wanted to crowd in her mouth and spill out in her well-thought-out argument for why she would never be a mother. She wasn't successful. The words tumbled right out anyway. "Call me selfish, but I only have one life. I'm damn well going to live it my way. And I shouldn't have to justify it to anyone. It's my choice. But then there was you. No matter how much I love you, I won't change my mind. I won't."

Standing, Nate went to her and stopped her pacing by gripping her shoulders. "Stop trying to convince me. Remember that the future is always changing, sweetheart. Who knows how you'll feel in ten years? Maybe we could travel now and then later we could—"

She put her fingertips against his lips. "The future might be changing, but my mind won't. Ever. This isn't negotiable." Her hand fell away from his face. "If you want to move back to the basement now, I understand."

Chapter 29

This was the most confusing, frustrating discussion Nate had ever had. He knit his brows and frowned at Dani. "Whoa there. How did we go from talking about whether we'll have kids to you wanting me to move out?"

"I don't *want* you to go...but once you realize what I'm saying, once it really settles in, you'll go. I just know it."

"Dani..."

"Everyone will understand," she continued. "It's no big deal."

"It sure as hell is to me!" He had to resist shaking her in frustration.

She stared up at him, her blue eyes brimming with tears. "I'm not changing my mind, and you deserve a woman who will give you the children you want."

"I can live without having kids."

After giving him one of her you-are-so-full-of-shit expressions, she shook her head.

"I can. Kids might be nice, but you're more important to me. If that means it's always just the two of us for the rest of our lives, fine. I love you."

"I won't let you make that kind of sacrifice."

"It isn't a sacrifice, sweetheart. Loving you is all I care about."

When she shook her head again, he grabbed her chin, forcing her to look him in the eye. "If you don't want kids, I understand. And I accept that choice. It doesn't mean we don't belong together."

"Nate…"

He wrapped his arms around her and held her close, rubbing his chin against her temple. "We'll travel together. With two salaries, we can pay the house off quicker and start our summer excursions that much sooner. There are tons of places I'd like to see, too. Rome. Tokyo. Australia."

"You don't know what you're saying. You've got to take some time to think about what I said."

"I don't need time," Nate said.

"Yes, you do," Dani insisted. "You're so damn young and—"

Letting out a heavy sigh, he shook his head. "I can't believe we're back to that. You're not that much older."

"There's a huge difference between twenty-four and thirty-two. At your age, you don't have enough life experience to even know what you want. I do. Ten years changes the way a person looks at the world."

"Not even nine."

"Jim Reinhardt warned me about being with you since I'm your boss."

That little announcement came out of left field and blindsided him. *"What?"*

"After the dance, some busybody parent called him and told him she saw us slow dancing."

"And he told you we couldn't date?"

She shrugged. "Not in so many words…"

Typical Dani. Hearing exactly what she wanted to hear. "Then what exactly did he say?"

"To keep our focus on the kids during school events."

"Which isn't even in the same universe as 'don't date each other.' Dani, I love you. I don't care if you're my boss or how old you are or whether you want kids. I want you. Only you."

She simply shook her stubborn head.

Instead of keeping the frustrating discussion going, especially since Dani was far too obstinate to ever give in, Nate kissed her. Through that kiss, he tried to show her the depth of his feelings as well as his fear of living a life without her. She responded by trying to turn her head. He growled, cupped her head, and held her right where he wanted her.

She didn't resist, slowly giving in and melting against him. Only when he'd gotten her cooperation did he gentle the kiss, nibbling on her lips before easing back. "I love you, Dani. That's all that matters."

Even though she looked skeptical, she replied in kind. "I love you, too."

"Will you be mad if I head out for a bit tonight? Robert invited me to have a beer with him, Ben, and Connor."

"That's fine. I wanted to relax and read anyway."

The party he was planning had taken on new meaning, and he hoped the guys had some good ideas about how to use the gathering of their friends and family to get Dani past this speed bump. "I won't be gone long. Besides, we can spend the rest of the afternoon together."

"It's fine." She sounded so damned defeated, but he wasn't sure there was anything he could do to revive her spirits. She'd made up her mind that she knew what was best for him, and until he could convince her otherwise, she'd probably be worried he was going to just…leave.

There was no way in hell he'd walk out on Dani. Yes, he was younger and technically she was his boss. Yes, their relationship had moved along pretty quick. And, yes, her decision not to have children had taken him totally by surprise.

None of that mattered. Nate loved her, and he had no intention of ever letting her get away.

* * *

"Hey, Nate!" Robert stood and waved his arm. "Over here!"

The place was crowded, and Nate had been having a hard time finding his friends. He waved back, relieved to see the men had grabbed a table near the back of the bar where they'd have a little bit of privacy.

Friends. Something new that he suddenly understood meant the world to him. Just another way that Dani had changed his life for the better.

If he lost her, would he also lose Robert, Ben, and Connor?

He took the empty chair, nodding at the guys. A waitress came over and took his order—a beer and some fish and chips. It felt like forever since he'd eaten.

"How was the trip?" Robert's tone bordered on amused.

"I take it Beth told you everything."

"You mean that your ex went along for the trip?" Robert laughed. "Oh yeah. The Ladies are on the warpath. If your Kat—"

"She's not *my* Kat," Nate grumbled as he took the silverware the waitress was passing to him. "I hope the Ladies get their pretty little hands on her. Then she won't be a problem anymore."

"Thought we were supposed to be talking about a party," Connor said.

"Absolutely," Nate replied.

"I got the hall booked." Robert passed Nate a piece of paper. "The church's rec area is ours for the Saturday before Thanksgiving."

"Thanks for booking it. Did you need a deposit?"

"Nah. We're all set."

Ben chimed in. "Do you think it's really a good idea to drop all this on her like that? I mean, Dani is a bit…um…"

Connor filled in the description Ben was searching for. "Control freak?"

With a nod, Ben said, "Yeah. A control freak. But in a good way."

Letting out a snort, Nate couldn't help but grin. "You don't have to be diplomatic. I know exactly how much she needs to be in charge. And damn if I don't love her for it. The woman keeps me on my toes."

He might be grabbing the reins for this, but it was for her own good. Grandpa Delgado was right—Dani needed a big gesture, proof that Nate loved her enough to make a lifelong commitment. After they were married, she could go back to being her type A self with Nate's blessings.

Their shared laughter spoke volumes of how his friends felt about their own wives.

"It's not like we don't all have our share of flaws," Ben said. "We should count ourselves damn lucky that the Ladies still put up with us."

With camaraderie running high, Nate shifted the topic, needing some friendly advice and hoping to draw on their varied life experiences. Only after he'd left Dani did her words finally hit him.

She didn't want children. Despite what he'd told her, he simply didn't know if he would be happy if he never had kids of his own.

Connor was a father—of twins. Robert had adopted Beth's niece and was preparing to welcome his own child into the world.

And Ben had a daughter from a first marriage but no children with Mallory. Their plethora of family dynamics could surely make them the right people to give Nate some sound counsel.

He jumped right in. "Dani told me she doesn't want to have kids."

"I suppose that's my fault," Robert said, a chuckle in his voice. "We left you two with Emma too long. She can be a handful."

Nate shook his head. "It's not that. She loves Emma. She just has tons of plans for her life that don't include kids." The waitress was back with his beer. After she left, he took a bracing swig so he could spit the rest out. "I always thought I'd have children of my own. I'm not sure how I feel about her shutting the door on that."

Silence settled between the men as the noise coming from the bar patrons swirled around them. The tension was enough to make Nate wish he'd kept his mouth shut. Clearly he'd overstepped some kind of informal boundary for what friends could talk about.

He was just about to apologize when Ben spoke. "Mallory can't have kids, not since the chemotherapy. Even if her ovaries still worked, she couldn't handle the hormonal changes of pregnancy."

Moments passed, and Nate was ready to ask him to explain when Ben added, "I would've loved to have a kid with Mallory, but it wasn't in the cards. I always thought I'd have another. A son, maybe. But when I married her, I had to let that go." He shrugged. "Having Amber made it easier. I already got to be a dad. You'll never have that chance."

"You know, it doesn't have to be a done deal," Robert added. "You and Dani are both so young…"

Nate snorted. "She can't seem to get past my age, either. Eight years younger. So what?"

"What I meant was that there are years and years ahead to change your minds."

It's not my *mind that needs changing.* "I don't want to lose her. Not over something like this."

"I don't know," Connor said. "It's a pretty big issue, and you're gonna ask her to marry you. If you two can't find a compromise…"

"What compromise is there?" Nate asked. "I might want to have a kid or two, but she's adamant that she'll never be a mom. Where could we possibly meet in the middle?" The more he thought about the impossible situation, the more upset he got.

Ben picked up his nearly empty glass and signaled to the waitress. "The way I see it, either you get her to change her mind…"

"Like *that* would ever happen with Dani," Robert teased.

"Or you change yours."

"Great. Just great." Nate nursed his beer until the waitress brought his food and Ben's refill. Although the fries were hot enough to burn his tongue, he ate as a way to keep from talking as the doubts that had been bubbling and brewing below the surface came to a rolling boil.

Despite the assurances he'd given Dani, he wasn't sure if he had been totally honest. To think that by being with the woman he loved might mean he would never have children—never even have the chance to try for a child—made his emotions churn.

There was anger. Although he loved her, he couldn't help but think it was selfish of her to make that choice with no thought at all for his wants or needs. The decision to have kids should be something a couple made together, not one either partner should slam the door on so the other person had no say at all.

There was disappointment, the same disappointment he'd felt when Kat had lost their baby. To think he'd never see his own features on a tiny face or hear his son's first laugh or watch his daughter's first steps made his heart ache.

And there was fear—the fear that all these things that he *might* want in his own future could cost him any future with Dani.

"Are you still getting married in Indiana?" Connor asked.

"Yep. Already got things worked out with the judge," Nate replied. "Thank heavens we have a whole week off for the holiday. The inn I booked wasn't nearly as expensive as I thought it would be."

"Well, then"—Robert cuffed him on the shoulder—"you won't have to get too pissed if she turns you down."

"Hell, Robert," Ben said. "That's why we're organizing this whole surprise party. Dani's not going to say no in front of everyone, especially Nate's family. She might feel like he's twisting her arm, but she'll agree to marry him. I know she will."

Robert thought it over for a moment. "You might be right... but is that what you want, Nate? To have her promise to marry you because she doesn't want to embarrass you?"

"No," he admitted. That wasn't what he wanted at all, a marriage born of obligation.

"If you're gonna pull the plug on this," Connor said, "now's the time."

"No, I want this. I do." *At least I think I do...*

Chomping on some more of his fish and chips, Nate decided he would follow through with the surprise party—and the marriage.

Dani was wrong. People changed their minds about important things all the time. And although she was stubborn, she was also compassionate. If he really wanted a child of his own, he would have to trust that she loved him enough that she wouldn't deny him something so important.

"Let's get our plans finalized. It's time for Dani and me to make it official."

Chapter 30

Getting Dani to the reception hall had been next to impossible, mostly because Nate had such a hard time coming up with a reason they needed to stop by there. Thankfully, Robert had provided him with a false errand, and Dani seemed to go along with the ruse.

Now he walked beside her up the concrete sidewalk, holding her hand and hoping he wasn't about to make the biggest mistake of his life. His conscience had been nagging him from the moment the plans had been finalized.

This party had seemed like such a great idea when he'd set it up with the guys. But as the days slipped by, drawing him closer and closer to Thanksgiving break, he became less and less sure of himself. With so much at stake, he couldn't afford to misstep. One slip, and Dani would seize the opportunity to run like the wind.

He couldn't—*wouldn't*—lose her.

The irony of the whole situation was that Nate had begun to understand exactly how her mind worked. The problem wasn't that she didn't love him; the trouble was that she loved him too much. She wouldn't trap him in a marriage that wouldn't fulfill all his needs, including what she believed was his desire to be a father.

Why couldn't she understand that without her, he'd never have a life at all?

Right before he opened the door, Nate thought about turning around and hurrying Dani back into the car. Until he got things figured out in his own mind, until he could say with absolute certainty that he wouldn't regret losing any opportunity to be a dad, any promise he made to her would be hollow.

She'd been correct; he needed to know his own mind first.

And right now, he just…didn't.

Robert took the choice away from him when he flung open one of the double glass doors and yelled, "Surprise, Dani!"

The grip she had on Nate's hand tightened like a vise when she stepped inside, probably from seeing the large banner that read: CONGRATULATIONS, DANI AND NATE!

"It's a surprise party," he whispered. "For us." Her brows gathered, so he tried to stammer out a better explanation. "O-our friends are helping us celebrate moving in together."

She didn't say anything, instead gaped at the people shouting and clapping as he walked with her into the enormous room, one large enough to hold all the people he'd figured should be there on the big day, including his mother and Mark.

The sound of a microphone squealing pierced the air, making everyone wince and the noise level of the numerous conversations drop considerably. "Welcome!" the DJ—one of Robert's former students who now owned an entertainment service— announced. "We're here to celebrate with Ms. Bradshaw…um… Danielle Bradshaw and Nate Ryan."

A cheer rose from the crowd, making Nate's stomach churn. If he was this nervous about asking her to marry him, how in the hell would he feel tomorrow when he stood before a minister and had to recite vows that would bind him to Dani for the rest of his life?

No. This wasn't a case of nerves about being Dani's husband. His concern was that she'd never forgive him for springing all this on her.

God, I'm an idiot. But there was no going back. The printouts of the judge's instructions and the inn reservations practically sizzled in his pocket, reminding him of all the work he and his friends—and even the Ladies Who Lunch—had put into this shindig. Of course, the Ladies weren't told about all his plans. They were in for a bombshell every bit as much as Dani.

"Are you surprised?" he asked, wondering if she was ever going to ease her taut grip on his hand.

"Very." Her voice was breathy.

"Everyone's here for us."

"No, really?" she said dryly.

He let the sarcasm pass, figuring she was entitled to a biting remark or two.

Jackie and Mark were standing together next to a table in the far corner as if they were uncomfortable. He could easily understand the feeling. Since the guys drew up the invitation list, there were quite a few people attending that Nate had only seen in passing—if he'd seen them at all.

He should have listened to his conscience.

Too late now, it chided.

"It'll be fun," Nate insisted.

She gave him a curt nod.

"Let's dance," the DJ announced. "But stay close. In about ten minutes, Nate has another surprise for Dani!" Eighties music blared over the speakers. The song made Nate's head ache.

"Another surprise?" she asked.

"Um...yeah. You'll love it." *At least I hope you do.*

As the Ladies came to Dani, surrounding her as they all spoke in fast, low voices, the other guests drifted back to the tables scattered throughout the hall. A few people started dancing.

Robert, Connor, and Ben came to stand at his side.

"That didn't go quite the way I'd hoped," he admitted, dragging his fingers through his hair.

"She's just stunned," Ben insisted. "Wait until you spring your other big surprise on her. She'll be putty in your hands."

"Says the carpenter named Carpenter," Connor teased.

Ben snorted. "I'm a contractor."

Nate was starting to believe following through with the second salvo of this blitzkrieg might be the last nail in the relationship's coffin. "Maybe I should leave well enough alone."

"And waste all that time and money?" Robert shook his head. "You're already standing on the high dive; you might as well jump in the deep end."

"I don't know," Connor said, his gaze shifting between Nate and Dani. "Dani looked kinda...pissed. You think shoving a ring under her nose might make things worse?"

"Honest to God," Nate said, "I really don't know anymore. She's been acting so different lately."

With a frown, Robert said, "She's just nervous—exactly like you are."

"Then maybe I should back off for a bit."

"Damn the torpedoes," Ben said. "Full speed ahead."

"And here comes the bride." Robert nodded at the Ladies heading their way.

Dani took Nate's hand when he held his out to her. "Hey, sweetheart."

She stared up at him, the concern clear in her eyes. "Are you okay? You look a little...green." She put the back of her free hand against his forehead. "You don't feel like you have a fever or anything."

"I'm fine."

"If you say so..."

The guys were right; there was no turning back now. He wasn't about to embarrass her in front of her friends and family by suddenly proclaiming he needed to solve this baby issue in his own mind before he could give Dani the kind of commitment she needed and deserved. No, he was a man who followed through, especially on personal commitments. No way in hell he'd do to Dani what Kat had done to him. They'd drive to Indiana tonight, and tomorrow they would be married.

End of story.

If he could only turn off the stupid and far-too-negative voice in his head telling him that to make a pledge like marriage in haste was a recipe for disaster.

"C'mon." Nate tugged on her hand. "I have another surprise for you."

"I can't wait," she drawled with enough sarcasm to make him glance back at her.

* * *

Dani was having a difficult time tamping down the urge to turn and run right out the door. Then she'd jump in her car and head straight home. But that wouldn't solve her problem. Besides, she was the one who hated public gestures of affection, especially surprise parties. He didn't know that.

Nate had clearly gone to a lot of trouble to plan this party. As she glanced around the room, she took in the faces of family and friends, including Jackie and Mark Brennan. Thankfully, Kat was nowhere in sight.

Where are Mom and Dad?

Duh. They weren't likely to fly here from the West Coast for a silly party. An engagement? Maybe. A wedding? Certainly. But not this.

Did Nate even invite them?

Of course he did. Beth, Mallory, and Jules were obviously a part of this. And why her friends didn't at least give her warning was beyond her.

Then she remembered Mallory and what the Ladies Who Lunch had put her through to help Ben win her heart. Nate was every bit as resourceful, but putting together something like this needed allies—the same allies Ben had called forward. This wasn't a spur-of-the-moment event, judging from the size of the crowd and the distance some of the partygoers had to have traveled. The Ladies would have insisted Dani's parents know what was happening.

She followed him to the dais where the DJ was working. Grabbing her around the waist, he lifted her to the platform, and then he hopped up to join her there. The DJ passed him the microphone.

Nate waited a moment for the murmurs to quiet down, a lot like he did when he had an unruly class. "I'd like to thank everyone for coming. But I've got one more thing I'm hoping we can all celebrate tonight." He handed the microphone back to the DJ and gestured to Robert.

With an enormous grin, Robert plucked a small box from his pocket—a velvet box the perfect size to hold an engagement ring.

Dani's heart plummeted to her feet, and she started trembling so fiercely, everyone had to notice. "Nate, what's happening?"

He winked at her. "I've got something special for you."

Her heart pounded like a jackhammer, her palms grew sweaty, and her mouth suddenly went dry. The walls began to press in on her, making her feel like a cornered animal.

Robert handed Nate the black velvet box. "Here you go, friend. Good luck."

The butterflies fluttering in her stomach went into overdrive. Why in the world would Robert have to wish Nate luck?

Nate took her left hand, gently kissed her knuckles, and then slowly went down on one knee. The women in the audience let out a collective sigh at the romantic gesture, the sound ringing much louder in Dani's ears than it should have. Funny, but she didn't even register the men's reactions, although she imagined there were tons of rolling eyes and a few snorts of masculine disgust.

"I think now is the perfect time to tell you just how much I love you. It's not often a guy finds the love of his life, and that's exactly what you are. The love of my life. Which means there's only one thing left for me to do. I've gotta make damn sure she doesn't get away."

Tears blurred her vision, both from her fear and from the wonderful things he was saying. "Nate...please..."

Nate squeezed her fingers. "Here, in front of all these people, I need to ask you a very important question." He swallowed hard. "Danielle Bradshaw, will you marry me?" His gruff voice sent shivers up her spine. "Will you promise to spend the rest of your life with me? 'Cause I want to be with you every day from now on."

Although her mind screamed at her, she couldn't turn him down. He'd be humiliated, and she'd never forgive herself.

It was a ring. Just an engagement ring. They weren't married yet. They'd have time to sort things out. And if they couldn't, they would quietly call off the engagement. People broke engagements all the time.

Since he'd put her back to the wall, Dani let him have his special moment. She loved him too much to do otherwise. "Yes, Nate. I'll marry you."

The attendees applauded and cheered while he popped open the velvet box and took out a beautiful engagement ring.

Gripping it between his thumb and index finger, he held it up. "Beth helped me pick it. I hope you like what we chose."

The diamond was a marquise cut, a small but very lovely stone standing alone on a platinum band. Exactly what Dani would've chosen for herself.

"I love it." Her voice quivered.

Nate slid the ring on her third finger, but he kept a tight hold of her hand. "There's more, sweetheart."

She arched an eyebrow, angry at herself for counting her chickens while they were still firmly planted in their shells. If he had something else up his sleeve, another way to twist her arm, she wasn't sure she could stand it. Only her love for him kept her feet glued to the spot. Any more pressure, and she'd run.

When he pulled a folded paper from his pocket, his hand trembled. Not a good sign at all, and one that tossed her body swiftly back into fight-or-flight.

"Since you've agreed to be my wife, I thought we'd avoid one of those long, drawn-out engagements."

"What are you—"

He handed her the paper.

She unfolded it and tried hard to make herself understand the dates and times before her. "I don't underst—"

"They're reservations, Dani. For tomorrow with Judge Shelton. He's gonna marry us."

Shit. Shit. Shit.

Breathing hard enough she feared she might hyperventilate, Dani dropped the paper and clutched his hand with both of hers. "Nate, wait. Please wait."

He acted as though he hadn't even heard her. "Then we're going to have a quick honeymoon at a quaint little place in Brown County."

The audience was going nuts, but Dani forced herself to tune them out. This was her future, not theirs. At that moment, the most important thing in her world was getting Nate to understand she wasn't about to go through with a rushed marriage. They had too many things to talk about and too many issues that had yet to be resolved.

What was wrong with him? He knew her so much better than this. *An ambush?* After all she'd told him about how she felt about Ben's very public proposal to Mallory? Sure, that discussion had happened back in August when he was first meeting the Ladies, but he should've remembered something that important.

Ben's proposal might have been horribly romantic, but he'd given Mallory no graceful way out. Had she turned him down, both of them would have been utterly humiliated in front of so many people. Which was exactly what Nate was doing to Dani. Luring her into a trap.

There'd be no chance for her to plan her own wedding, to use any of the ideas she'd been collecting since she'd been a teenager. No choosing the proper dress. No asking Beth to be her matron of honor. No Ladies getting makeup and hair done in a salon on her wedding day. She'd have absolutely no control over one of the biggest events of her entire life.

Did Nate ever bother listening to anything she'd said?

Evidently not, considering he'd just put her smack dab into Mallory's shoes.

All of her worry and concern were quickly being trumped by anger. Couldn't he feel how violently her hands were shaking? How could he not know she'd hate this? "Please, Nate," she whispered. "We should talk in private."

His eyes narrowed. "Talk? About what? I love you, Dani. I want to marry you. You want to marry me. Why wait?"

If he wasn't going to keep his voice down, neither was she. "Why wait? Are you serious?"

He had the gall to nod.

She pulled her hands back and folded her arms under her breasts. "Because we have a bunch we should discuss first."

"We'll have plenty of time to talk driving to Indiana. Plus, we have three whole days together out there. You said you loved me... You do, don't you?"

The annoyance in his voice was as big a surprise as this stupid party. "I do love you. I'm just not ready to hop in the car and go get married."

"Why not?" Since the crowd now stood stone silent, Nate's shouts echoed through the hall. "If you love me, it shouldn't matter when we get married."

"It does matter, and you damn well know it. What about kids, Nate?"

"What about them?" His nonchalant shrug was directly opposed to the anger in his eyes. "We've got *years* to decide that." He'd dropped his voice back to a whisper.

Too late. Her temper was in full flight. "There's nothing to be decided. I'm not having children. If you want some, you're gonna have to marry someone else."

"Dani, be reasonable..."

When he reached for her, she took a step back. Her jaw ached from clenching it. "How dare you do this to me?"

"Do what?"

"Embarrass me like this!"

"I didn't want to embarrass you. I wanted to marry you!" Nate looked out at the audience as if just realizing they were there. Then he glanced back at her. "Let's go outside and talk. Okay?"

She shook her head, not bothering to tell him she'd put the same request to him not a full minute ago. Now there was no way to fix this. Nate couldn't make this humiliation right with a couple of words. Her heart hurt as she began to truly open her eyes. For Nate to pull a stunt like this meant he wasn't the man she thought he was. And the fact that he wouldn't accept her choice of remaining childless told her this relationship was doomed anyway.

She might as well end it now.

Tears spilled over her lashes, but she swiped them away with the back of her hands. The new diamond scratched her cheek. She jerked the ring from her finger and held it out to him. "I love you, Nate. I do. But I can't marry you. Ever."

Nate shook his head. "Stop it, Dani. We need to talk about this."

"Take the ring back! Please! Just take it!"

"No!"

Dani let out a frustrated growl, jumped off the dais, and marched right up to Robert. "Take this. Please."

Robert opened his hand and let her drop the ring onto his palm.

"Please see that he gets a refund." Then she faced the people who stood as quiet as corpses. "I'm sorry you had to witness this, everyone. I really am." She took a steadying breath so she could end this. "Please drink, dance, and have fun. I'll pick up the bar tab. Go get drunk. It's what I'm planning to do."

With as much dignity as she could manage, Dani walked through the double doors and out into the night.

Chapter 31

Nate sat on the dais while the DJ finished packing up his equipment. He was on his fourth beer, one that he realized was empty when he tried to take another pull. While he wanted to fling the empty bottle against the wall and savor it smashing into shards—just like Dani had slammed his heart against the same wall and broken it into a million pieces—he refrained. Instead, he looked around the empty room and sighed.

The crowd had fled quickly after Dani's rather regal exit. She'd marched out of the hall like a queen—back as straight as an arrow, head held high. Not a single glance back at what she was leaving behind. And why would she? She'd been in the right. His own stupidity and impatience had created this entire debacle.

The only people left were the clearly rattled DJ, Ben, Connor, Mark, Jackie, and a septuagenarian janitor who peeked out of his office door every now and then, probably to see if they'd finally left. The Ladies and Robert had gone to help a visibly upset Beth, which probably meant it had been too soon for her to be out after her bout of severe morning sickness. That, or she was so disgusted with Nate she didn't even want to talk to him. She was, after all, Dani's best friend. No doubt she'd be privy to a whole lot of rehashing about this fiasco for years to come.

"Hey." Connor leaned back against the platform, crossing his arms over his chest. "You okay?"

Ben took Nate's other side. "Need a ride home?"

Nate shrugged. "If she took the car, I guess I do."

Striding over to stand in front of him, his mother set her hands on her hips, glaring at him exactly like she had when he'd been younger and had done something naughty. "No worries. I'll make sure he gets home."

"Stupid question," Connor said, "but does he even *have* a home now?"

Ben winced. "Hadn't thought about that." His gaze caught Nate's. "Think she'll kick you out?"

"*I* would," Nate replied. "But knowing Dani, she'll have my stuff back in the basement before I can get back to the house. Then she'll want to pretend we're nothing more than colleagues."

"There's the rub," Jackie said.

"You mean still having to work together?"

"No," Jackie said. "What I mean is do you really know her as well as you think you do?"

Mark joined the impromptu gathering. "I'd say after tonight the answer to that is a resounding *no*."

"All done here," the DJ said.

Since Nate had already paid the guy, he simply nodded and then watched him use a dolly to roll the last of his junk out the door.

After popping off a text message, Connor slid his phone into his pocket. "I should be going. Jules will need help with the twins. You okay, Nate?"

Not really. "Fine."

"We should all get together soon. Okay?"

Although he doubted the Ladies would appreciate their men remaining his friends, Nate nodded.

Ben had been staring at Jackie since she'd planted herself in front of them. No doubt she was every bit as intimidating to him as she had been to her former students. God knew that withering frown had set Nate's stomach churning on far too many occasions.

It was clear Jackie was going to dive right into a major scold, one Nate believed he deserved, so he gave Ben an out. "I'm sure Mallory's waiting for you."

As he rubbed the back of his neck, he said, "This is all my fault. Maybe I should call Dani or something…"

Nate shook his head. "This was my idea, Ben."

"But I was the one who encouraged you. I guess I'd hoped that things would work out for you two the way they did for Mallory and me."

"Not everyone gets a happy ending," Nate said.

"Is there anything I can do?" Ben asked.

"Nah."

"Just give her some time. I'm sure this will blow over."

Scoffing, Nate shook his head.

"It will," Ben insisted. "Every one of us has screwed up at one time or another, but the Ladies forgave us. Dani will forgive you, too."

Afraid to let even a spark of hope flare in his heart, Nate frowned. "I'll see you later, Ben."

With a hangdog expression, Ben left Nate alone with his mother and stepfather. "You guys should probably get on the road. It's getting awfully late and—"

"Nathaniel," Jackie said in that tone that instantly made him feel as though he were nine years old again, "if you think we're going anywhere right now, you're not nearly as smart as I always thought."

Mark just shook his head.

"You know what, Mom? I'm not up for getting scolded any more tonight." Nate raked his fingers through his hair. "I screwed up, and I know it. You don't need to rub my nose in it."

"For pity's sake…" She held her hand out for him to grasp; then she tugged him to his feet. "It seems you're having all sorts of trouble understanding women lately. I suppose I should blame myself. First…" Pulling him into her arms, she hugged him. "I'm sorry things turned out so shitty."

A grown man shouldn't have tears pool in his eyes just from having his mother hug him, but damn if that wasn't exactly what happened. Nate hugged her back. "Thanks, Mom."

Pushing him back to arm's length, Jackie leveled a determined smile at him. "Next, we see what we can do to fix this."

"Fix this?" Mark knit his brows. "Dani is too much like you."

"Exactly," Jackie said with a decisive nod that brought a smile to her husband's lips.

Whatever the two of them were sharing through a simple look, Nate couldn't comprehend, although he'd always hoped that he and Dani could have that kind of relationship—one where the partners could communicate without words. "I'm confused. Care to explain what you two seem to know that I don't?"

"You're marrying someone a lot like your mom," Mark replied. "God help you."

"Tell me about it. I've felt like Sisyphus from the moment Hurricane Dani blew into my life."

"That's a whole lotta metaphors," Jackie said.

Nate shrugged. "Yeah, well, what can I say? I teach literature."

Since Mark hated to be left out of a conversation, it was no surprise when he asked, "Who is this Sissy Face?"

"Sisyphus," Nate clarified. "He's a poor guy stuck rolling a stone uphill forever."

After he barked a laugh, Mark smiled at his wife. "Sounds as if Nate has a pretty good understanding of what being married to a woman like you will be like. God only knows why we love you both as much as we do."

Her scowl was pure bluster. "Watch it there, Brennan, or you're going to be sleeping in the guest room for an entire month."

While he normally enjoyed their lighthearted teasing, Nate needed them to focus. "I love Dani because I only feel alive when I'm with her. I need her spirit and her comfort and her friendship. She's my other half."

"Like I said," Mark said, affectionately cuffing Nate's neck, "sounds like you understand what marrying a woman like her will be like."

"She won't take me back," Nate insisted. "Not after this stupid stunt."

"Your heart was in the right place, honey," his mom said. "You and Dani are meant to be together."

"I should remind you two," Mark said, "that every time people poke their noses into relationship trouble, they only make things worse."

"Not this time," Jackie said with a shake of her head. "Nate needs us. So does Dani. And if you think I'm going to let these two break up without doing a single thing to stop it, you've got another think coming."

"Mom's right," Nate admitted. "Especially about you, Mark."

His stepfather merely arched an eyebrow.

"Dani *is* a lot like Mom. I figure you know how to handle her, so maybe you'll have some good ideas on how to make this right with Dani."

Mark let out a heavy sigh before he nodded. "I'll tell you this, Nate... Getting that woman back in your life isn't going to be easy. But it's more than worth it."

When the men got to their feet, Jackie stopped them with an outstretched palm. "I do need to ask you one thing first, Nate."

"Ask away."

"What about this baby stuff? From what I gathered, Dani doesn't want any kids, right?"

Nate nodded.

"Is that something you can live with?"

"Much as I hate to say this," Mark said with a wink at his wife. "Your mom's right. That's a big decision to make, and you should know what you want before you put Dani through any more heartache."

"You know what's funny?" Nate asked. "The moment I realized she was really walking out, that she wasn't going to marry me, I had my answer." It had suddenly been crystal clear, as though all his uncertainty had vanished at the thought of Dani not being in his life.

"Well?" Jackie flipped her wrist. "Spill!"

"I don't want to be a father if it means losing Dani. Without her, I don't even have a life."

Mark clapped him hard on the shoulder. "Spoken like a man in love."

"Now," Jackie added, "you just need to tell *her* that."

"But first, you need to get something to eat and then get some sleep," Mark said. "We've got a great place to stay for tonight. If there's no extra room in that hotel, you can sleep on the couch in our suite."

"I should go see how Dani's doing," Nate insisted.

Mark shook his head. "If I've learned anything from being married to your mom it's that the best thing to do when her temper has skyrocketed is give her time. Let her cool off. Until then, talking is a waste of your breath."

* * *

After she'd carried the last pile of Nate's clean clothes to the basement, Dani stopped to take a good look around. She hadn't been down there in just about forever. Nate was responsible for keeping it clean, so she didn't venture into the basement at all anymore.

Setting the clothes next to the other folded garments she'd already brought down, she wished she hadn't finished all the laundry. Although it was a stupid thought, she wanted to still have a shirt he'd worn. Then she could comfort herself with his scent on the long, lonely nights that she would be facing for the rest of her life.

The sheets. She breathed a sigh of relief. His pillowcase would bear his pleasant smell.

He'd be back in this basement soon. Having already resigned herself to sharing the house with him, Dani had to admit—if only to herself—that she would still enjoy spending time with him. At least she would once the agony eased.

It's like a Band-Aid, Dani. You ripped it off; now the pain will stop.

A snort slipped out. Now she was lying to herself.

Eyes burning with tears, she whirled around and ran up the stairs, slamming the door she'd seen him walk through a thousand times. Then she leaned back against it and chewed hard on her bottom lip so she wouldn't cry.

After the stunt Nate pulled, no one would fault her if she kicked him out. Between Jules and Connor, one of them could find him a place to rent. If she had any sense at all, Dani would have already set all his stuff out on the driveway. Shit, some women would've poured gasoline on the pile and set it ablaze.

Easy there. He didn't do anything wrong.

She kept reminding herself that. Some women surely thought she was the stupidest female in the whole world. Who wouldn't love a romantic proposal followed by a whirlwind wedding and honeymoon in the country?

Me. That's who.

None of it mattered anyway. Nate surely hated her now. After all, she'd marched right out of there, snubbing him in front of family and friends. How could he ever forgive her for that? Had his shoes been on her feet, she would carry that grudge for the rest of her life—would probably leave some mean comment in her will just to have one last lick at him.

Sorrow weighed heavily on her shoulders. In her typical fashion, she'd overreacted and made a dicey situation so much worse than it had to be. Why couldn't she be more like the other Ladies?

Every single one of them had struggled through what seemed like impossible difficulties finding their mates. Dani had been there all along, watching the three of them resist like fish caught on hooks. Their men had been patient and given them time to adjust, to get used to the idea of going from being a single to being a couple.

And what had Nate done?

He'd sprung a trap on her, and Dani had wiggled free before she was caught forever.

So why was she so damned sad?

Because she loved Nate Ryan with every piece of her heart. And she'd showed him exactly how much she cared by running away like a frightened rabbit when she should have thrown her arms around him, kissed him, and then driven straight to Indiana.

No, no, no. She couldn't marry him. Especially not now. There were too many obstacles between them, too many problems that had absolutely no solutions.

Or were those "problems" actually nothing more than excuses to allow her to blame something other than herself for her current predicament?

For the first time since she got home, Dani checked her cell phone. There were thirty-six text messages. Not a single one from Nate. Of course, she hadn't expected him to text. Or call. Or ever talk to her again. Even though she was going to allow him to stay in the basement, he would most likely want to put as much distance between the two of them as he could.

"Fucked your life up something royal, eh, Dani girl?" she said to herself.

One by one, she read and deleted the texts. Colleagues were worried about her, and there was no doubt that gossip was burning up the wireless networks in Cloverleaf. Some friends shared sentiments ranging from concern to dismay to amusement. Several offered prayers in support, which probably couldn't hurt.

Mallory left a long voice mail and a couple of texts, as did Juliana. Beth left five voice mails and ten increasingly frantic text messages. After firing off quick texts to Mallory and Jules, Dani focused on Beth. If anyone could talk her down off the ledge, it was Beth.

"Dani!" Beth's voice buzzed in her ear. "Robert and I have been so worried."

"I'm fine."

"No, you're not. Want me to come over?"

"Why?"

"So we can talk."

"I told you, Beth. I'm fine."

Beth snorted. "I know you a heck of a lot better than that."

With a weighty sigh, Dani said, "I'm really not in the mood to talk. Besides, what's done is done."

Beth clucked her tongue as though scolding a student. "We both know that's nonsense. Nothing's ever done. You and Nate—"

"After tonight, there is no me and Nate. There'll never be a me and Nate again."

"That's not true," Beth insisted. "Look, I know tonight was… rough."

A laugh slipped out, one that quickly turned to a sob that Dani bit back.

"But it's not the end of the world," Beth said. "Shoot, it's not even the end of you being with Nate. He loves you."

It wasn't until she was already shaking her head that Dani realized Beth couldn't see her. "He loved me. Not loves. *Loved*."

"Love doesn't die because of a little tiff."

"A little tiff? Good God, Beth. You were there tonight. How can you call it a little tiff?" The tears spilled over Dani's lashes, and if she didn't end this call quickly, she was going to lose her precious control. "I need to go."

"Why the rush? Oh, don't bother answering that. I know darn well why you want to hang up. If you have to talk about what happened and deal with it, you're gonna break down and finally cry. Which, I'll have you know, is probably the best thing in the world for you right now. In case you haven't figured it out, none of the Ladies knew about the proposal plans. We thought it was just a party. Trust me, had we known, we would have put the kibosh on it before it ever happened." A long pause was followed by. "Crap. Hang on…"

At least the sounds of Beth gagging gave Dani something else to think about—something other than how she'd ruined her entire life this evening by acting like a five-year-old. There was some solace in knowing her friends hadn't been a part of the surprise proposal. "What's wrong? Are you still morning sick?"

Slow moments passed, and just about the time Dani was considering jumping in her car and hurrying over to help Beth, Robert's voice came on the line. "Hey, Dani. Beth's kinda… indisposed."

Dani could hear Beth's voice shouting from a distance, but she couldn't understand what her friend was saying.

"Is she okay?" Dani asked.

"Just sick. Again. How are you doing?"

"Fine. I'm more worried about Beth."

"She'll be all right in time. I guess the question is, will *you* be all right?"

"Doubt it," Dani replied. "I fucked up, and I don't think there's any way to fix it."

"Is that what you want?" Robert asked. "To fix things with Nate?"

Even though every single problem that had sent Dani running from that reception hall was still an obstacle, her answer came swiftly. "Yes. I do."

"Well, then. Tell him that."

As if… "It's not that easy, Robert."

"Bullshit. Look, I've gotta go take care of my wife. Take a piece of advice, okay?"

"Spit it out."

"That man loves you. I'm pretty sure that despite what happened tonight, you love him, too. Don't throw that all away just because you're afraid."

Chapter 32

Nate shook Mark's hand and then hugged his mother. They waited by Mark's SUV, which was parked next to the curb in front of Dani's house. He was taking a big chance in having them drop him off without first checking if Dani would allow him to return to living in the basement. Maybe once his parents left, she'd have pity on him and let him stay, at least until he could find a new place.

"We should wait." Jackie nodded at the house. "She was looking out of the bay window."

"That's our...um, *her* bedroom."

"Think she'll let you in?" Mark asked.

With a lopsided grin, Nate said, "Like I said earlier, I have no idea how she'll react. But there's only one way to find out. Besides, I have to talk to her. I can't give up without a fight."

"Remember," Mark said, "patience and forgiveness—the best things you can give her."

Jackie nodded. "This might take a while, Nate. Slow, steady steps should help you win her back."

"Or it could be in the blink of an eye," Mark countered. "Just be ready for anything. It'll all work out in the wash."

Although he wasn't entirely sure he believed them, Nate nodded. "I'll try to keep that in mind." He gave his mother another hug, suffered through Mark cuffing him hard on the shoulder, and then headed to the garage door. He was about to punch in the code when the door began to rise.

"That's a good sign," Jackie called before she slipped into the passenger seat.

With a smile, Nate ducked under the slowly rising door and headed into the garage. After a bracing breath, he opened the door and stepped inside the mudroom. He shed his jacket and entered the kitchen.

Dani was waiting for him, leaning back against the island with her arms crossed under her breasts and a forlorn frown on her face.

He wasn't sure what to think about that, whether she was angry he'd shown up or was still upset about last night. The strange thing was that his physical response to her closeness was immediate. Devastating. The desire to take her into his arms, to soothe away any hurt he'd inflicted, was almost impossible to resist. He wanted to kiss her senseless. He wanted to strip off both of their clothes. And he wanted to take her now, right there against the wall.

This was more than trust, more than need.

This was love, the kind a man never got over.

Her wary gaze brought him quickly back to his senses. If he did everything he wanted to do, he'd never be able to stay the course the way everyone had advised him. So instead of attacking her as he longed to, he stuck with the game plan he'd formed with his mother and Mark. Steady the course. One step at a time.

Makes me sound like an alcoholic.

"Hi." His voice was deep and gravelly.

She didn't erupt as he'd thought she would, although her brows knit in confusion, most likely at his tone, the one he always had when she'd aroused him. Then she simply said, "Hi."

Having been prepared to weather an emotional storm, Nate wasn't sure whether he should breathe a sigh of relief or start to panic. Going on instinct, he addressed his first problem. "I was wondering… should I be talking to Connor about finding a new place to rent?"

Thankfully, she shook her head.

"So I can stay in the basement?"

She nodded.

If she'd only say something, *anything*, maybe then he could gauge her mood. His only clue was an enigmatic frown that told him next to nothing. "For how long?"

"Pardon?"

"I mean… can I stay for the rest of the school year? Or only until Connor can find me someplace else to go?"

"For as long as you want to, although…" She kept talking, but her words became a mumble far too soft for him to hear.

"What did you say?"

"Nothing." Bottom lip quivering, she pushed away from the island. "Never mind." Then she headed toward the staircase at a brisk pace.

Whatever she'd said had clearly been important, perhaps even offering him some insight as to whether this battle to win her back would be fruitless.

He *had* to know.

Nate hurried after her, grabbing her upper arm just as she reached the first step. "Wait. Please. I need to know what you said."

Dani shook her head, but she didn't try to jerk her arm away, nor did she give his restraining hand a withering stare. If he judged her reaction correctly—especially when she turned back to face him—she didn't truly want to leave.

He tossed the game plan right out the window right then and there. The tension—the same pull that had been there from that very first kiss—practically made the air around them crackle. There could be no slow winning back of her trust, no gentle nudging her back into a relationship. No drawn-out courtship to pull her back to his side. The confrontation was now. His love for her would allow no less.

"Please, sweetheart." He inwardly winced at the endearment, but it slipped out of him so casually. So habitually. And it was exactly what she was to him, the best and sweetest part of his heart. "Come sit down and talk to me. Please."

Her teeth worried her bottom lip. "I…I…" She dropped her gaze to the stairs. "I can't."

Words crowded in his mind, apologies and pleas and questions flooding his thoughts until he wasn't at all sure where to begin. The one thought that trumped the rest was simple.

So Nate spoke that thought aloud. "I love you, Dani."

Her head popped up, her eyes wide.

"I mean it. I love you. I always will."

She shook her head as her whole body trembled. "You don't mean it. Not after last night—"

"I'm really sorry about that. I should've known better. I'd like to at least try to make it up to you."

"You're sorry? *You're* sorry?"

"I sure as hell am," he replied, hoping she heard the conviction in his voice. "It was wrong of me to pressure you into making that important a decision. I can only hope one day you'll forgive me for being such an idiot."

Her blue eyes searched his. "You're apologizing? To *me*?"

"Well, yeah…At least I'm trying to."

Tears spilled over her lashes as she laughed, a haunting sound that hit him like a blow to the chest.

"I know I hurt you," Nate said, stroking her upper arms now. "I'll try to make up for that every day for the rest of our lives. If you'll let me."

* * *

Dani couldn't find a single word to utter. She was just so shocked at what Nate was saying.

He was apologizing to her. After the humiliation she'd put him through last night, *he* was apologizing to *her*!

Her heart suddenly felt full yet also as light as a feather. For the first time since she'd fallen in love with this wonderful man, she truly believed that he loved her in return. There was no other reason he would try to accept responsibility for her mistake.

Everything inside her was screaming for him, needing to show him the depth of her devotion. She looped her arms around his neck and planted her lips against his.

Although she'd expected he would stiffen and maybe even push her away, he didn't. Instead, a low, needful growl rose from his chest, and he wrapped his arms around her and lifted her off the stair.

Dani moaned against his lips before stroking her tongue across his, returning his thrust with a parry that found her tongue in his mouth. She tried to tell him with her body what she simply couldn't find the words to say. With her kiss, she begged for his forgiveness and let him know that he had hers. And her heart as well.

There would be time to talk. After. But at that moment, she needed him, needed his touch, his kiss. She needed him deep inside her body.

Nate turned and pinned her against the door to his basement. In between heated kisses, he jerked her sweater over her head and cast it aside. Then he opened the clasp on her bra and helped her shrug it away. His heated palms covered her breasts as his mouth claimed hers again.

Slipping her hands between them, she fumbled with Nate's khakis—the same ones he'd worn the night before. After unbuckling his belt, popping the waistband button, and unzipping him, she shoved the pants and his briefs over his hips. They fell around his ankles. She stopped kissing him long enough to rip open his dress shirt, loving how they both laughed when the buttons rained down on the floor tiles like hailstones.

Framing his face in her hands, Dani stared into Nate's eyes as he unfastened her jeans. "I want you."

His hands slid over her hips as he pushed her garment down her body. "I want you, too. You're all I'll ever need, sweetheart."

He kissed her, smiling as she tried to kick her jeans aside. He nibbled the tender skin on her neck, working his way down to her collarbone and then to one breast. When he drew the hardened nipple deep into his mouth, she tunneled her fingers through his hair and arched into him. After torturing her with his tongue and teeth, he moved to her other breast to continue his sweet torment.

Body on fire, she clung to him, letting him pull her higher and higher. "Nate. Now."

As he pressed his body against hers, she marveled in the myriad sensations. The heat of his cock pressing against her lower belly. The cold of the wood on the skin of her back. The taste of his kiss as his tongue slid in and out, mimicking the act she so desperately wanted.

His actions became less controlled, fiercer. He held her waist as he lifted her so she could wrap her legs around his hips as he slid his erection inside her, a swift thrust that made her gasp in surprise and splendor.

Dani squeezed Nate hard with her thighs as she held tight to his shoulders. His strength amazed her, the sleek muscles rolling beneath her fingertips. He set a rough cadence, slamming into her again and again as he buried his face against her neck, his breaths every bit as choppy as hers.

The wave of heat began in her core and spread like wildfire through her entire body. She cried out, calling to him to join her.

A few more deep thrusts, and he groaned as he buried himself to the hilt, shuddering as he came.

* * *

Nate sauntered out of the master bathroom, still gloriously naked. A thrill of delight made Dani smile. That gorgeous body belonged to her, and she'd never be stupid enough to let him go again.

She lifted the sheet so he could slide into bed beside her. After their spontaneous combustion in the kitchen, he'd carried her to the bedroom. She'd made a hasty trip to the bathroom before he took a turn cleaning up.

After leaning back against the headboard, he tugged her against his side. She rested her cheek on his shoulder, trying to figure out the best way to start this conversation. If she waited too much longer, the tenderness between them could easily grow awkward.

"I love you, Nate."

"After what just happened, I'd sure as hell hope so," he teased, sliding his fingers through her loose hair. "I love you, too. And thank you for forgiving me so easily."

Dani sat up to look into his eyes. "But I didn't."

"Didn't what?"

"Forgive you."

The only thing that would have made him appear more confused was if he'd scratched his head. "You don't forgive me?"

"I don't have to," she insisted. "What happened last night—"

"Was entirely my fault. I should never have tried to trap you like that. I knew better. I did. I was just so damned afraid of losing you. I shouldn't—"

She stopped him by putting her hand over his mouth. "Stop. Please. Just listen to me for a minute. Okay?"

Although he took a moment or two to think it over, he nodded. As she pulled her hand back, he grabbed it and pulled her index finger into his mouth, rolling his tongue around it before finally releasing her.

The action sent the desire inside her soaring, but she still had so much to say to him. While she might wish they could make love again and forget this difficult conversation, there were so many things she needed to tell him.

Dani took a deep breath and tried to explain all she was feeling. "What you did last night for me was the most romantic thing in the world."

"What?"

"Just listen, Nate." He nodded, so she pressed on. "It was sweet and romantic and I'm thoroughly ashamed of myself for being such a bitch about it." She shook her head when he opened his mouth, and he quickly closed it again. "After all the time we've had together, I have to admit something to you. Until last night, I always thought in the back of my mind that what we had wasn't going to be permanent."

"I proposed to you, Dani. I wanted to marry you. How could you not think that would last?"

"Marriage isn't always forever, and we both know that. And before you ask, it wasn't because of you. It was my own fears that made me doubt you and kept me from giving you my complete trust."

Picking up her hand, he gave it a squeeze. "I hear a *but* in that statement. Does that mean you trust me now?"

She nodded. "With all my heart."

"Care to tell me what I did to earn that trust?"

"I wish I knew," she confessed with a shrug. "It was so strange…I was so angry at you, but not because you sprang that proposal and the hasty wedding plans on me. Because when you did, I realized I'd been doing nothing up to that point but playing house with you."

She tried to explain what she was just coming to understand herself. She might have considered Nate as her mate, but something deep down told her it had all been a lie, that their union would never be reality. She could see what would've happened so clearly, how she would have kept putting off the wedding date and finding ways to postpone that moment of true commitment. "When we were together, I was happy to keep things the way they were. Status quo. Sure, everyone knew we were together, and I loved you. But then you pushed me to make it…*real*. To commit. To put my entire trust in you, to hand you my heart." Dani brushed away the tears that had wet her cheeks. "I ran away to protect myself from admitting exactly how much I loved you, how much I needed you."

The harshness of Nate's features eased, and he smoothed the back of his hand against her face. "I'll protect your heart. Always."

"I know that now. I knew it last night the moment I walked in this house and you weren't here. Without you, this isn't a home. You were everywhere I looked, and I wanted to run right back to you and tell you so. I just didn't think you'd ever forgive me."

Leaning closer, he brushed a kiss over her mouth. "And I didn't think you'd ever forgive me."

"There was nothing to forgive you for," Dani said with a shake of her head. "Nothing at all."

He gripped her chin. "I tried to trap you into getting married before you were ready. I hope you'll pardon me for doing that to you."

"I do."

"I mean it, Dani. I knew it wasn't the right thing to do. I was just so damned scared of losing you. When you walked out, I wanted to kick myself because I thought I'd lost you forever. You know something else?" He waited a moment, then said, "I answered a really important question for myself last night—the one about having kids of my own."

Her heart skipped a beat before it started pounding a rough rhythm. "What was the answer?"

"I figured out that I wanted *you*, that any children I had with any other woman would never make me happy. All I want is you."

"Do you mean that?"

"Hell, yeah."

"Would you be surprised that I thought about that, too?" she asked.

He shook his head. "But you've already made up your mind."

"I have," Dani said. "Although I realized something else. I'm young. Not as young as you, of course." She tossed him a wink. "But young enough to realize things change. Who knows? Maybe my biological clock will start ticking. Don't get your hopes up," she cautioned when he grinned. "I'm only saying that I'm not going to be stubborn simply for the sake of being stubborn. We'll have to take it one day at a time."

"That's all I could ever ask," Nate said, kissing her forehead. "You know what's ironic about this whole damn thing?"

She arched a brow.

"That in trying to keep from losing you, I lost you. And while you tried to protect your heart, you actually gave it away."

This time, she kissed him. "Aren't we a bundle of contradictions?"

"You know what? Getting married doesn't matter. Not really. What matters is *us*. And if you never want to get married, fine. All I want is for you to be happy."

"Well, then…" She ran her hands up his arms and across his shoulders before pressing her breasts against his chest. "There's one thing you can do to make me very, very happy."

Pulling her on top of him, he smoothed his hands down her back to cup her bottom. "Name it."

"Marry me."

"You mean it?"

"Damn right I do," she said with a nod. "Let's get married."

"Then give me a minute." Nate rolled Dani onto her back and jumped out of bed. He was out the bedroom door and hurrying down the stairs before she could find her voice.

"Nate! Where are you going?" she finally called.

"I need to get something." His voice echoed up the stairwell.

"The shades are all open," she cautioned. "Don't let the neighbors see you."

The sound of him bounding up the stairs made her smile. That smile froze on her face when she saw the velvet box in his hand.

Without a word, he took the ring and held it out to her. "Do you mean it, sweetheart? You want to get married? You really do?"

She nodded.

Nate crawled back onto the mattress, kneeling before her as he picked up her left hand and slid the cool metal onto her third finger. "This doesn't mean we have to set a date or anything. I don't want to push. Not again."

"How about this week? We can get some airline tickets, head to Vegas, and just drive around 'til we find a kitschy little wedding chapel. Something fun. What do you say to that?"

Cupping her neck, he pulled her close and kissed her, a long, deep kiss full of love. "What I'll say is, 'I do.'"

Chapter 33

Nate waited patiently at the front of the Las Vegas wedding chapel. His nerves were steady and calm as he waited to make Dani his wife.

They'd laughed when they saw the place on their trip to the clerk's office to get their marriage license. With no wedding venue in mind, they figured they'd glance through a few brochures and pick something funny, someplace they could laugh about whenever they reminisced about the occasion. When they saw the themed wedding chapel, they knew they'd found the right location. Dani had made a fast call to see if they could get an appointment sometime that day while he'd filled out most of the paperwork. Thankfully, there was an open slot that she quickly booked.

The place was so corny, so silly, and so…perfect. It offered everything from an Elvis impersonator performing the ceremony to dressing the bride, groom, and guests as zombies, vampires, even aliens. But as they flipped through the book of possible scenarios, one was exactly what they wanted—something so off-the-beaten-path that no one would ever believe them until they saw pictures. Since their courtship had been nothing but unusual, there was no better choice for their wedding than to make it as over-the-top as possible.

Once they'd chosen the right one, the hosts hustled them into changing rooms with costumes and jewelry for them to put on. Then Nate was escorted to the front of the chapel to wait for his bride.

As he stood there, he tried hard not to laugh aloud at the scene around him. The wedding officiate was a dead lookalike for Captain Jack Sparrow. Every now and then he'd growl out a very pirate-like, "Argh," before he let loose with a full, boisterous belly laugh. The two witnesses to the ceremony were the hosts, a husband and wife in their sixties who owned the place and seemed to enjoy the wedding almost as much as the bride and groom. They were both in full pirate regalia and grinning like kindergarteners at recess.

Nate's own outfit was every bit as crazy—pirate garb all the way to the hat, the sword belted at his hip, and the clip-on earring. The only thing he put aside was the eye patch. He wanted to see Dani in all her pirate glory.

The music began—a rather jaunty accordion tune one would expect to hear at a bar frequented by pirates. She appeared at the entrance, wearing a white off-the-shoulder peasant blouse and a red skirt that swirled around her knee-high black boots as she walked. A thick black leather belt circled her waist, and damn if she didn't have a dagger tucked in that belt. Her blond hair had been pulled into a high ponytail that was tied with a red silk scarf. The look was completed by two very large gold hoop earrings.

She was perfect.

In slow, steady steps, she joined him at the altar, which had been piled with candles and a small treasure chest full of fake gold pieces that were also scattered all around. He held out a hand, and a happiness he'd never known settled on him when she put her hand in his.

* * *

Dani knew Nate was handsome. But dressed as a pirate?

He was magnificent.

His shirt was white muslin, and he wore a black leather vest and pants with thick stripes of black and red. His dark leather boots came to the knee, and a red sash was tied around his slim waist. He swept his hat off his head when she started down the aisle, tucking it under his arm in a sign of respect that made tears blur her eyes.

This wedding would give them such wonderful stories to tell everyone back home. Their students would demand pictures, and the newly married Mr. and Mrs. Ryan would be more than happy to prove that they had truly been married in a pirates' den.

She'd also show it to Jim Reinhardt, and if he held any concerns, she'd resign as department head. Nate was more important to her than being in charge of the English department.

She said her vows in a firm voice that she hoped gave him no doubt as to how much she loved him and how much she wanted to be his wife. Funny how things were so clear to her now, how walking away had almost been the worst mistake of her life. That's what love had done for Dani; it had helped her learn what truly mattered in life. And what didn't.

Nate's voice was every bit as strong when he gave her his vows. She paid more attention to the way his thumb rubbed over her knuckles and how he couldn't stop smiling through the ceremony than what he actually said. The words didn't matter. The fact that they would be man and wife was the only important thing.

"I now pronounce you husband and wife," Captain Sparrow said before doffing his hat and giving them a formal bow.

Nate tugged her into his arms, smiling down at her before he kissed her, a bit longer and more passionately than the situation called for. Dani didn't mind. Her life was complete now that he was her husband.

That was all that mattered.

* * *

"Déjà vu," Dani said, squeezing Nate's hand as they walked into the reception hall—the same one she'd run away from just three weeks ago.

"I know, right?" As he opened the door, he tossed her a smile with that wonderful dimple. "But I'm glad we're back."

"Me too."

The door closed behind them as a cheer rose from the crowd, most of them the guests from the earlier party that she tried daily to put out of her mind. At least the circumstances were happier now, and if Nate could forgive her, Dani was just going to have to learn to forgive herself.

Nate's parents came over to the couple first.

"I have to admit," Jackie said, "that I'm enjoying this party a helluva lot more than the last one." Her wink took the sting out of the remark. Then she gathered Dani into her arms and gave her a tight hug. "I knew you two belonged together. Welcome to the family."

"Thanks."

Mark embraced her next. "We're happy to call you our daughter."

If they kept saying wonderful things like that, Dani was going to burst into tears. "Thank you both."

The next half hour was spent meeting and greeting the guests, and Dani feared she'd never be able to sneak away and thank the Ladies. They'd planned this reception right after she and Nate had returned from their short honeymoon. From what they told her, their husbands went to a lot of trouble to get in touch with everyone who'd witnessed the proposal fiasco to invite them to this new and much happier occasion.

Mallory was setting out plates by the three-tiered cake that Ben was fussing over as though to add a few finishing touches. Jules was working with Connor to set up a large screen and projector. Beth and Robert were helping guests find their tables.

They'd gone to so much trouble and expense, Dani wasn't sure she'd ever be able to truly express her appreciation. But she'd try. Her friends—these sisters of her heart and the men they loved—were the reason she'd found the courage to make a commitment to Nate. They'd shown her that marriages could succeed and that love didn't have to fade away. She only hoped she and her husband would be half as happy as the Ladies and their men.

About the time Dani figured she'd welcomed enough guests that she could go hunt Beth down, her friend suddenly appeared at her side.

"It's time to eat," Beth said.

Dani gave her a fierce hug. "I can't thank you, Mallory, and Jules enough for doing this for us."

Beth blew a teasing raspberry. "We're all glad you and Nate worked things out. As far as the party goes, the guys just repeated a lot of the same plans they'd made for the first party. You should be thanking them more than us. I'm just sorry your parents couldn't make it." She nodded at the front table. "Did you see the cake Ben made?"

"It's gorgeous."

"Why don't you and Nate go sit at the head table? Then we can start dinner—and the show."

"Show?" Dani cocked her head. "What kind of show?"

"It's a surprise." After a quick kiss on the cheek, Beth hurried away.

And what a surprise it was. After the meal had been served, Connor fired up the projector and showed the Ryans' pirate wedding in its entirety, much to the delight of the attendees. How he'd obtained a copy was beyond her, until she saw Nate's grin. "You didn't."

"I did."

She had to admit, it made a great show.

* * *

The Ladies Who Lunch weren't able to get together as a group until the crowd finally began to dwindle. Dani had grabbed a piece of cake to enjoy. Nate had fed her a small bite earlier, but then they'd been so busy talking to people, she'd never had a proper serving. She was making up for that now, and thanks to Ben, she had a slice with gobs of icing.

Beth joined her at the table first, holding her own small piece of cake.

"That won't bother your stomach?" Dani asked.

"Not sure." Beth shrugged. "But if it does, at least I get to enjoy the sugar buzz first."

Not long after, Mallory and Jules took a seat, eating dessert and nursing their drinks.

Setting aside her fork, Dani smiled at her friends. "You're all so wonderful. Thank you for doing this."

In typical fashion, all three waved away the compliment.

Jules lifted her champagne glass in toast. "We're all happy for you."

"We couldn't have picked anyone better for you than Nate." Mallory inclined her head at their husbands. All four were holding longneck beers, chatting and laughing in clear companionship. "He fits."

With a nod, Beth said, "He does, doesn't he? The guys like him. And so do the Ladies."

"That makes me so happy," Dani said. "The three of you are so damned important to me that I can't imagine what it would be like to have a husband none of you wanted to spend time with."

"He's like the last puzzle piece," Jules said.

Mallory nodded. "Like I said, he *fits*."

"You realize the circle's complete now, don't you?" Beth asked.

Dani didn't even have to ask what she meant. As usual, she just knew. "It really is. The four of us are always going to be the Ladies Who Lunch, but now? Now, we're so much more than that."

"We're four families." A smirk colored Jules's features. "Even if the kids aren't here right now."

"Thank God for your manny," Beth said, patting Jules's hand.

"Four *happy* families," Mallory added. "Of all shapes and sizes."

"Well, then..." Dani picked up her own champagne glass. "I have a toast for all of us."

Mallory and Jules lifted their champagne glasses. Although Beth only had milk, she grabbed it and joined them.

"To friendship. To family. And most of all to *love*—the one thing that truly makes life worth living."

Please turn the page for an excerpt from the first book
in Sandy James's Ladies Who Lunch series,

The Bottom Line.

Available now!

Chapter 1

*O*ne more change.

After a year of unrelenting upheaval, Mallory Hamilton was ready to get her life back. She only needed one more change.

Giving her short hair another quick tweak, she set the gel aside. Rascal, her tabby cat, jumped up on the vanity counter, where he knew he didn't belong. But Mallory had learned from experience, some silly rules were made to be broken.

She ran her hand down his back as he arched up to get more of her touch. The cat's fur was soft and warm, and she wanted nothing more than to crawl back into bed and let Rascal snuggle against her side like a living heating pad.

"Did you finish your breakfast?" she asked her pet.

Rascal's reply was more purring.

Mallory took one last look in the mirror, smiled, and walked out of the bathroom. Her cat padded beside her, twitching his tail in the air.

The summer had been hot and very dry, matching her mood quite well. Everyone patted her on the shoulder and told her they admired her strength. Truth was she wasn't strong. She was numb. Her life had taken a one-eighty turn so fast, she hadn't had the chance to catch her breath. There simply hadn't been time to cry. Now that the ordeal had ended, she saw no reason to indulge herself in an emotional breakdown. Crying wouldn't change a damned thing.

She'd lost things she couldn't get back, and that was that.

The doorbell rang as she finished buttoning her shirt.

Rascal hopped on the bed, stretching out on the rumpled quilt and kneading his claws against the cloth. Before she headed downstairs, Mallory jerked the shade up so that the sunlight hit his striped brown fur.

"Have a nice nap. I need to talk to the contractor about fixing up this dump."

And her home really *was* a dump.

The doorbell rang again.

"Coming!"

She had to push the front door with her hip to hold it tight while she flipped open the dead bolt. The squeak when she opened the door grated on her nerves. She promised herself she would go to the hardware store and get some oil after the contractor left.

Dressed in a sky-blue polo and jeans, a thirtysomething guy with short dark hair glanced up from the iPad he held in his hand. His sexy smile took her by surprise.

"Are you Mallory?" he asked.

"Yes. I'm Mallory Hamilton. You're Ben? The contractor Robert Ashford sent?"

"Yes, ma'am. He said you wanted some work done on your place." He fished in his shirt pocket and produced a white business card, which he handed to her. "If you show me which projects you'd like done, I can give you an estimate. Then we can talk about a timetable."

She blinked twice when she read the name, but she didn't laugh. She hadn't truly felt like laughing in a very long time.

"Your last name's Carpenter? Seriously? You're a carpenter named Carpenter?"

"I'm a *contractor* named Carpenter." His words were clipped.

She opened the door wider, sorry that she might have offended him. No doubt he'd grown tired of dealing with rude comments about his name. "Please come in. I'll show you around."

His brown eyes wandered the foyer. "DIY?"

"Pardon?"

Ben nodded at the coat closet with no door, then at the floor. "Do-it-yourself. The laminate flooring isn't tight enough. I assume the door's in the garage because it was too long to close after you put the floor in."

She nodded. "Along with the trim. The chair rail for the dining room. The sink for the half bath. And—"

He held up a hand. "How about you take me room to room and show me what you'd like done?"

"Gladly."

The downstairs wasn't too bad, except for the great room. The fireplace mantel was only partly stained, and the gas logs had never been installed. That's what the contractor was for.

He followed her up the stairs into the master bedroom. "And in here?"

"Doesn't it speak for itself?"

When he smiled, he had laugh lines that framed his eyes. "It does, but I want to know what *you* think needs to be done."

She pointed at the exposed beam at the apex of the cathedral ceiling. "It's fake, and the corners have split away from the drywall. I like the way it looks in general, so I'd like to see if you can save it."

He nodded and entered more information on his tablet.

"The window needs...*something*. I can hear the wind whistle when storms blow through."

"Any water when it rains?"

"No."

Ben pulled the drape back. "They're newer windows. When did you have them put in?"

"Not sure. Maybe three years ago?"

"They're in good shape, but they weren't caulked properly. Next?"

Mallory led him into the bathroom and froze, utterly mortified. So accustomed to being alone now, she never bothered hiding anything she used on a daily basis. She swept her arm across the counter, scooping up all her stuff and dropping it into the deep vanity drawer.

Without missing a beat, Ben flipped the switch to the exhaust fan, which did nothing in response. "You'll need a new fan. Do you want to keep these light fixtures? They're a bit...dated."

His calm acceptance eased her embarrassment. "They suck."

He chuckled. "Light fixtures are easy to switch out. I'll bet you're tired of six big, naked bulbs staring you in the eye first thing in the morning."

Nothing else naked stared at her, but the lightbulbs still had to go. "Yeah...you're right. I'll need new ones for all three baths."

More taps on his iPad that were probably adding up to a pretty penny.

Didn't matter. She couldn't take her house anymore. Not the way it was.

She needed it to be *her* home now.

The rest of the tour took a good hour. Every disaster she showed him raised her anxiety, especially when his response was to draw his lips into a grim line and nod curtly. Dollar signs flashed in her head. She didn't even want to know what he found in the crawl space or the attic.

They ended up right where they began, and for some reason, the foyer looked worse this time than it had when she'd invited him inside. Her stomach was tied into nervous knots, and she was on the verge of a full-blown panic attack. But she was going to do this.

She *had* to do this.

"So what do you think? Can all this be fixed?" Her voice quivered.

Ben kept working on his tablet.

"I know this house is…old and a big mess, but—"

He finally glanced up. "Relax. There's nothing really *wrong* with the place."

Mallory snorted. "*Everything's* wrong with this place. But it's all I've got and I sure can't afford to move."

In all honesty, she probably could afford to move—she simply didn't want to. The commute was less than ten minutes, and she was close to everything she needed. The library. The pharmacy. Her friends. A SuperTarget.

His gaze wandered the foyer. "The way I see it, this place has a few scars. That's all. Just scars."

"Scars?" She hated that word more than anyone would ever know.

"Yeah. Cosmetic stuff mostly, but the bones are good. Just give it time—give *me* time."

His words pounded through her brain, a steady rhythm that made her insides somersault and her head ache.

A few scars.

Cosmetic stuff mostly.

Give it time.

"What's the bottom line?" she asked, holding a tight lid on her emotions.

"Bottom line is I'll fix things for you, Mrs. Hamilton. I promise."

Those few simple words worked magic by easing her anxiety. Perhaps it was his sincerity. Perhaps it was his smile. Perhaps it was the funny coincidence of his name. "I believe you."

"I need to check some prices, see if I can call in some favors, and get you a price. You realize it's an estimate, right? That when I get to work, I might find more problems hiding underneath the skin?"

She nodded. What was below the surface always caused her the most trouble. With her luck lately, Ben Carpenter would find everything from termite infestation to dry rot.

* * *

Ben Carpenter's temper rose to a boil the moment he saw Amber sitting on the front porch of his rented town house. Since it was the last week before she started eighth grade, she was supposed to be spending time with her mother. Then she'd come back home Sunday before classes began.

Damn you, Theresa.

His daughter's elbows were propped on her knees, and her chin rested on her hands. She'd gathered her long dark hair into a ponytail, and she wore her usual jeans and T-shirt. A pink backpack lay at her feet.

Throwing the truck into park, he sighed. Not at having his daughter home where she belonged, but because his bitch of an ex-wife had abandoned their kid. Again.

"Hey, ladybug," he said, resisting the urge to gather her into his arms. "Why didn't you call me and tell me you were coming back early?"

Ever since she'd become a teenager, Amber had started keeping her distance. He just hadn't figured out whether it was a teenage thing or if she didn't want to hug her father anymore. She never hugged Theresa, but then again if Theresa were his mother, he'd not only be reluctant to hug her, he'd run away to join the circus.

At least Amber always knew she was safe with her father. He tried to make a stable home, even if they could only afford a rental. She'd decorated her bedroom herself and made it reflect her eclectic personality. Posters of anything from androgynous singers to muscular athletes lined the walls. Since he remembered how important his own privacy had been at that age, he didn't hover.

Amber looked up at him with brown eyes that held enough red to show she'd been crying. "Her phone got turned off 'cause she didn't pay for it." Each word dripped with disdain he was accustomed to hearing whenever Amber spoke of Theresa. "She took mine. Said I was too young to have my own phone."

Of course she took Amber's phone—he paid for it.

"What happened this time?" Ben asked.

"Some of her stupid friends were going to Vegas." She stood and picked up her backpack, slinging the strap over her shoulder. "She didn't say when she was coming back. Just dropped me off, telling me she didn't want to see you. Do you know how many of my friends' texts I've missed?"

He gave her ponytail a playful tug. "Why didn't you let yourself in?"

"I couldn't remember the new code."

"I'm sorry. I wish I hadn't had to change—"

"It's not your fault, Dad. It's hers. She was the one who let herself in and took your checkbook."

Once she followed him into the house, Amber dropped her pack inside the door, flopped on the couch, and grabbed the remote. Then she flipped through channels.

"Well, at least you're home now, ladybug."

What kind of mother does something like this?

"Pizza or Chinese?" he asked, picking up the phone. "If I'd known you were coming back so soon, I could've shopped."

"You never know when I'm coming home."

"Touché."

Amber's gaze shifted from the flat-screen to him. "You know, I hear people say that all the time, but I don't know what it means."

He found a smile. His daughter was, above all other things, the most curious creature on the face of the planet. From the time she could speak, her favorite word was "why," usually followed by a question that revealed an intelligence beyond her years. Most kids outgrew that curiosity. Not Amber. If anything, it grew exponentially with each passing year.

"I think it's a fencing term or something. Flip open the laptop and Google it."

She turned back to whatever show she'd been watching. "I don't want to know that bad. And get Chinese. Sweet-and-sour pork. I had pizza delivered last night when Theresa didn't come home 'til ten."

"Theresa?"

"I stopped calling her Mom."

"Why?"

"'Cause she doesn't act like a mom."

She had him there.

After calling for supper delivery, Ben sat down in his recliner with his iPad and scrolled through the list of things he'd need to do to make Mallory Hamilton's house decent.

Her house reeked of "hubby just moved out." Half the master closet was empty, and she'd barely begun to spread her things into the vacated space. Only one toothbrush in the holder, but there was toothpaste spatter on the backsplash over the second sink. She still had a light line on the third finger of her left hand where her ring had blocked the sun.

What kind of idiot would leave such a nice woman? Pretty, too, although she wore her light brown hair awfully short. At least it suited her round face and drew attention to her best feature—her big, brown doe eyes.

The least Ben could do was fix her home. Her husband—or was it ex-husband?—obviously had no idea how to finish any of the numerous projects he'd begun. Most of what he'd done would have to be started over, but Ben hadn't lied to her when he'd said the house had good bones.

It was a sturdy, roomy home built in the days when houses were supposed to last. No cheap vinyl siding or slab foundation. The crawl space was dry, the floor joists sturdy and well put together. The attic needed more insulation, but it was also clean and dry and the roof had plenty of life left. Once he finished working on repairs, she could stay in that house and make new memories or sell the place for a nice profit. Either option would give her a fresh start, which she surely needed.

Back to that estimate…

After fiddling with the costs, he came to a final figure when the doorbell rang.

Amber popped up and came to stand at his side, holding out her hand and grinning. "Cough it up, Dad."

He pulled out his wallet and handed her some cash. As she

went to the door, he frowned at the nearly empty wallet, which matched his nearly empty bank account.

Ever since the economy turned sour, finding jobs hadn't been easy. Ben was grateful to friends and customers who recommended him to potentials, but work was still sketchy at best.

He hadn't told Mallory Hamilton how much he needed this job. If she knew how desperate he was getting she might not hire him.

While Amber took the food to the kitchen island and started setting out containers, he e-mailed his estimate to Mallory, sending it off with a wish and a prayer.

About the Author

Sandy James lives in a quiet suburb of Indianapolis with her husband. She's a high school social studies teacher who especially loves psychology and United States history. Since she and her husband own a small stable of harness racehorses, they often spend time together at the two Indiana racetracks.

Learn more at:
SandyJames.com
Twitter: @SandyJamesBooks
Facebook.com/SandyJamesBooks

www.ingramcontent.com/pod-product-compliance
Ingram Content Group UK Ltd.
Pitfield, Milton Keynes, MK11 3LW, UK
UKHW022259280225
455674UK00001B/101